PENGUIN TWENTIETH-CENTURY CLASSICS

SOMETHING CHILDISH AND OTHER STORIES

Katherine Mansfield was born in Wellington, New Zealand, in 1888 and died in Fontainebleau in 1923. She came to England for the latter part of her education and, after 1908, never returned to New Zealand. Her first writing (apart from some early sketches) was published in the *New Age*, to which she became a regular contributor. Her first book, *In a German Pension*, was published in 1911. In 1912 she began to write for *Rhythm*, edited by John Middleton Murry, whom she later married. For the next few years her writing was mainly experimental, but with the publication of *Prelude* in 1916 she showed herself to have evolved her own distinctive voice as a fiction writer. She contracted tuberculosis in 1917 and from that time led a wandering life in search of health. Her second book of collected stories, *Bliss*, was not published until 1921. Her third collection, *The Garden Party*, appeared a year later. It was her last book to be published in her lifetime. After her death two more collections of stories were published, as well as her *Letters* and later her *Journal*.

Claire Tomalin writes in her biography of Katherine Mansfield: 'It was largely through her adventurous spirit, her eagerness to grasp at experience and to succeed in her work, that she became ensnared in disaster ... If she was never a saint, she was certainly a martyr, and a heroine in her recklessness, her dedication and her courage.'

Suzanne Raitt was educated in England and the United States and, after six years lecturing in the English department at Queen Mary and Westfield College, University of London, is currently an Associate Professor at the University of Michigan.

She is the author of *Virginia Woolf's 'To the Lighthouse'* (Harvester Key Texts Series) and *Vita and Virginia: The Work and Friendship of V. Sackville-West and Virginia Woolf* (Clarendon Press). She edited Virginia Woolf's *Night and Day* for World's Classics and is currently co-editing a collection of essays on women's fiction and the Great War with Trudi Tate and working on a critical biography of May Sinclair for Oxford University Press.

KATHERINE MANSFIELD

*Something Childish
and Other Stories*

EDITED WITH AN INTRODUCTION
AND NOTES BY SUZANNE RAITT

PENGUIN BOOKS

PENGUIN BOOKS

Published by the Penguin Group
Penguin Books Ltd, 27 Wrights Lane, London w8 5tz, England
Penguin Books USA Inc., 375 Hudson Street, New York, New York 10014, USA
Penguin Books Australia Ltd, Ringwood, Victoria, Australia
Penguin Books Canada Ltd, 10 Alcorn Avenue, Toronto, Ontario, Canada m4v 3b2
Penguin Books (NZ) Ltd, 182–190 Wairau Road, Auckland 10, New Zealand

Penguin Books Ltd, Registered Offices: Harmondsworth, Middlesex, England

First published by Constable & Co. 1924

Published in Penguin Books 1996
1 3 5 7 9 10 8 6 4 2

Introduction and Notes copyright © Suzanne Raitt, 1996
All rights reserved

The moral right of the editor has been asserted

ACKNOWLEDGEMENTS
The editor is grateful to the Society of Authors
as the literary representative of the Estate of
Katherine Mansfield for permission to quote from
unpublished drafts of 'The Little Primitives', 'Late Spring',
'The Wrong House' and 'A Strange Mistake'.

Set in 10/12 pt Monotype Garamond
Typeset by Datix International Limited, Bungay, Suffolk
Printed in England by Clays Ltd, St Ives plc

Except in the United States of America, this book is sold subject
to the condition that it shall not, by way of trade or otherwise, be lent,
re-sold, hired out, or otherwise circulated without the publisher's
prior consent in any form of binding or cover other than that in
which it is published and without a similar condition including this
condition being imposed on the subsequent purchaser

Contents

Introduction

'Did K. M. do something to deserve this cheap posthumous life?' wondered Virginia Woolf on 6 March 1923, barely two months after Katherine Mansfield's death in France from tuberculosis. Katherine's ghost had been seen at the house in which she had stayed on her last visit to England in August 1922. Dorothy Brett, to whom the house belonged, was a deaf painter, whose relationship with Katherine had been shadowed at the end by her flirtation with Katherine's husband, John Middleton Murry. And yet, noted Virginia, 'now [Brett] idolises her', sitting there 'deaf, injured, solitary, brooding over death, & hearing voices'.[1] For Virginia, this kind of posthumous longevity was a cheap travesty; yet she too sometimes seemed to see Katherine, 'that strange ghost, with the eyes far apart, & the drawn mouth, dragging herself across her room'.[2] The two volumes of stories, *The Doves' Nest and Other Stories* (1923) and *Something Childish and Other Stories* (1924), which Murry edited and published after his wife's death, speak strangely of Katherine's haunting, of her life after death. 'Katherine did *not* want to die,' said her brother-in-law fifty-seven years after she died. He believed she had entered the body of Murry's second wife, Violet le Maistre, whose handwriting and physical appearance bore an increasingly close resemblance to Katherine's. Like Katherine, Violet died in her thirties of tuberculosis. She welcomed the disease, telling Murry, 'I wanted you to love me as much as you loved Katherine – and how could you, without this?'[3]

Katherine's ghost is still with us today. Like the most troublesome of phantoms, she walks in many forms: as modernist, as feminist, as white-colonial writer, as wronged wife, as bisexual, and as medical and psychological case-study. To many readers she is familiar as the author of delicately sensuous stories, evocative of a turn-of-the-century New Zealand, but with a vein of satire and sentimentality. Her stories have been reprinted over and over again in different editions and different selections. Particular stories persist: 'Prelude', 'At the Bay', 'Je ne Parle pas Français', 'The Garden Party', 'The Fly'. The interest of the present collection lies partly in the fact that almost none of its stories is well-known. This was the last of the five collections to be published, and the reader might be forgiven for assuming that, by the time he came to putting it together, Middleton Murry, already working with stories Katherine had herself left uncollected during her lifetime, might have been scraping the bottom of the barrel. Is this the Katherine who persists as an embarrassment, the Katherine of whose now much an-thologized 'Bliss' Virginia Woolf could write: 'I dont [sic] see how much faith in her as woman or writer can survive that sort of story'? Yet Virginia's faith did survive, as though the 'superficial smartness', the 'callousness & hardness' of Katherine's writing stayed with her to goad her, not easily thrown aside as the volume itself could be. There is an uneasy theatricality about Virginia's dismissal of 'Bliss': 'I threw down Bliss with the exclamation, "She's done for!"'[4] Katherine's early death at the age of thirty-four only made such gestures even more difficult. The ghost that Brett hoped to see was perhaps merely the spectre of her own guilty and obscene survival.

So what now are we to make of Katherine Mansfield? This volume in particular raises the question, for it contains stories which span a lengthy period – from the earliest of her collected stories, 'The Tiredness of Rosabel' (1908), to a late story written for Clement Shorter of the *Sphere*, 'Sixpence' (1921) – and cover a wide range of her work. There are three of the early New Zealand stories ('The Woman at the Store', 'Ole Underwood' and 'Millie') and the trio of dialogues she wrote in 1917 for Orage's *New Age* ('Late at Night', 'Two Tuppenny Ones, Please' and 'The Black Cap'), as well as a number of satirical sketches in the mode of the *In a German Pension* collection of 1910 ('The Journey to Bruges', 'A Truthful Adventure', 'Pension Séguin', 'Violet' and 'Bains Turcs'). Collected here also are the autobiographical sketches 'An Indiscreet Journey' and 'Carnation' and three stories, along the lines of 'Prelude', which examine little girls' experiences in their families, 'How Pearl Button was Kidnapped', 'New Dresses' and 'The Little Girl'. And this list does not take account of stories such as 'Something Childish but very Natural', 'Spring Pictures', 'A Suburban Fairy Tale', 'See-Saw', 'This Flower', 'The Wrong House' and 'Poison'. Nor does it reflect the cat-egorial complexity, the hybrid nature of an apparently simple story like 'Pearl Button', which engages at once with a Maori context and with a modernist-feminist one. As a collection *Something Childish* is awkward and diverse, presenting a rag-bag Katherine Mansfield, a discontinuous, restless *oeuvre*. 'Nothing of any worth can come from a disunited being,' she wrote discontentedly in February 1922. 'I am a *sham*.'[5] *Something Childish* seems to reflect this feeling of inauthenticity, this exasperated search for an origin and a home. Katherine's self-imposed exile from New Zealand was only the first of many such exiles. First she and Murry, and then she alone, continually moved around England and Europe in search initially of financial and domestic stability, and then of health. Katherine was not at home in her body or in the world. '*Silence* . . . sick persons feel it building up about them, trying to thrust its way into the place of the other.'[6] This sense of intrusion, of illegitimate displacements, was one that would echo not only through Katherine's life, but also through the responses of those who had loved her to Murry's relationship with her manuscripts and papers after her death. For *Something Childish* is only one of the many volumes Murry continued to publish and reissue long after Katherine's bodily ghost had faded from the world.

The posthumous publications began with the appearance in June 1923 of *The Doves' Nest and Other Stories*, five months after Katherine's death. Many of the stories that Murry included are fragments; strangely, he chose to publish them before the finished stories that would appear a year later in *Something Childish*. In the Introductory Note to the latter volume (omitted from the Constable *Collected Stories* but reinstated here), Murry addressed the objection that 'Katherine Mansfield, were she still alive, would not have suffered some of these stories to appear' (p. 5). Indeed, Katherine herself had never published nine of them, all written well before her death (see Note on the Text). Murry's self-justification in his Introductory Note is based on Katherine's own recognition, as he records it, that one day it would be appropriate to publish a collected edition of her works; but the context in which he reports that remark suggests that she was referring not to unpublished stories, but to the early stories in *In a German Pension*, which she had always refused to reprint.[7] With typical clumsiness, Murry's defence only increases the sense that the spirit of Katherine's wishes has been violated, as though he and Katherine were struggling for possession even after her death. Katherine had herself observed that Murry's distaste for her illness partly reflected a dislike of being upstaged by it: 'I, as a tragic figure, outfaced or threatened to outface him . . . He was the one who really wanted *all* the tragedy.'[8] By keeping the dead Katherine in view, Murry also intensified the image of himself as her desolate widower, with an agonizing duty to keep her memory alive. 'Have I kept faith with my darling?' he asked himself in 1950, three marriages later. 'I feel deep in my soul a great joy, because I know that I have . . . I feel strangely that I am in touch with her.'[9] After Katherine's death Murry's financial insecurity was greatly eased by the regular receipt of her royalties – increased, of course, by the periodic publication of new volumes; he commented when he bought the farm in which he and his fourth wife would live that 'it is Katherine who has bought this farm for us.'[10] But to accuse him of failing to carry out her wishes would be to misunderstand the extent to which Murry was in touch with Katherine's own ambivalence about what she might leave behind. It is her anxiety as much as his that reverberates through her posthumous publications.

Katherine left three separate sets of instructions about her literary remains. On 9 September 1919 she wrote to Murry, as she prepared once again to go south for the winter: 'All my Mss. I simply leave to you.' On 7 August 1922, still fearing that she would die of heart disease, she made a more equivocal request:

My heart has been behaving in such a curious fashion that I can't imagine it means nothing. So, as I should hate to leave you unprepared, I'll just try and jot down what comes into my mind. All my manuscripts I leave entirely to you to do what you like with. Go through them one day, dear love, and destroy all you do not use. Please destroy all letters you do not wish to keep and all papers. You know my love of tidiness. Have a clean sweep.

In a formal will made on 14 August 1922 she issued the following instructions: 'All manuscripts note books papers letters I leave to John M. Murry likewise I should like him to publish as little as possible and to tear up and burn as much as possible. He will understand that I desire to leave as few traces of my camping ground as possible.'[11] All three texts leave to Murry the decision as to which papers to burn. Katherine's instinct towards secrecy ('One thing I am determined upon. And that is *to leave no sign.*') struggled with her instinct to hoard and keep papers.[12] Yet she routinely prepared for a journey with a ritual purging: 'Tidied all my papers. Tore up and ruthlessly destroyed much. This is always a great satisfaction. Whenever I prepare for a journey I prepare as though for death.'[13] When her lifelong companion L. M. (Ida Baker) offered

Katherine the letters she had written to L. M. between 1906 and 1908, and between 1914 and 1916, Katherine dismissed them with a curt 'burn them *all*.'[14] Katherine demonstrates all the confusion of the terminally ill, unwilling to relinquish control and yet fearing exposure or erasure: 'Often I reproach myself for my "private" life – which, after all, were I to die, *would* astonish even those nearest to me.'[15] Subsequent biographies by Antony Alpers and Claire Tomalin, detailing Katherine's lovers, her miscarriage and her gonorrhoea, have shown that Katherine's revelations to her intimates were usually partial. By leaving Murry as many personal papers as she did she ensured both that he might come to know a new Katherine after her death and that he would remain preoccupied with her for most of his life.

Murry's reputation as an editor is ambiguous. On the one hand, later editors of Katherine's almost illegible manuscripts have acknowledged his accuracy and care.[16] But Murry's understanding of his own role was not simply to transcribe what he found in the endless notebooks and papers his wife left behind, but to tidy, punctuate, reorder and categorize.[17] He also applied this method to the stories he reprinted and published for the first time: punctuation is rationalized, paragraph breaks are introduced, and dashes and ellipses converted into full stops. Typographically Katherine's writing, as edited by Murry, loses some of its breathlessness, its speed and carelessness. More recently editorial fashions have changed, and the current edition of Katherine's *Collected Letters*, edited by Vincent O'Sullivan and Margaret Scott (3 vols., Clarendon, 1984–93), for the first time precisely reproduces all the irregularities of Katherine's spelling, punctuation and layout. The reader is struck by the density of words on the page, by the writer's impatience with grammatical convention. Murry's sanitization is particularly significant in relation to the stories in which Katherine may be presumed to have given such matters some thought. L. M. claimed that 'she never allowed anyone to alter her work by so much as a comma.'[18] In the present volume, however, I have chosen to keep to the text of the collection as it first appeared in 1924, since as a collection it is almost as much Murry's work as Katherine's.

Murry's editorial work on Katherine's stories was followed by a series of volumes devoted to her private papers: the *Journal* in 1927, two volumes of *Letters* in 1928, the *Scrapbook* in 1939, the *Letters to John Middleton Murry* in 1951 and a 'definitive' and expanded edition of the

Journal in 1954. Publication of her poems and personal papers had been his first thought, almost as soon as Katherine died. Katherine's sister Charlotte wrote to another sister, Vera, in January 1923 that Murry was convinced Katherine's manuscripts would make 'a tremendous stir in literature . . . Constable will take anything he can give them.'[19] To many of Katherine's friends, however, this institutionalization of Katherine as a literary figure betrayed the woman they had known. Immediately after Katherine's death L. M. helped Murry with 'deciphering and typing [Katherine's] more difficult manuscripts', but meeting him some time later, she was anxious to tell him what she thought of his handling of the bequest. 'As he by then was printing everything of Katherine's he could get hold of, including all her private, personal papers, I was angry and told him it was very wrong.'[20] The rift was permanent, and the two did not meet again. D. H. Lawrence, to whom Katherine had been so close when the Lawrences and the Murrys were neighbours on and off between 1914 and 1916, was anxious that Katherine was being mis-represented on aesthetic grounds. 'She was a good writer they made out to be a genius. Katherine knew better herself, but her husband, J. M. Murry, made capital out of her death,' he said in 1925.[21] Lytton Strachey felt that Murry's editing of the first version of the journals falsified Katherine's character: 'why that foul-mouthed, virulent, brazen-faced broomstick of a creature should have got herself up as a pad of rose-scented cotton wool is beyond me.'[22] But all the texts – journals, letters and stories – continued to sell and to receive admiring and respectful reviews.

Objections to Murry's cultivation of his wife's posthumous reputa-tion were on three counts. Firstly, Murry simply published and praised too much. T. S. Eliot wrote of Katherine's 'inflated reputation'; Sylvia Lynd, a friend of the Murrys', of Murry's 'boiling Katherine's bones to make soup'.[23] Critics in a New Zealand that was increasingly closely identified with Katherine's work in European eyes expressed feelings of irritation and shame. 'Mr Middleton Murray [sic] has already done his best to compromise [Katherine] in the minds of the reading public by cramming her incontinently down their throats on every possible occa-sion,' wrote one critic in the *New Zealand Artists' Annual* of 1928.[24] It was thought that both the amount of publicity and the quality of some of the writing Murry was publishing could diminish her in the eyes of her public.

Related to this fear was an anxiety about the terms on which Katherine and her writing were being reconstructed. This was Murry's Katherine, finally more or less under his control and metamorphosed by the pressure of his guilt and grief. Paradoxically, of course, in publishing so much, Murry was also handing her over to readers whose responses he could not predict. But he was defensive, in the Introductions to the *Journal*, the *Letters* and elsewhere, about what seemed to others a betrayal of Katherine's trust and confidence. She was 'a writer whose life and work were one and inseparable', he commented. 'Her letters are essential to a real understanding of her work.'[25]

For some, it was exactly in this identification of the woman with the work, the dissolving of the one into the other, that Murry's betrayal lay. For such as these, Murry's posthumous Katherine – the Katherine who engaged in 'a sustained effort at self-purgation'[26] – was indeed the spectre of a Katherine he had already cheapened during her lifetime. Leonard Woolf:

I think that in some abstruse way Murry corrupted and perverted and destroyed Katherine both as a person and a writer. She was a very serious writer, but her gifts were those of an intense realist, with a superb sense of ironic humour and fundamental cynicism. She got enmeshed in the sticky sentimentality of Murry and wrote against the grain of her own nature.[27]

At the centre of Murry's presentation of Katherine as writer and as woman was a particular sentimentalizing version of her native New Zealand. In the biography of Katherine that he and Ruth Elvish Mantz published in 1933 Murry stressed the way in which Katherine's brother, killed in the war in 1915, became symbolic for her of the country and the childhood she had lost. Murry contended that Katherine's 'genius' was 'deeply rooted in her own country', and drew attention to the journal entry of early 1916 in which she wrote that 'I want to write about my own country till I simply exhaust my store.'[28] For Murry this sense of a 'sacred debt' to her homeland became entwined with his belief in Katherine's gradual self-refinement, her 'progress towards [a] condition of inward clarity'.[29] He wrote that she needed to become reconciled with her own image of New Zealand:

If she could overcome in herself her old resentment against her own country, if her bitterness against it could be dissolved 'in forgiveness of ancient injustice', if she could cease to feel that she personally had been wronged by New Zealand, then the truth and beauty of Life would emerge in it and through her.[30]

'New Zealand' thus ceases to be a newly independent country, a site of racial and cultural conflict, and becomes merely a feature in Katherine's psychic geography. Murry and other critics have taken the modernist family stories, like 'Prelude' and 'At the Bay', as emblematic of Katherine's writerly transactions with her country of origin. The current volume, however, which includes the much earlier, more brutal, stories like 'The Woman at the Store' alongside the portraits of family life in 'New Dresses' and 'The Little Girl', epitomizes the fractured and ambivalent nature of Katherine's relationship with New Zealand and of New Zealand's relationship with her. As Linda Hardy has argued, Katherine Mansfield has functioned in New Zealand writing 'not as a point of origin, nor as the founding term of a national culture, but as a phantasmatic and sometimes troubling sign of displacement'.[31] This insight is true also in reverse: New Zealand for Katherine was both the 'founding term' of her being and a sign of her continual displacement, a reminder that she had no home. Murry, troubled perhaps by his own failure to house Katherine adequately ('how I *loathe* hotels. I know I shall die in one.'),[32] emphasized her internal home-coming, as he saw it, insisting that, if she had no material home, she did at least recover a sense of imaginative belonging.

The present collection includes eight of the stories – 'How Pearl Button was Kidnapped', 'New Dresses', 'The Woman at the Store', 'Ole Underwood', 'The Little Girl', 'Millie', 'The Wrong House' and 'Sixpence' – that Ian Gordon identified as 'New Zealand stories' when he compiled his anthology of Katherine's work, *Undiscovered Country*, in 1974 (Longman). 'How Pearl Button was Kidnapped' is placed second in this volume, after the early 'The Tiredness of Rosabel'. Opening the collection with this London-based story of a young milliner's material deprivation and sexual longings sets up a particular framework for the reading of the New Zealand stories which follow (although not directly and not in sequence). 'Rosabel' is a story about weariness, frustration and the image of an unattainable but endlessly pleasurable world elsewhere. It is a 'psychological sketch',[33] the kind of plotless, symbolist story which the *Yellow Book* published in the 1890s. Rosabel's craving for beauty and luxury means that she disregards physical hunger, going without dinner in order to buy a bunch of violets. The slogans and advertisements that surround her as she sits on the bus – 'How many times had she read these' – suggest that even her desires have been bought. She is physically excited by the clichés in her neighbour's cheap romance; her neighbour, smiling, is simply lost in the book.

The story emphasizes the compulsive nature of such romantic fantasies. Rosabel's thought processes, fluctuating between memory and fantasy, are reproduced without authorial comment, apart from when Rosabel imagines her lover taking her in his arms. Suddenly the real and the phantasmatic body coincide: 'The real Rosabel, the girl crouched on the floor in the dark, laughed aloud, and put her hand up to her hot mouth.' The image of the 'hot mouth' embodies for the reader the intensely sexual nature of Rosabel's responses, which the narrator, whose distancing voice closes the story, will attribute to 'that tragic optimism, which is all too often the only inheritance of youth'. Such an ending breaks the identification between the reader and Rosabel, now exposed as deluded and 'nervous'. Having constructed romantic fantasy as simply an effect of capitalism – Rosabel meets the man she fantasizes about when she sells him a hat – the story further suggests that satisfaction in such a context is inevitably impossible. The girl and Harry cannot find a hat they like and finally buy one not because it pleases them, but because it looks 'adorable' on Rosabel. It is her image, not the hat, that is for sale. Harry, with a 'tinge of insolence', asks if she has ever been painted. Rosabel answers 'shortly', but her real flash of anger is towards the girl, for owning not only the hat that should be Rosabel's, but also the man.

On the face of it this is a proto-feminist story about a working-class woman and the inequity of a socio-economic system that forces Rosabel to choose between violets and dinner, while others can buy a hat simply to wear to lunch (they get the flowers – in this case the 'black velvet rose' *and* the food). But it is also, and much more subtly, a story about the politics and the ambivalent pleasures of fantasy. Is Rosabel's fantasy to be celebrated, immersing her as it does in the 'great wet world' and the heat of desire? Or is she cheated? Is her fantasy pernicious, condemning her as it does to an evening without proper nourishment? Is it itself complicit in exactly the system that degrades her, since she dreams not only of masculine attention, but also of wealth and luxury? And written as the story was on the eve of Katherine's final departure from New Zealand at the age of twenty, does it anticipate some of Katherine's own psychic transactions with a country that had given her as a child and an adolescent just the kind of affluent life of which Rosabel dreams?

The next story in the collection, 'How Pearl Button was Kidnapped', was one of the stories that Murry originally published in 1912 in his periodical *Rhythm*. Reading 'Pearl Button' after 'Rosabel' (which Katherine herself never published) encourages the reader to see it as a parallel story of escape and re-imprisonment. Like Rosabel, Pearl Button lives in a 'House of Boxes' dominated by the routines of commercial life. 'Don't the men go to offices?' she asks her Maori 'kidnappers'. Pearl goes with them willingly because they seem to promise a life of colour, vitality and beauty. She soon discovers a new sensuous pleasure in being carried by one of the women: 'she had a nice smell – a smell that made you bury your head and breathe and breathe it . . .' Her visit to the Maori introduces her to an anarchic world where she is the centre of attention, and where it does not matter that she spills pear juice down her dress. But like Rosabel's, Pearl's pleasures are transient: the police, agents of social control, arrive to take her home.

The word 'Maori' is never mentioned in the story, and some commentators have assumed that Pearl's kidnappers are gypsies.[34] But many textual details identify them as Maori: the characteristic Maori flax basket or 'kete', the greenstone ornament or 'tiki' round the woman's neck and the long braids of the girl in the house by the sea. Ian Gordon suggests that Katherine was drawing on her journal and memories of the camping trip she took through the North Island of New Zealand, during which she made extensive notes on the Maori people she observed and stayed with.[35] She had certainly much more invested in the image of the Maori than most critics have allowed. The stories that clearly seek to represent Maori culture ('Kezia and Tui', 'Maata') are rarely included in anthologies, and 'Pearl Button' itself has been read by one of Katherine's best critics, Kate Fullbrook, as 'pure allegory', and the 'dark people' described as '"people" of the unconscious'.[36]

This repression of Katherine's relationship with the indigenous culture of her homeland is an indication of the 'problem' she poses both for European critics, intent on reclaiming her for modernism, and for critics of a New Zealand tradition.[37] As Linda Hardy puts it, Katherine Mansfield cannot legitimate New Zealand culture in the way that

Shakespeare can English culture: for a start, her grandparents were born in England, and her parents in Australia. In Hardy's words, 'Mansfield has always been associated, in New Zealand, with an orientation toward Europe, and away from that indigenous, Maori culture to which [Janet] Frame is not alone in assigning a unique priority and authenticity.'[38] We have already seen that Katherine too, in 'Pearl Button', implied that the Maori lived close to the wildness and fertility of the earth, that they were the ones who were able, unlike Pearl's parents, to help her find the sea. But Pearl is caught between two tides of blue: 'a great big piece of blue water was creeping over the land' and 'little blue men came running, running towards her with shouts and whistlings.' The narrow strip of land where Pearl stands, between the Maori village by the sea and the colonial city, symbolized by the encroaching crowds of police, is emblematic of the colonial predicament. Pearl can never truly belong to the Maori, and the Maori, although they seem to represent the possibility of a more authentic way of life, look 'in a frightened way towards the House of Boxes' and scream when the police arrive. There is no space between where Pearl can play safely, and in *The Urewera Notebook* Katherine expresses her own sense of discomfort at that transitional space: 'give me the Maori and the tourist but nothing between,' as though she was herself impatient with the 'hybrid' nature of the white settler and the anglicized Maori. In Te Whaiti in 1907 she wrote:

This place proved utterly disappointing after Umuroa which was fascinating in the extreme – The Maoris here know some English and some Maori not like the other natives – Also these people dress in almost English clothes compared with the natives [t]here – and they wear a great deal of ornament in Umuroa and strange hair fashions – I found nothing of interest here.[39]

As a metropolitan white colonial Katherine needed the Maori visibly to represent an autonomous indigenous culture, a culture which could guarantee her a New Zealand which she at once owned and repudiated.

It is important to relocate Katherine in a white-settler society which was still, as she travelled in the interior of the North Island, encountering armed resistance from Maori groups. Katherine associated Maoris with violence. Thinking of the Maori princess, Maata Mahupuku, with whom she had a brief affair, she wrote: 'I alone in this silent clockfilled room have become powerfully – I want Maata – I want her as I have had her – terribly . . . I feel savagely crude.'[40] An image of violence surfaces more publicly in a May 1919 *Athenaeum* review of Somerset Maugham's *The Moon and Sixpence*: 'Strickland cut himself off from the body of life, clumsily, obstinately, savagely, hacking away, regardless of torn flesh, and quivering nerves, like some old Maori warrior separating himself from a shattered limb with a piece of sharp shell.'[41] For Katherine, Maori could symbolize a primal violence and a primitive sexuality.

It is perhaps too simple to dismiss these images as the projections of a racist imagination, although that is undoubtedly partly what they are. From an early date Katherine Mansfield was preoccupied with a sense of New Zealand's difference from Europe; but it was a difference that she could not easily articulate. Commenting on Jane Mander's *The Story of a New Zealand River* in a review of 1920, she noted that 'as is almost invariably the case with novels that have a colonial setting, in spite of the fact that there is frequent allusion to the magnificent scenery, it profiteth us nothing . . . she leans too hard on England.'[42] For Katherine, New Zealand was too easily a place of negation, 'a little land with no history'.[43] Clumsily she tried to project her sense of her own difference from the Europeans with whom she mixed by dressing up as a Maori: 'There was something almost eerie about it, as though of a psychic transformation rather than a mere impersonation,' wrote her first husband, George Bowden (the marriage, in 1909, lasted for only a day).[44] This kind of psychic mobility could signify Katherine's difference to others, but also to herself. For in spite of the occasional pathos of her self-descriptions ('I am the little Colonial walking in the London garden patch – allowed to look, perhaps, but not to linger.'),[45] she also embraced her 'outsider's' perspective, criticizing England with the authority of a visitor:

I love my typical English husband for all the strangeness between us. I *do* lament that he is not warm, ardent, eager, full of quick response, careless, spendthrift of himself, vividly alive, *high-spirited*. But it makes no difference to my love. But the lack of these qualities in his country I HATE – These and others – the lack of its *appeal* – that is what I chiefly hate. I would not care if I never saw the English country again.[46]

The biting satire of the Bavarian sketches published in 1910 in *In a German Pension* could perhaps be read as a displaced attack on England from a woman who had only recently made it her home.

Of course, as with any long relationship, Katherine's feelings towards

New Zealand and towards England were not constant. Some of her shock and wonder at the harshness of the New Zealand pioneers' lives are expressed in the other stories in this volume (apart from 'Pearl Button') which derive from her experiences on the 1907 trip: 'The Woman at the Store' and 'Millie'. If the compilation of the *Something Childish* volume bears witness to Murry's feelings about Katherine after her death, 'The Woman at the Store' marks the initial moment of their friendship, since this was the first of Katherine's stories that Murry, as the young editor of *Rhythm*, ever published, in 1912. Because of it he asked to be introduced to her, and then swiftly became her lodger and finally her lover.

The New Zealand of 'The Woman at the Store' is far from the lush seascape of 'Pearl Button'. This is the country that Katherine herself had ridden through, with its tussock grass, its pumice dust, and its

great masses of charred logs – looking for all the world like strange fantastic beasts a yawning crocodile, a headless horse – a gigantic gosling – a watchdog – to be smiled at and scorned in daylight – but a veritable nightmare in the darkness.[47]

Two men and a woman, riding through the outback for a purpose which is never made clear, stop off for the night at a small trading post where a woman and child live. The discomfort of the journey and the harshness of the landscape symbolize the unforgiving nature of the life in which the woman has found herself, and the sinister revelation of the child's drawing at the end of the story is anticipated at the beginning: 'the sky was slate colour, and the sound of the larks reminded me of slate pencils scraping over its surface.' Just as the child silently spies on the narrator bathing in the stream, so the landscape seems at once expressionless and voyeuristic. Bodies seem to dry out and decay: Jo's red-spotted handkerchief looks as though 'his nose has been bleeding on it,' the woman's body is 'nothing but sticks and wires', the cabbages in her garden smell of 'stale dish-water' and flies buzz round the bedroom.

All these vivid details contribute to the impression that the guilt is not only the woman's, but also the country's. When the narrator dozes off near the beginning she dreams that her mother is scolding her for wearing the pattern off the carpet: the woman's decorative appearance and sexual dexterity have similarly been erased by the pointlessness and loneliness of her life. The child too is 'diseased', with her 'whitish hair and weak eyes'. In true symbolist fashion, as the storm gathers so does the feeling of dread:

There is no twilight in our New Zealand days, but a curious half-hour when everything appears grotesque – it frightens – as though the savage spirit of the country walked abroad and sneered at what it saw. Sitting alone in the hideous room I grew afraid.

The woman has been brutalized by her environment and, in spite of the detective-story thrill of the tale, there is an acute sense of the woman's vulnerability at the hands of historical change and the process of industrialization. As Jim explains, when she and her husband opened the store originally, the coach passed once a fortnight, 'and she had no end of a time!' But once the railway was opened people stopped using the road, and the only people who come through now are 'Maoris and sundowners' or tramps. The woman's violence is explicable not simply in symbolic but also in social terms.

'Millie', published about a year after 'The Woman at the Store' in *Rhythm*'s successor, the *Blue Review*, similarly looks at the plight of the settler woman. Millie's identification with the young fugitive grows out of her sense of her own exposure to the 'burning mirror' of the afternoon sun, her own inarticulate feeling of sorrow. In this story England is explicitly evoked in the print of *Garden Party at Windsor Castle*. The inappropriateness of such an image and Millie's languid reaction to it – 'too much side' – suggest Millie's lack of interest in both her environment and her own life (she 'had almost forgotten her wedding day') and the inescapability of images such as these in colonial New Zealand. The fatuousness of the print is implicitly linked to the homicidal violence of 'the young English "johnny"' as the other side of the same coin.

The youth of the boy hiding behind the woodpile arouses long-suppressed feelings in Millie. The reader is encouraged by an earlier reference to her childlessness to interpret these feelings as maternal rather than sexual, although Millie's decision to hide him reflects her angry thought that 'men is all beasts' who brutalize women and children alike. Her meeting with the fugitive offers Millie the chance of a new intimacy, however fleeting, that stirs her to an awareness of an emotional life she has been denied. 'A strange dreadful feeling gripped Millie Evans' bosom – some seed that had never flourished there, unfolded and struck deep roots and burst into painful leaf.' The boy who brought death to a man brings life to Millie, and she feeds him as though he were her own.

The puzzling ending of the story, when Millie's plans fail and she watches with 'a strange mad joy' as her husband and his friends ride off in pursuit of the boy, could be interpreted in a number of ways. Millie, capable of a momentary tenderness, has none the less been so deadened by her blank and silent life that she no longer has the capacity to sustain emotions of affection or pity (early in the story she says of her husband 'he's softer than me'). She is also seized by a primitive excitement at the thought of the chase and the final killing, as though, living so far from the urbane society represented by *Garden Party at Windsor Castle*, she has reverted to a bestial state of being. Katherine also perceived women as capable of intense sadism and vindictiveness:

that extraordinary vindictive feeling, that relish for little laughter – that comes over women in pain . . . They don't want to spare the one whom they love. If that one loves them with a kind of blind devotion . . . they long to torment him, and this tormenting gives them real positive relief.[48]

Both 'The Woman at the Store' and 'Millie' engage with what Katherine saw as the peculiar dynamics of women's emotional violence, their desire to hurt. In these stories New Zealand becomes the perfect expression of such feminine cruelty and vulnerability; a third story, 'Ole Underwood', also published in *Rhythm* during those early months of her association with Murry, tells the story of a figure who used to terrify Katherine as a child as she walked to school. The New Zealand that Katherine recalled in her mid-twenties was a dangerous place full of racial and sexual conflict. The rawness of these early stories evolved later on into the suppressed violence of portraits like 'At the Bay' and 'The Garden Party'. Haunting those pictures of upper-middle-class colonial life are the ghosts of women like Millie, on whose sacrifice and perversity the affluence of families like the Beauchamps (Katherine's original name) depended.

The writing and publication of the early New Zealand stories marked a significant shift in Katherine's development as an author. The effect of Murry's publication of early stories in two 'haphazard'[49] collections after the end of her life was to occlude the links that Katherine had formed with a succession of different periodicals. Both Murry and Katherine's editor Ian Gordon note that Katherine's early connection with Orage's *New Age* produced her as a particular kind of writer, sardonic and detached.[10] It may have partly been Katherine's restlessness with this image that prompted her to send first a 'Fairy Story' (which Murry rejected) and then 'The Woman at the Store' to *Rhythm* in late 1911, when the magazine was only a few months old. 'The Woman at the Store' is the pivot upon which one of her many transitions turned: a pivot not only in terms of her personal life, since it introduced her to Murry, but also in terms of her development as a writer, since it signalled her shifting cultural allegiances. Katherine's relationships with the different periodicals that published her work – represented in this collection by *New Age*, *Rhythm*, *Blue Review* and *Sphere* – demonstrate the extent to which any writing, but perhaps especially writing in this period, is shaped by the context in which it is published. Just as Murry constructed her in one context when she was dead, so he constructed her in another when she was alive. Or maybe it would be truer to say that she constructed him, for her role in administering, shaping the editorial policy and bearing the financial burdens of *Rhythm* and *Blue Review* is sometimes overlooked in critical accounts of her work at this period. Yet her writing appeared more often than Murry's in the journal they edited together, and their joint editorials speak directly of Katherine's self-reconstruction as a European writer. It is in relation to Millie's New Zealand, which first appeared in *Rhythm*'s pages, that comments like the following, from a *Rhythm* editorial, must be read. Katherine and Murry have characterized the 'mob' as those who are content with the cultural 'known', who prefer to inhabit the 'poverty' of the familiar:

The land whereon these people live is barren and desolate, lying parcelled and monotonous in the midst of an unknown sea. The artists sail in stately golden ships over this familiar and adventurous ocean ... The tiny land folk call to them and beckon them to shore; but the artists see the land that it is barren and miserable, and they sail onwards.[11]

Ambivalence towards New Zealand and a justification of Katherine's leaving it resonate through this account of a far-off island without culture. *Rhythm*'s endorsement of an avant-garde aesthetic (it was founded in response to the Post-Impressionist exhibition of 1910) meant for Katherine a considered repudiation of the New Zealand her teachers at Queen's College in Harley Street had perceived as wild and uncouth.[12] *Rhythm* published the work of Holbrook Jackson, Frank

Harris, Gilbert Cannan, Pablo Picasso, Henri Gaudier-Brzeska and D. H. Lawrence. It was thus a context in which Katherine could feel herself truly part of a European cultural élite, without dependence on the paternal advice of A. R. Orage, editor of the *New Age*, who had fostered her writing in the past. But this symbolic maturity also swiftly introduced her to the chill side of independence: in late 1912 the publisher of *Rhythm* fled, leaving large debts in Murry's name, and Katherine arranged to pay her entire allowance direct to the printers until the debt was cleared. Indeed, *Rhythm*'s financial difficulties displaced Katherine and Murry from their first home together, Runcton Cottage near Chichester, after only a couple of months there. The European identity for which Katherine had turned her back on New Zealand delivered her straight into the instability of the modern publishing industry to which her own writing was so closely linked.

Her shift from the *New Age* to *Rhythm* was not absolute, however. She returned briefly to the *New Age* in 1917 when, at Orage's suggestion, and after a hilarious Christmas performance of a playlet she had written at Ottoline Morrell's house in Garsington, she briefly abandoned prose in favour of dialogue. Orage had lost many of his regular contributors to the war and appealed to old allies like Katherine to help him out. She wrote and gave him 'Late at Night', 'Two Tuppenny Ones, Please' and 'The Black Cap', each a strange mixture of satire and poignancy. The stories with which she began her involvement with *Rhythm* bear witness to her debt to Orage's lover, Beatrice Hastings, who regularly wrote feminist polemics for the *New Age*. 'Millie' and 'The Woman at the Store' are as much indictments of women's isolation and oppression within marriage as they are critiques of settler society. Something of her uncertainty about that indictment comes out in the title story of the present collection which, according to Murry, was the first piece she wrote after the beginning of their relationship. He states that before their meeting 'despair and hopelessness' had inspired her writing. Under the influence of their love 'her work began to change. At first the readjustment was so confusing to her that she could not write at all.' When 'Something Childish but very Natural' did finally emerge it was, in his words, 'saturated with wistful and childlike idealism'.[33]

Leonard Woolf's comment that Katherine became trapped in Murry's 'sticky sentimentality' is endorsed by remarks such as these, which suggest that Murry was a woefully (or wilfully) inadequate reader of Katherine's work. To a modern-day reader, 'Something Childish' is clearly about something much more troubling than childlike idealism. Edna can even be seen as a successor to Millie, with her 'all men is beasts', though Edna's way of putting it is much more subdued: 'it's not that I'm frightened of you – it's not that – it's only a feeling, Henry, that I can't understand myself even.' Edna's sexual ambivalence – her fear of losing the 'childishness' of their relationship – leads logically, even 'naturally', to her ultimate rejection of their mutual fantasy. Murry's desperate recuperation of the story as a meditation on idealism, and his failure to interpret Katherine's own resistance to the piece (it is one of those she never published) has its own poignancy; but it also speaks of Katherine's power to hurt. For 'Something Childish' is far from being an innocent story about fantasy and reality, as more readers than Murry have read it.[14] It is rather an attempt to explore women's sexual reluctance (although according to Alpers it was Murry who was at first uncomfortable with the idea of a full sexual relationship).[15] Whether or not Katherine intended to address difficulties in her own relationship in this, the first story that came directly out of it, is impossible to determine, but she certainly anticipated in it some of her own future experiences: she and Murry were both sustained almost until her death by the fantasy that when she was well they would live together like children in a little house in the country.

'Something Childish' was an attempt to step back from the explicit sexual critiques of 'The Woman at the Store' and 'Millie' into a more oblique and careful style which would still allow Katherine to explore the question of sex within marriage. Her willingness to expose women's sexual hesitancy and fear did not mean, however, that she saw herself as a feminist. Indeed, although Kate Fullbrook claims that feminism 'came [to Katherine] as a matter of course',[16] at many points in her life and writing she displays a powerful hostility to feminists, as in the following unpublished sketch:

I longed to take them [the feminists] home and show them my babies and make their hair soft and fluffy, and put them in teagowns and then cuddle them – I think they would never go back to their Physical Culture, or the Society for the Promotion of Women's Rights.[17]

The aggressive nature of this fantasy of infantilization is reiterated in one of the five '*dame seule*' stories included here, 'A Truthful Adventure', in which the woman traveller denies any interest in the campaign for women's franchise. The awkward and painful tone of all these stories, with their defensive portrayal of the woman traveller's vulnerability and isolation, perhaps grows out of a reluctance explicitly to engage in a feminist critique. The narrator in all five stories approaches her travels with a sardonically detached air, but she muddles the station platform and cannot get a porter to help her ('A Journey to Bruges'), has unwanted companions foisted on her and annoys the boatman ('A Truthful Adventure'), chooses the wrong hotel ('Pension Séguin'), cannot shake off an old schoolfriend ('Violet') and is plagued by the complaints of a stranger ('Bains Turcs'). All these stories ironically dramatize the threatening and annoying encroachment of the outside world on the woman who travels alone. Even Edna in 'Something Childish' encounters sexual interest on the train. However, the tone of the *dame seule* stories is not poignant but self-mocking and satirical, even brittle. It is as though Katherine was not yet ready (as she would be in later stories like 'Miss Brill' and 'The Daughters of the Late Colonel') to confront the true extent of women's helplessness and exposure in the world of tickets and train stations. Katherine was reluctant even in her early healthy days to see herself as a victim and by the end her anger and determination to resist the disease meant that she often disassociated herself from her illness altogether. 'Consumption doesn't belong to me. It's only a horrid stray dog who has persisted in following me for four years,' she wrote to William Gerhardi a year before her death.[18]

Her characteristic repudiation of her own physical fragility – more than once she undertook major journeys when she was simply too weak to travel – was bound up with her ambivalence about the vulnerability of femininity itself. In 1919 she wrote bitterly of 'this illness – getting worse and worse, and turning me into a woman.'[19] Womanhood, and especially girlhood, is seen over and over again in her stories as an uncertain and constraining condition which incites both women and men to violence. Helen, in 'New Dresses', is both frightened and anarchic, her mother Anne vindictive and unfair, and her sister Rose smug and pitiless. Kezia in 'The Little Girl' is similarly terrified by the father whom she ultimately perceives as vulnerable, just like herself. The family is seen in these two stories as the arena in which the violence of sexual difference is played out, often through intergenerational conflict. Masculinity is depicted as an authoritarian and brutalizing force which continually reminds women and girl-children of their physical in-adequacy. After a beating from her father, 'next time [Kezia] saw him she whipped both hands behind her back, and a red colour flew into her cheeks.' For the child every encounter with her father is a beating. So, for Katherine, feminization was an apt metaphor for the debilitating progress of her illness as it lashed her into immobility and submission. By the same token it took a fatal disease to subdue her into acknow-ledgement of her inferior gender, a trajectory that took in infantilization along the way:

We [she and Murry] had been for two years drifting into a relationship, different to anything I had ever known. We'd been *children* to each other, openly con-fessed children, telling each other everything, each depending equally upon the other. Before that I had been the man and he had been the woman and he had been called upon to make no real efforts. He'd never really 'supported' me. When we first met, in fact, it was I who kept him, and afterwards we'd always acted (more or less) like men-friends. Then this illness – getting worse and worse, and turning me into a woman.[60]

In this 1919 journal entry Katherine seems to be criticizing their mutual ideal of childlike, sexless innocence as an illusion exposed by oncoming death. But if we think back to 'Something Childish' we can see that even at the very outset of her relationship with Murry Katherine had her doubts about being children together, although there the idyll is interrupted not by death but by sex. Sex, like death, reminds the body of its own limits, exposes the hollowness of the body that cannot age.

Increasingly Katherine railed against Murry for at once ignoring and hastening her death. Most of all she blamed him for changing. 'In the sea drowned souls sang all night,' she wrote in 1920 from a cottage in Ospedaletti in Italy. 'J. and I are no longer as we were. I love him but he rejects my *living* love. This is anguish. These are the worst days of my whole life.'[61] As she weakened, too tired to do more than 'crawl and creep' about the garden, she began a story about death, another of those that she suppressed and Murry published, called here 'The Wrong House' but originally 'A Strange Mistake'. A funeral procession mis-takenly calls at the wrong house, terrifying its elderly resident. The story opens with an image of Mrs Bean, knitting and sighing, and listening to the clock chime. Death is already present in the photographs she has been shown at the mission of 'repulsive little black objects with bellies shaped like lemons'. The racist terms of her repulsion only partly disguise the fact that it is death as much as the colour of the children's skin that disgusts her. This image of starvation is countered throughout the story by Mrs Bean's desperate thoughts of the chicken her maid Dollicas will cook for supper, as though death can be kept away by eating. As the glass coach stops at the door, in a grotesque parody of the 'Cinderella' story, Mrs Bean is aware that even Dollicas has abandoned her – 'Dollicas surely would have known' – and her terror at her own mortality delivers her into a kind of tomb, 'a cave whose walls were darkness'. When the maid returns, her mistress is 'dazed' and the mission vest she has been knitting lies trampled on the floor, as though in recognition of the inadequacy of her attempts to stave off death.

This meditation on death's random cruelty and her own horror was one of the starkest pieces Katherine ever wrote. Still, her characteristic feeling for metaphor, her feeling for the nightmarishness of everyday life, come through. Like Mrs Bean, Katherine was deserted and left alone to listen to the sea and wait. 'Broke my watch glass . . . The roaring of the sea was insufferable.'[62] When death finally did come it was in the shape of Murry. In her excitement at his arrival in Gurdjieff's Institute in Fontainebleau, where she spent the last months of her life, she bounded up the stairs too fast and collapsed with blood pouring from her mouth. All the doctors could do was to provide hot-water bottles. A fitting tribute, perhaps, to someone who always hated, and refused to give, false comfort.

NOTES ON THE INTRODUCTION

1. *The Diary of Virginia Woolf*, Anne Olivier Bell, ed. (5 vols., Hogarth Press, 1977–84), II, 6 March 1923, p. 238. (Hereafter referred to as *Diary*.)

2. *Diary*, II, 17 October 1924, p. 317.

3. Katherine Middleton Murry, *Beloved Quixote: The Unknown Life of John Middleton Murry* (Souvenir, 1986), pp. 44, 49.

4. *Diary*, I, 7 August 1918, p. 179.

5. *The Journal of Katherine Mansfield*, John Middleton Murry, ed. (Constable, 1954), pp. 293–4. (Hereafter referred to as *Journal*.)

6. *The Scrapbook of Katherine Mansfield*, John Middleton Murry, ed. (Constable, 1939), p. 190.

7. See Introductory Note (p. 5): 'When she was urged to allow *In a German Pension* to be republished, she would always reply: "Not now . . . When the time for a collected edition comes –".'

8. *Journal*, p. 185.

9. Cited in Katherine Middleton Murry, *Beloved Quixote*, p. 42.

10. Cited in C. K. Stead, Introduction to *Katherine Mansfield: Letters and Journals*, C. K. Stead, ed. (Penguin, 1977), p. 11.

11. Cited in Antony Alpers, *The Life of Katherine Mansfield* (Oxford University Press, 1982), pp. 298, 365, 366.

12. *Journal*, p. 254; and see Ian A. Gordon, Introduction to Katherine Mansfield, *The Urewera Notebook* (Oxford University Press, 1978), pp. 14–16.

13. *Journal*, p. 292.

14. Ida Baker, *Katherine Mansfield: The Memories of LM* (Michael Joseph, 1971), pp. 126–7.

15. *Journal*, p. 165.

16. See *Katherine Mansfield: Letters and Journals*, p. 13.

17. See Gillian Boddy, 'Editing the Notebooks of Katherine Mansfield: Some Preliminary Observations', in *Editing in Australia*, Paul Eggert, ed. (New South Wales University Press, 1990), pp. 191–7, p. 193.

18. Ida Baker, *Katherine Mansfield: The Memories of LM*, p. 73.

19. Cited in Boddy, 'Editing the Notebooks of Katherine Mansfield', *Editing in Australia*, p. 191.

20. Ida Baker, *Katherine Mansfield: The Memories of LM*, pp. 207–8.

21. Cited in Claire Tomalin, *Katherine Mansfield: A Secret Life* (Viking, 1987), p. 240.

22. Cited in Michael Holroyd, *Lytton Strachey: A Biography* (2nd edn, Penguin, 1979), p. 928.

23. Cited in Claire Tomalin, *Katherine Mansfield*, pp. 240–41.

24. Cited in Dennis McEldowney, 'The Multiplex Effect: Recent Biographical Writing on Katherine Mansfield', *Ariel*, 16 (October 1985), pp. 111–24, p. 112.

25. John Middleton Murry, *Katherine Mansfield and Other Literary Studies* (Constable, 1959), p. 71.

26. Ibid., p. 81.

27. Leonard Woolf, *Beginning Again: An Autobiography of the Years 1911–1918* (Hogarth, 1964), p. 204.

28. Ruth Elvish Mantz and John Middleton Murry, *The Life of Katherine Mansfield* (Constable, 1933), p. 2; *Journal*, pp. 93–4.

29. John Middleton Murry, *Katherine Mansfield and Other Literary Studies*, p. 81.

30. Ibid., pp. 83–4.

31. Linda Hardy, 'The Ghost of Katherine Mansfield', *Landfall*, 43 (December 1989), pp. 416–32, p. 420.

32. Katherine Mansfield to Ottoline Morrell, *The Letters of Katherine Mansfield*, John Middleton Murry, ed. (2 vols., Constable, 1928), I, 24 May 1918, p. 177.

33. Clare Hanson and Andrew Gurr, *Katherine Mansfield* (St Martin's Press, 1981), p. 29.

34. Rhoda B. Nathan, *Katherine Mansfield* (Continuum, 1988), p. 121.

35. See Ian A. Gordon, Introduction to Katherine Mansfield, *The Urewera Notebook*, pp. 28–9.

36. Kate Fullbrook, *Katherine Mansfield* (Harvester Wheatsheaf, 1986), pp. 41, 43.

37. See, for example, W. H. New, *Dreams of Speech and Violence: The Art of the Short Story in Canada and New Zealand* (University of Toronto Press, 1987), p. 113: 'The problem, in writing a history of New Zealand short fiction, is Katherine Mansfield.'

38. See Linda Hardy, 'The Ghost of Katherine Mansfield', *Landfall*, 43, p. 427.

39. Katherine Mansfield, *The Urewera Notebook*, p. 61.

40. Cited in Antony Alpers, *The Life of Katherine Mansfield*, p. 49.

41. Cited in *The Critical Writings of Katherine Mansfield*, Clare Hanson, ed. (Macmillan, 1987), pp. 51–2.

42. Ibid., p. 102.

43. 'To Stanislaw Wyspianski', *Katherine Mansfield: Letters and Journals*, p. 39.

44. George Bowden, 'A Biographical Note on Katherine Mansfield' (1948), cited in C. A. Hankin, *Katherine Mansfield and Her Confessional Stories* (Macmillan, 1983), p. 93.

45. *Journal*, p. 157.

46. Ibid., pp. 158–9.

47. Katherine Mansfield, *The Urewera Notebook*, p. 34.

48. *Journal*, p. 111.

49. Ian A. Gordon, Introduction to *Undiscovered Country: The New Zealand Stories of Katherine Mansfield* (Longman, 1974), p. xiii.

50. John Middleton Murry, Introductory Note to Katherine Mansfield, *Poems* (2nd edn, Constable, 1930), p. xiii: '[Orage] wanted her to write nothing but satirical prose'; Katherine Mansfield, *The Urewera Notebook*, p. 30.

51. Katherine Mansfield and John Middleton Murry, 'Seriousness in Art', *Rhythm*, 6 (July 1912), cited in *The Critical Writings of Katherine Mansfield*, p. 25.

52. See *Journal*, p. 105: '[the Principal of Queen's] asked any young lady in the room to hold up her hand if she had been chased by a wild bull, and as nobody else did I held up mine (though of course I hadn't). "Ah," he said, "I am afraid you do not count. You are a little savage from New Zealand."'

53. John Middleton Murry, *Katherine Mansfield and Other Literary Studies*, p. 75.

54. Cherry Hankin, 'Fantasy and the Sense of an Ending in the Work of Katherine Mansfield', *Modern Fiction Studies*, 24 (Autumn 1978), pp. 465–74, p. 471.

55. See Antony Alpers, *The Life of Katherine Mansfield*, p. 140.

56. Kate Fullbrook, *Katherine Mansfield*, p. 22.

57. Cited in Clare Hanson, Introduction to *The Critical Writings of Katherine Mansfield*, p. 19.

58. Katherine Mansfield to William Gerhardi, *The Letters of Katherine Mansfield*, II, 21 November 1921, p. 157.

59. *Journal*, p. 183.

60. Ibid.

61. *Journal*, p. 192.

62. Ibid.

Further Reading

MANSFIELD'S WRITING

The Letters of Katherine Mansfield, John Middleton Murry, ed. (2 vols., Constable, 1928)

The Scrapbook of Katherine Mansfield, John Middleton Murry, ed. (Constable, 1939)

Katherine Mansfield's Letters to John Middleton Murry 1913–1922, John Middleton Murry, ed. (Constable, 1951)

The Journal of Katherine Mansfield (Definitive Edition), John Middleton Murry, ed. (1st edn, Constable, 1927; Definitive edn, Constable, 1954)

Katherine Mansfield: Letters and Journals, C. K. Stead, ed. (Penguin, 1977)

The Urewera Notebook, Ian A. Gordon, ed. (Oxford University Press, 1978)

[Contains text of the diary Mansfield kept during the camping trip in North Island in November and December 1907, which inspired the 'New Zealand stories' in this volume: 'The Woman at the Store', 'Ole Underwood' and 'Millie'.]

The Stories of Katherine Mansfield, Antony Alpers, ed. (Oxford University Press, 1984)

The Collected Letters of Katherine Mansfield, Vincent O'Sullivan and Margaret Scott, eds., 3 vols. (Clarendon, 1984–93)

The Critical Writings of Katherine Mansfield, Clare Hanson, ed. (Macmillan, 1987)

[Contains essays, reviews and journal extracts, with a useful Introduction.]

BIOGRAPHIES

Alpers, Antony, *The Life of Katherine Mansfield* (Oxford University Press, 1982)

Baker, Ida, *Katherine Mansfield: The Memories of LM* (Michael Joseph, 1971)

Mantz, Ruth Elvish and Middleton Murry, J., *The Life of Katherine Mansfield* (Constable, 1933)

Tomalin, Claire, *Katherine Mansfield: A Secret Life* (Viking, 1987)

CRITICAL DISCUSSIONS

Carter, Angela, 'The Life of Katherine Mansfield', *Nothing Sacred: Selected Writings* (Virago, 1982), pp. 158–61

Fullbrook, Kate, *Katherine Mansfield* (Harvester Wheatsheaf, 1986)

Hankin, Cherry, 'Fantasy and the Sense of an Ending in the Work of Katherine Mansfield', *Modern Fiction Studies*, 24 (Autumn 1978), pp. 465–74

—*Katherine Mansfield and Her Confessional Stories* (Macmillan, 1983)

Hanson, Clare, *Short Stories and Short Fictions, 1880–1980* (Macmillan, 1985)

Hanson, Clare and Gurr, Andrew, *Katherine Mansfield* (St Martin's Press, 1981)

Hardy, Linda, 'The Ghost of Katherine Mansfield', *Landfall*, 43 (December 1989), pp. 416–32

Ihimaera, Witi, *Dear Miss Mansfield* (Viking, 1987)

Kaplan, Sydney Janet, *Katherine Mansfield and the Origins of Modernist Fiction* (Cornell University Press, 1991)

Nathan, Rhoda B., *Critical Essays on Katherine Mansfield* (G. K. Hall, 1993)

Pratt, Mary Louise, 'The Short Story: The Long and the Short of It', *Poetics*, 10 (1981), pp. 175–94

Wevers, Lydia, 'The Short Story', *The Oxford History of New Zealand Literature in English*, Terry Sturm, ed. (Oxford University Press, 1991), pp. 215–22

Note on the Text

Something Childish and Other Stories was first published posthumously in Britain on 21 August 1924 (Mansfield died on 9 January 1923).[1] Her husband, John Middleton Murry, was responsible for putting together and editing the collection. Of the twenty-five stories he included, nine had remained unpublished during Mansfield's lifetime ('The Tiredness of Rosabel', 'Something Childish but very Natural', 'An Indiscreet Journey', 'Spring Pictures', 'A Suburban Fairy Tale', 'See-Saw', 'This Flower', 'The Wrong House' and 'Poison'). The others had already been published by Mansfield in a variety of periodicals, including *Rhythm*, *New Age*, *Blue Review*, the *Nation* and *Sphere* (details of periodical publication are given in the Notes). Of the unpublished stories, Murry published 'The Tiredness of Rosabel', 'Something Childish but very Natural', 'A Suburban Fairy Tale', 'See-Saw' and 'Poison' mostly in his own periodical, *Adelphi*, during the time between Mansfield's death and the publication of the *Something Childish* volume nineteen months later. Holograph and typescript versions of a few of the stories ('The Tiredness of Rosabel', 'Spring Pictures', 'A Suburban Fairy Tale', 'Carnation', 'See-Saw', 'This Flower', 'The Wrong House' and 'Poison') exist in the Newberry Library, Chicago, the Alexander Turnbull Library (National Library of New Zealand) and the British Museum. The British edition of this volume was reprinted in 1929, 1932 and 1936. The first American edition, entitled *The Little Girl and Other Stories*, was published on 19 October 1924 and reprinted later in 1924 and in 1931. In 1945 all five volumes of Katherine Mansfield's stories were republished together in a Constable edition, *The Collected Stories of Katherine Mansfield*. There have also been a number of selections published, some of which include one or more of the *Something Childish* stories.

The present volume follows the text of the first British edition since, although Murry made some alterations to the versions of the stories his wife had already published, *Something Childish* as an anthology is his work as well as hers. Minor changes have been introduced in order that this edition conforms to Penguin house style: three-point ellipses, single external quotation marks, the elision of full points after contractions, and spaced N-dashes. In addition, story titles have been put within quotes, volume titles and French phrases in italics, obsolete spellings modernized and inconsistencies and obvious errors silently corrected. It is not always clear that Mansfield had necessarily authorized the original punctuation of the stories, some of which may have gone into print without being submitted to her for final approval. When Murry was preparing many of the stories for publication in *Something Childish*, he substantially altered the punctuation of both previously published and unpublished versions, adding commas, introducing paragraph breaks, substituting commas for dashes and introducing ellipses and hyphens. The cumulative effect is a much more standard prose style, with more orthodox punctuation and spelling. Mansfield's more experimental and informal prose has far fewer paragraph breaks, is denser on the page and gives a greater impression of breathlessness and informality. It has not been possible here to include details of every change, but I have included, in the notes to 'The Woman at the Store', a sample paragraph of the original version so that interested readers can get an impression of Mansfield's original prose. Murry also occasionally changed words or names of characters, and I have given details of such changes in the notes. Where there are other substantial differences between the periodical, typescript or holograph versions of the stories and the text as it appears here, I have included information about variants in the Notes.

In 1984 Antony Alpers edited a new selection of Mansfield's stories for Oxford University Press, *The Stories of Katherine Mansfield*, which in most cases reprints the periodical versions. Readers who are interested to see the stories as they first appeared should consult this volume, which reprints all the *Something Childish* stories apart from 'New Dresses', 'A Suburban Fairy Tale', 'See-Saw', 'This Flower' and 'The Wrong House'.

1. I am indebted here, and throughout the edition, to B. J. Kirkpatrick's excellent *A Bibliography of Katherine Mansfield* (Clarendon, 1989).

Facsimile of title page of first edition

SOMETHING
CHILDISH
AND OTHER STORIES
BY
KATHERINE
MANSFIELD

*A little bird was asked: Why are your
songs so short? He replied: I have many
songs to sing, and I should like to sing
them all.*
ANTON TCHEHOV

CONSTABLE & CO. LTD.
LONDON

To H. M. Tomlinson

Introductory Note

Most of the stories and sketches in this collection were written in the years between the publication of Katherine Mansfield's first book, *In a German Pension*, in 1911 and the publication of her second, *Bliss and Other Stories*, in 1920. There are a few exceptions. The first story, 'The Tiredness of Rosabel', was written in 1908 when Katherine Mansfield was nineteen years old, and the three stories following also were written before *In a German Pension* was published: while 'Sixpence' and 'Poison' were written after *Bliss* had appeared. 'Sixpence' was excluded from *The Garden Party and Other Stories* by Katherine Mansfield because she thought it 'sentimental'; 'Poison' was excluded because I thought it was not wholly successful. I have since changed my mind: it now seems to me a little masterpiece.

I have no doubt that Katherine Mansfield, were she still alive, would not have suffered some of these stories to appear. When she was urged to allow *In a German Pension* to be republished, she would always reply: 'Not now; not yet – not until I have a body of work done and it can be seen in perspective. It is not true of me now: I am not like that any more. When the time for a collected edition comes –' she would end, laughing. The time has come.

The stories are arranged in chronological order.

J. M. M.

The Tiredness of Rosabel

At the corner of Oxford Circus Rosabel bought a bunch of violets, and that was practically the reason why she had so little tea – for a scone and a boiled egg and a cup of cocoa at Lyons[1] are not ample sufficiency after a hard day's work in a millinery establishment. As she swung on to the step of the Atlas 'bus,[2] grabbed her skirt with one hand and clung to the railing with the other, Rosabel thought she would have sacrificed her soul for a good dinner – roast duck and green peas, chestnut stuffing, pudding with brandy sauce – something hot and strong and filling. She sat down next to a girl very much her own age who was reading *Anna Lombard*[3] in a cheap, paper-covered edition, and the rain had tear-spattered the pages. Rosabel looked out of the windows; the street was blurred and misty, but light striking on the panes turned their dullness to opal and silver, and the jewellers' shops seen through this, were fairy palaces. Her feet were horribly wet, and she knew the bottom of her skirt and petticoat would be coated with black, greasy mud. There was a sickening smell of warm humanity – it seemed to be oozing out of everybody in the 'bus – and everybody had the same expression, sitting so still, staring in front of them. How many times had she read these advertisements – 'Sapolio[4] Saves Time, Saves Labour' – 'Heinz's Tomato Sauce'[5] – and the inane, annoying dialogue between doctor and judge concerning the superlative merits of 'Lamplough's Pyretic Saline.'[6] She glanced at the book which the girl read so earnestly, mouthing the words in a way that Rosabel detested, licking her first finger and thumb each time that she turned the page. She could not see very clearly; it was something about a hot, voluptuous night, a band playing, and a girl with lovely, white shoulders. Oh, Heavens! Rosabel stirred suddenly and un-fastened the two top buttons of her coat ... she felt almost stifled. Through her half-closed eyes the whole row of people on the opposite seat seemed to resolve into one fatuous, staring face ...

And this was her corner. She stumbled a little on her way out and lurched against the girl next her. 'I beg your pardon,' said Rosabel, but the girl did not even look up. Rosabel saw that she was smiling as she read.

6

Westbourne Grove looked as she had always imagined Venice to look at night, mysterious, dark, even the hansoms were like gondolas dodging up and down, and the lights trailing luridly – tongues of flame licking the wet street – magic fish swimming in the Grand Canal. She was more than glad to reach Richmond Road, but from the corner of the street until she came to No. 26 she thought of those four flights of stairs. Oh, why four flights! It was really criminal to expect people to live so high up. Every house ought to have a lift, something simple and inexpensive, or else an electric staircase like the one at Earl's Court[7] – but four flights! When she stood in the hall and saw the first flight ahead of her and the stuffed albatross head on the landing, glimmering ghost-like in the light of the little gas jet, she almost cried. Well, they had to be faced; it was very like bicycling up a steep hill, but there was not the satisfaction of flying down the other side . . .

Her own room at last! She closed the door, lit the gas, took off her hat and coat, skirt, blouse, unhooked her old flannel dressing-gown from behind the door, pulled it on, then unlaced her boots – on consideration her stockings were not wet enough to change. She went over to the wash-stand. The jug had not been filled again to-day. There was just enough water to soak the sponge, and the enamel was coming off the basin – that was the second time she had scratched her chin.

It was just seven o'clock. If she pulled the blind up and put out the gas it was much more restful – Rosabel did not want to read. So she knelt down on the floor, pillowing her arms on the window-sill . . . just one little sheet of glass between her and the great wet world outside!

She began to think of all that had happened during the day. Would she ever forget that awful woman in the grey mackintosh who had wanted a trimmed motor-cap[8] – 'something purple with something rosy each side' – or the girl who had tried on every hat in the shop and then said she would 'call in to-morrow and decide definitely.' Rosabel could not help smiling; the excuse was worn so thin . . .

But there had been one other – a girl with beautiful red hair and a white skin and eyes the colour of that green ribbon shot with gold they had got from Paris last week. Rosabel had seen her electric brougham[9] at the door; a man had come in with her, quite a young man, and so well dressed.

'What is it exactly that I want, Harry?' she had said, as Rosabel took the pins out of her hat, untied her veil, and gave her a hand-mirror.

'You must have a black hat,' he had answered, 'a black hat with a feather that goes right round it and then round your neck and ties in a bow under your chin, and the ends tuck into your belt – a decent-sized feather.'

The girl glanced at Rosabel laughingly. 'Have you any hats like that?'

They had been very hard to please; Harry would demand the impossible, and Rosabel was almost in despair. Then she remembered the big, untouched box upstairs.

'Oh, one moment, Madam,' she had said. 'I think perhaps I can show you something that will please you better.' She had run up, breathlessly, cut the cords, scattered the tissue paper, and yes, there was the very hat – rather large, soft, with a great, curled feather, and a black velvet rose, nothing else. They had been charmed. The girl had put it on and then handed it to Rosabel.

'Let me see how it looks on you,' she said, frowning a little, very serious indeed.

Rosabel turned to the mirror and placed it on her brown hair, then faced them.

'Oh, Harry, isn't it adorable,' the girl cried, 'I must have that!' She smiled again at Rosabel. 'It suits you, beautifully.'

A sudden, ridiculous feeling of anger had seized Rosabel. She longed to throw the lovely, perishable thing in the girl's face, and bent over the hat, flushing.

'It's exquisitely finished off inside, Madam,' she said. The girl swept out to her brougham, and left Harry to pay and bring the box with him.

'I shall go straight home and put it on before I come out to lunch with you,' Rosabel heard her say.

The man leant over her as she made out the bill, then, as he counted the money into her hand – 'Ever been painted?' he said.

'No,' said Rosabel, shortly, realising the swift change in his voice, the slight tinge of insolence, of familiarity.

'Oh, well you ought to be,' said Harry. 'You've got such a damned pretty little figure.'

Rosabel did not pay the slightest attention. How handsome he had been! She had thought of no one else all day; his face fascinated her; she could see clearly his fine, straight eyebrows, and his hair grew back from his forehead with just the slightest suspicion of crisp curl, his laughing, disdainful mouth. She saw again his slim hands counting the money into hers ... Rosabel suddenly pushed the hair back from her face, her forehead was hot ... if those slim hands could rest one moment ... the luck of that girl!

Suppose they changed places. Rosabel would drive home with him, of course they were in love with each other, but not engaged, very nearly, and she would say – 'I won't be one moment.' He would wait in the brougham while her maid took the hat-box up the stairs, following Rosabel. Then the great, white and pink bedroom with roses every-where in dull silver vases. She would sit down before the mirror and the little French maid would fasten her hat and find her a thin, fine veil and another pair of white suède gloves – a button had come off the gloves she had worn that morning. She had scented her furs and gloves and handkerchief, taken a big muff and run down stairs. The butler opened the door, Harry was waiting, they drove away together ... *That* was life, thought Rosabel! On the way to the Carlton[10] they stopped at Gerard's,[11] Harry bought her great sprays of Parma violets, filled her hands with them.

'Oh, they are sweet!' she said, holding them against her face.

'It is as you always should be,' said Harry, 'with your hands full of violets.'

(Rosabel realised that her knees were getting stiff; she sat down on the floor and leant her head against the wall.) Oh, that lunch! The table covered with flowers, a band hidden behind a grove of palms playing music that fired her blood like wine – the soup, and oysters, and pigeons, and creamed potatoes, and champagne, of course, and afterwards coffee and cigarettes. She would lean over the table fingering her glass with one hand, talking with that charming gaiety which Harry so appreciated. Afterwards a matinee, something that gripped them both, and then tea at the 'Cottage.'[12]

'Sugar? Milk? Cream?' The little homely questions seemed to suggest a joyous intimacy. And then home again in the dusk, and the scent of the Parma violets seemed to drench the air with their sweetness.

'I'll call for you at nine,' he said as he left her.

The fire had been lighted in her boudoir, the curtains drawn, there were a great pile of letters waiting her – invitations for the Opera, dinners, balls, a week-end on the river, a motor tour – she glanced through them listlessly as she went upstairs to dress. A fire in her bed-room, too, and her beautiful, shining dress spread on the bed – white tulle[13] over silver, silver shoes, silver scarf, a little silver fan. Rosabel knew that she was the most famous woman at the ball that night; men paid her homage, a foreign Prince desired to be presented to this English wonder. Yes, it was a voluptuous night, a band playing, and *her* lovely white shoulders . . .

But she became very tired. Harry took her home, and came in with her for just one moment. The fire was out in the drawing-room, but the sleepy maid waited for her in her boudoir. She took off her cloak, dismissed the servant, and went over to the fireplace, and stood peeling off her gloves; the firelight shone on her hair, Harry came across the room and caught her in his arms – 'Rosabel, Rosabel, Rosabel' . . . Oh, the haven of those arms, and she was very tired.

(The real Rosabel, the girl crouched on the floor in the dark, laughed aloud, and put her hand up to her hot mouth.)

Of course they rode in the park next morning, the engagement had been announced in the *Court Circular*,[14] all the world knew, all the world was shaking hands with her . . .

They were married shortly afterwards at St George's, Hanover Square,[15] and motored down to Harry's old ancestral home for the honeymoon; the peasants in the village curtseyed to them as they passed; under the folds of the rug he pressed her hands convulsively. And that night she wore again her white and silver frock. She was tired after the journey and went upstairs to bed . . . quite early . . .

The real Rosabel got up from the floor and undressed slowly, folding her clothes over the back of a chair. She slipped over her head her coarse, calico nightdress, and took the pins out of her hair – the soft, brown flood of it fell round her, warmly. Then she blew out the candle and groped her way into bed, pulling the blankets and grimy 'honeycomb' quilt[16] closely round her neck, cuddling down in the darkness . . .

So she slept and dreamed, and smiled in her sleep, and once threw out her arm to feel for something which was not there, dreaming still.

And the night passed. Presently the cold fingers of dawn closed over her uncovered hand; grey light flooded the dull room. Rosabel shivered, drew a little gasping breath, sat up. And because her heritage was that tragic optimism, which is all too often the only inheritance of youth, still half asleep, she smiled, with a little nervous tremor round her mouth.

(1908)

How Pearl Button was Kidnapped

Pearl Button swung on the little gate in front of the House of Boxes. It was the early afternoon of a sunshiny day with little winds playing hide-and-seek in it. They blew Pearl Button's pinafore frill into her mouth, and they blew the street dust all over the House of Boxes. Pearl watched it – like a cloud – like when mother peppered her fish and the top of the pepper-pot came off. She swung on the little gate, all alone, and she sang a small song. Two big women came walking down the street. One was dressed in red and the other was dressed in yellow and green. They had pink handkerchiefs over their heads, and both of them carried a big flax basket[1] of ferns. They had no shoes and stockings on, and they came walking along, slowly, because they were so fat, and talking to each other and always smiling. Pearl stopped swinging, and when they saw her they stopped walking. They looked and looked at her and then they talked to each other, waving their arms and clapping their hands together. Pearl began to laugh.

The two women came up to her, keeping close to the hedge and looking in a frightened way towards the House of Boxes.

'Hallo, little girl!' said one.

Pearl said, 'Hallo!'

'You all alone by yourself?'

Pearl nodded.

'Where's your mother?'

'In the kitching, ironing-because-its-Tuesday.'

The women smiled at her and Pearl smiled back. 'Oh,' she said, 'haven't you got very white teeth indeed! Do it again.'

The dark women laughed, and again they talked to each other with funny words and wavings of the hands. 'What's your name?' they asked her.

'Pearl Button.'

'You coming with us, Pearl Button? We got beautiful things to show you,' whispered one of the women. So Pearl got down from the gate and she slipped out into the road. And she walked between the two dark women down the windy road, taking little running steps to keep up, and wondering what they had in their House of Boxes.

They walked a long way. 'You tired?' asked one of the women, bending down to Pearl. Pearl shook her head. They walked much further. 'You not tired?' asked the other woman. And Pearl shook her head again, but tears shook from her eyes at the same time and her lips trembled. One of the women gave over her flax basket of ferns and caught Pearl Button up in her arms, and walked with Pearl Button's head against her shoulder and her dusty little legs dangling. She was softer than a bed and she had a nice smell – a smell that made you bury your head and breathe and breathe it . . .

They set Pearl Button down in a log room full of other people the same colour as they were – and all these people came close to her and looked at her, nodding and laughing and throwing up their eyes. The woman who had carried Pearl took off her hair ribbon and shook her curls loose. There was a cry from the other women, and they crowded close and some of them ran a finger through Pearl's yellow curls, very gently, and one of them, a young one, lifted all Pearl's hair and kissed the back of her little white neck. Pearl felt shy but happy at the same time. There were some men on the floor, smoking, with rugs and feather mats round their shoulders. One of them made a funny face at her and he pulled a great big peach out of his pocket and set it on the floor, and flicked it with his finger as though it were a marble. It rolled right over to her. Pearl picked it up. 'Please can I eat it?' she asked. At that they all laughed and clapped their hands, and the man with the funny face made another at her and pulled a pear out of his pocket and sent it bobbling over the floor. Pearl laughed. The women sat on the floor and Pearl sat down too. The floor was very dusty. She carefully pulled up her pinafore and dress and sat on her petticoat as she had been taught to sit in dusty places, and she ate the fruit, the juice running all down her front.

'Oh!' she said in a very frightened voice to one of the women, 'I've spilt all the juice!'

'That doesn't matter at all,' said the woman, patting her cheek. A man came into the room with a long whip in his hand. He shouted something. They all got up, shouting, laughing, wrapping themselves up in rugs and blankets and feather mats. Pearl was carried again, this time into a great cart, and she sat on the lap of one of her women with the driver beside her. It was a green cart with a red pony and a black pony. It went very fast out of the town. The driver stood up and waved the whip round his head. Pearl peered over the shoulder of her woman. Other carts were behind like a procession. She waved at them. Then the country came. First fields of short grass with sheep on them and little bushes of white flowers and pink briar rose baskets – then big trees on both sides of the road – and nothing to be seen except big trees. Pearl tried to look through them but it was quite dark. Birds were singing. She nestled closer in the big lap. The woman was warm as a cat, and she moved up and down when she breathed, just like purring. Pearl played with a green ornament[2] round her neck, and the woman took the little hand and kissed each of her fingers and then turned it over and kissed the dimples. Pearl had never been happy like this before. On the top of a big hill they stopped. The driving man turned to Pearl and said, 'Look, look!' and pointed with his whip.

And down at the bottom of the hill was something perfectly different – a great big piece of blue water was creeping over the land. She screamed and clutched at the big woman, 'What is it, what is it?'

'Why,' said the woman, 'it's the sea.'

'Will it hurt us – is it coming?'

'Ai-e, no, it doesn't come to us. It's very beautiful. You look again.'

Pearl looked. 'You're sure it can't come,' she said.

'Ai-e, no. It stays in its place,' said the big woman. Waves with white tops came leaping over the blue. Pearl watched them break on a long piece of land covered with garden-path shells. They drove round a corner.

There were some little houses down close to the sea, with wood fences round them and gardens inside. They comforted her. Pink and red and blue washing hung over the fences, and as they came near more people came out, and five yellow dogs with long thin tails. All the people were fat and laughing, with little naked babies holding on to them or rolling about in the gardens like puppies. Pearl was lifted down and taken into a tiny house with only one room and a verandah. There was a girl there with two pieces of black hair down to her feet.[3] She was setting the dinner on the floor. 'It *is* a funny place,' said Pearl, watching the pretty girl while the woman unbuttoned her little drawers for her. She was very hungry. She ate meat and vegetables and fruit and the woman gave her milk out of a green cup. And it was quite silent except for the sea outside and the laughs of the two women watching her. 'Haven't you got any Houses of Boxes?' she said. 'Don't you all live in a row? Don't the men go to offices? Aren't there any nasty things?'

They took off her shoes and stockings, her pinafore and dress. She walked about in her petticoat and then she walked outside with the grass pushing between her toes. The two women came out with different sorts of baskets. They took her hands. Over a little paddock, through a fence, and then on warm sand with brown grass in it they went down to the sea. Pearl held back when the sand grew wet, but the women coaxed, 'Nothing to hurt, very beautiful. You come.' They dug in the sand and found some shells which they threw into the baskets. The sand was wet as mud pies. Pearl forgot her fright and began digging too. She got hot and wet, and suddenly over her feet broke a little line of foam. 'Oo, oo!' she shrieked, dabbling with her feet, 'Lovely, lovely!' She paddled in the shallow water. It was warm. She made a cup of her hands and caught some of it. But it stopped being blue in her hands. She was so excited that she rushed over to her woman and flung her little thin arms round the woman's neck, hugging her, kissing . . .

Suddenly the girl gave a frightful scream. The woman raised herself and Pearl slipped down on the sand and looked towards the land. Little men in blue coats – little blue men came running, running towards her with shouts and whistlings – a crowd of little blue men to carry her back to the House of Boxes.

(1910)

'You got three-quarters of an hour,' said the porter. 'You got an hour mostly. Put it in the cloak-room, lady.'

A German family, their luggage neatly buttoned into what appeared to be odd canvas trouser legs, filled the entire space before the counter, and a homoeopathic[1] young clergyman, his black dicky[2] flapping over his shirt, stood at my elbow. We waited and waited, for the cloak-room porter could not get rid of the German family, who appeared by their enthusiasm and gestures to be explaining to him the virtue of so many buttons. At last the wife of the party seized her particular packet and started to undo it. Shrugging his shoulders, the porter turned to me. 'Where for?' he asked.

'Ostend.'

'Wot are you putting it in here for?'

I said, 'Because I've a long time to wait.'

He shouted, 'Train's in 2.20. No good bringing it here. Hi, you there, lump it off!'

My porter lumped it. The young clergyman, who had listened and remarked, smiled at me radiantly. 'The train is in,' he said, 'really in. You've only a few moments, you know.' My sensitiveness glimpsed a symbol in his eye. I ran to the book-stall. When I returned I had lost my porter. In the teasing heat I ran up and down the platform. The whole travelling world seemed to possess a porter and glory in him except me. Savage and wretched I saw them watch me with that delighted relish of the hot in the very much hotter. 'One could have a fit running in weather like this,' said a stout lady, eating a farewell present of grapes. Then I was informed that the train was not yet in. I had been running up and down the Folkestone express. On a higher platform I found my porter sitting on the suitcase.

'I knew you'd be doin' that,' he said, airily. 'I nearly come and stop you. I seen you from 'ere.'

I dropped into a smoking compartment with four young men, two of whom were saying good-bye to a pale youth with a cane. 'Well, good-bye, old chap. It's frightfully good of you to have come down. I knew you. I knew the same old slouch. Now, look here, when we come back we'll have a night of it. What? Ripping of you to have come, old man.' This from an enthusiast, who lit a cigar as the train swung out, turned to his companion and said, 'Frightfully nice chap, but – lord – what a bore!' His companion, who was dressed entirely in mole, even unto his socks and hair, smiled gently. I think his brain must have been the same colour: he proved so gentle and sympathetic a listener. In the opposite corner to me sat a beautiful young Frenchman with curly hair and a watch-chain from which dangled a silver fish, a ring, a silver shoe, and a medal. He stared out of the window the whole time, faintly twitching his nose. Of the remaining member there was nothing to be seen from behind his luggage but a pair of tan shoes and a copy of *The Snark's Summer Annual*.[3]

'Look here, old man,' said the Enthusiast, 'I want to change all our places. You know those arrangements you've made – I want to cut them out altogether. Do you mind?'

'No,' said the Mole, faintly. 'But why?'

'Well, I was thinking it over in bed last night, and I'm hanged if I can see the good of us paying fifteen bob[4] if we don't want to. You see what I mean?' The Mole took off his pince-nez and breathed on them. 'Now I don't want to unsettle you,' went on the Enthusiast, 'because, after all, it's your party – you asked me. I wouldn't upset it for anything, but – there you are – you see – what?'

Suggested the Mole: 'I'm afraid people will be down on me for taking you abroad.'

Straightway the other told him how sought after he had been. From far and near, people who were full up for the entire month of August had written and begged for him. He wrung the Mole's heart by enumerating those longing homes and vacant chairs dotted all over England, until the Mole deliberated between crying and going to sleep. He chose the latter.

They all went to sleep except the young Frenchman, who took a little pocket edition out of his coat and nursed it on his knee while he gazed at the warm, dusty country. At Shorncliffe the train stopped. Dead silence. There was nothing to be seen but a large white cemetery. Fantastic it looked in the late afternoon sun, its full-length marble angels appearing to preside over a cheerless picnic of the Shorncliffe departed on the brown field. One white butterfly flew over the railway lines. As we crept out of the station I saw a poster advertising the *Athenaeum*.[5] The Enthusiast grunted and yawned, shook himself into existence by rattling the money in his trouser pockets. He jabbed the Mole in the ribs. 'I say, we're nearly there! Can you get down those beastly golf-clubs of mine from the rack?' My heart yearned over the Mole's immediate future, but he was cheerful and offered to find me a porter at Dover, and strapped my parasol in with my rugs. We saw the sea. 'It's going to be beastly rough,' said the Enthusiast, 'Gives you a head, doesn't it? Look here, I know a tip for sea-sickness, and it's this: You lie on your back – flat – you know, cover your face, and eat nothing but biscuits.'

'Dover!' shouted a guard.

In the act of crossing the gangway we renounced England. The most blatant British female produced her mite of French: we '*S'il vous plaît*'d' one another on the deck, '*Merci*'d' one another on the stairs, and '*Pardon*'d' to our heart's content in the saloon. The stewardess stood at the foot of the stairs, a stout, forbidding female, pock-marked, her hands hidden under a businesslike-looking apron. She replied to our salutations with studied indifference, mentally ticking off her prey. I descended to the cabin to remove my hat. One old lady was already established there.

She lay on a rose and white couch, a black shawl tucked round her, fanning herself with a black feather fan. Her grey hair was half covered with a lace cap and her face gleamed from the black drapings and rose pillows with charming old-world dignity. There was about her a faint rustling and the scents of camphor[6] and lavender. As I watched her, thinking of Rembrandt[7] and, for some reason, Anatole France,[8] the stewardess bustled up, placed a canvas stool at her elbow, spread a newspaper upon it, and banged down a receptacle rather like a baking tin . . .

I went up on deck. The sea was bright green, with rolling waves. All the beauty and artificial flower of France had removed their hats and bound their heads in veils. A number of young German men, displaying their national bulk in light-coloured suits cut in the pattern of pyjamas, promenaded. French family parties – the female element in chairs, the male in graceful attitudes against the ship's side – talked already with that brilliance which denotes friction! I found a chair in a corner against a white partition, but unfortunately this partition had a window set in it for the purpose of providing endless amusement for the curious, who peered through it, watching those bold and brave spirits who walked 'for'ard' and were drenched and beaten by the waves. In the first half-hour the excitement of getting wet and being pleaded with, and rushing into dangerous places to return and be rubbed down, was all-absorbing. Then it palled – the parties drifted into silence. You would catch them staring intently at the ocean – and yawning. They grew cold and snappy. Suddenly a young lady in a white woollen hood with cherry bows got up from her chair and swayed over to the railings. We watched her, vaguely sympathetic. The young man with whom she had been sitting called to her.

'Are you better?' Negative expressed.

He sat up in his chair. 'Would you like me to hold your head?'

'No,' said her shoulders.

'Would you care for a coat round you? . . . Is it over? . . . Are you going to remain there?' . . . He looked at her with infinite tenderness. I decided never again to call men unsympathetic, and to believe in the all-conquering power of love until I died – but never put it to the test. I went down to sleep.

I lay down opposite the old lady, and watched the shadows spinning over the ceilings and the wave-drops shining on the portholes.

In the shortest sea voyage there is no sense of time. You have been down in the cabin for hours or days or years. Nobody knows or cares. You know all the people to the point of indifference. You do not believe in dry land any more – you are caught in the pendulum itself, and left there, idly swinging. The light faded.

I fell asleep, to wake to find the stewardess shaking me. 'We are there in two minutes,' said she. Forlorn ladies, freed from the embrace of Neptune, knelt upon the floor and searched for their shoes and hairpins – only the old and dignified one lay passive, fanning herself. She looked at me and smiled.

'*Grâce de Dieu, c'est fini,*' she quavered in a voice so fine it seemed to quaver on a thread of lace.

I lifted up my eyes. '*Oui, c'est fini!*'

'*Vous allez à Strasbourg, Madame?*'

'No,' I said. 'Bruges.'

'That is a great pity,' said she, closing her fan and the conversation. I could not think why, but I had visions of myself perhaps travelling in the same railway carriage with her, wrapping her in the black shawl, of her falling in love with me and leaving me unlimited quantities of money and old lace ... These sleepy thoughts pursued me until I arrived on deck.

The sky was indigo blue, and a great many stars were shining: our little ship stood black and sharp in the clear air. 'Have you the tickets? ... Yes, they want the tickets ... Produce your tickets!' ... We were squeezed over the gangway, shepherded into the custom house, where porters heaved our luggage on to long wooden slabs, and an old man wearing horn spectacles checked it without a word. 'Follow me!' shouted the villainous-looking creature whom I had endowed with my worldly goods. He leapt on to a railway line, and I leapt after him. He raced along a platform, dodging the passengers and fruit wagons, with the security of a cinematograph[9] figure. I reserved a seat and went to buy fruit at a little stall displaying grapes and greengages. The old lady was there, leaning on the arm of a large blond man, in white, with a flowing tie. We nodded.

'Buy me,' she said in her delicate voice, 'three ham sandwiches, *mon cher*!'

'And some cakes,' said he.

'Yes, and perhaps a bottle of lemonade.'

'Romance is an imp!' thought I, climbing up into the carriage. The train swung out of the station; the air, blowing through the open windows, smelled of fresh leaves. There were sudden pools of light in the darkness; when I arrived at Bruges the bells were ringing, and white and mysterious shone the moon over the Grand' Place.[10]

(1910)

A Truthful Adventure

'The little town lies spread before the gaze of the eager traveller like a faded tapestry threaded with the silver of its canals, made musical by the great chiming belfry. Life is long since asleep in Bruges; fantastic dreams alone breathe over tower and mediaeval house front, enchanting the eye, inspiring the soul and filling the mind with the great beauty of contemplation.'

I read this sentence from a guide-book while waiting for Madame in the hotel sitting-room. It sounded extremely comforting, and my tired heart, tucked away under a thousand and one grey city wrappings, woke and exulted within me . . . I wondered if I had enough clothes with me to last for at least a month. 'I shall dream away whole days,' I thought, 'take a boat and float up and down the canals, or tether it to a green bush tangling the water side, and absorb mediaeval house fronts. At evensong I shall lie in the long grass of the Béguinage' meadow and look up at the elm trees – their leaves touched with gold light and quivering in the blue air – listening the while to the voices of nuns at prayer in the little chapel, and growing full enough of grace to last me the whole winter.'

While I soared magnificently upon these very new feathers Madame came in and told me that there was no room at all for me in the hotel – not a bed, not a corner. She was extremely friendly and seemed to find a fund of secret amusement in the fact; she looked at me as though expecting me to break into delighted laughter. 'To-morrow,' she said, 'there may be. I am expecting a young gentleman who is suddenly taken ill to move from number eleven. He is at present at the chemist's – perhaps you would care to see the room?'

'Not at all,' said I. 'Neither shall I wish to-morrow to sleep in the bedroom of an indisposed young gentleman.'

'But he will be gone,' cried Madame, opening her blue eyes wide and laughing with that French cordiality so enchanting to English hearing. I was too tired and hungry to feel either appreciative or argumentative. 'Perhaps you can recommend me another hotel?'

'Impossible!' She shook her head and turned up her eyes, mentally counting over the blue bows painted on the ceiling. 'You see, it is the season in Bruges, and people do not care to let their rooms for a very short time' – not a glance at my little suitcase lying between us, but I looked at it gloomily, and it seemed to dwindle before my desperate gaze – become small enough to hold nothing but a collapsible folding tooth-brush.

'My large box is at the station,' I said coldly, buttoning my gloves.

Madame started. 'You have more luggage . . . Then you intend to make a long stay in Bruges, perhaps?'

'At least a fortnight – perhaps a month.' I shrugged my shoulders.

'One moment,' said Madame. 'I shall see what I can do.' She disappeared, I am sure not further than the other side of the door, for she reappeared immediately and told me I might have a room at her private house – 'just round the corner and kept by an old servant who, although she has a wall eye,[2] has been in our family for fifteen years. The porter will take you there, and you can have supper before you go.'

I was the only guest in the dining-room. A tired waiter provided me with an omelette and a pot of coffee, then leaned against a sideboard and watched me while I ate, the limp table napkin over his arm seeming to symbolise the very man. The room was hung with mirrors reflecting unlimited empty tables and watchful waiters and solitary ladies finding sad comfort in omelettes, and sipping coffee to the rhythm of Mendelssohn's Spring Song[3] played over three times by the great chiming belfry.

'Are you ready, Madame?' asked the waiter. 'It is I who carry your luggage.'

'Quite ready.'

He heaved the suitcase on to his shoulder and strode before me – past the little pavement cafés where men and women, scenting our approach, laid down their beer and their post-cards to stare after us, down a narrow street of shuttered houses, through the Place van Eyck,[4] to a red-brick house. The door was opened by the wall-eyed family treasure, who held a candle like a miniature frying-pan in her hand. She refused to admit us until we had both told the whole story.

'*C'est ça, c'est ça,*' said she. 'Jean, number five!'

She shuffled up the stairs, unlocked a door and lit another miniature frying-pan upon the bed-table. The room was papered in pink, having a pink bed, a pink door and a pink chair. On pink mats on the mantelpiece obese young cherubs burst out of pink eggshells with trumpets in their mouths. I was brought a can of hot water; I shut and locked the door. 'Bruges at last,' I thought as I climbed into a bed so slippery with fine linen that one felt like a fish endeavouring to swim over an ice pond, and this quiet house with the old 'typical' servant, – the Place van Eyck, with the white statue surrounded by those dark and heavy trees, – there was almost a touch of Verlaine[5] in that . . .

Bang! went a door. I started up in terror and felt for the frying-pan, but it was the room next to mine suddenly invaded. 'Ah! home at last,' cried a female voice. '*Mon Dieu*, my feet! Would you go down to Marie, *mon cher*, and ask her for the tin bath and some hot water?'

'No, that is too much,' boomed the answer. 'You have washed them three times to-day already.'

'But you do not know the pain I suffer; they are quite inflamed. Look only!'

'I have looked three times already; I am tired. I beg of you come to bed.'

'It would be useless; I could not sleep. *Mon Dieu, mon Dieu*, how a woman suffers!' A masculine snort accompanied by the sounds of undressing.

'Then, if I wait until the morning will you promise not to drag me to a picture gallery?'

'Yes, yes, I promise.'

'But truly?'

'I have said so.'

'Now can I believe you?'

A long groan.

'It is absurd to make that noise, for you know yourself the same thing happened last evening and this morning.'

. . . There was only one thing to be done. I coughed and cleared my throat in that unpleasant and obtrusive way of strange people in next door bedrooms. It acted like a charm, their conversation sifted into a whisper for female voice only! I fell asleep.

'Barquettes for hire. Visit the Venice of the North[6] by boat. Explore the little known and fascinating by-ways.' With the memory of the guide-book clinging about me I went into the shop and demanded a boat. 'Have you a small canoe?'

'No, Mademoiselle, but a little boat – very suitable.'

'I wish to go alone and return when I like.'

'Then you have been here before?'

'No.'

The boatman looked puzzled. 'It is not safe for Mademoiselle to go without a guide for the first time.'

'Then I will take one on the condition that he is silent and points out no beauties to me.'

'But the names of the bridges?' cried the boatman – 'the famous house fronts?'

I ran down to the landing stage. 'Pierre, Pierre!' called the waterman. A burly young Belgian, his arms full of carpet strips and red velvet pillows, appeared and tossed his spoil into an immense craft. On the bridge above the landing stage a crowd collected, watching the proceedings, and just as I took my seat a fat couple who had been hanging over the parapet rushed down the steps and declared they must come too. 'Certainly, certainly,' said Pierre, handing in the lady with charming grace. 'Mademoiselle will not mind at all.' They sat in the stern, the gentleman held the lady's hand, and we twisted among these 'silver ribbons' while Pierre threw out his chest and chanted the beauties of Bruges with the exultant abandon of a Latin lover. 'Turn your head this way – to the left – to the right – now, wait one moment – look up at the bridge – observe this house front. Mademoiselle, do you wish to see the Lac d'Amour?'[7]

I looked vague; the fat couple answered for me.

'Then we shall disembark.'

We rowed close into a little parapet. We caught hold of a bush and I jumped out. 'Now, Monsieur,' who successfully followed, and, kneeling on the bank, gave Madame the crook of his walking-stick for support. She stood up, smiling and vigorous, clutched the walking-stick, strained against the boat side, and the next moment had fallen flat into the water. 'Ah! what has happened – what has happened!' screamed Monsieur, clutching her arm, for the water was not deep, reaching only to her waist mark. Somehow or other we fished her up on to the bank where she sat and gasped, wringing her black alpaca skirt.

'It is all over – a little accident!' said she, amazingly cheerful.

But Pierre was furious. 'It is the fault of Mademoiselle for wishing to see the Lac d'Amour,' said he. 'Madame had better walk through the meadow and drink something hot at the little café opposite.'

'No, no,' said she, but Monsieur seconded Pierre.

'You will await our return,' said Pierre, loathing me. I nodded and turned my back, for the sight of Madame flopping about on the meadow grass like a large, ungainly duck, was too much. One cannot expect to travel in upholstered boats with people who are enlightened enough to understand laughter that has its wellspring in sympathy. When they were out of sight I ran as fast as I could over the meadow, crawled through a fence, and never went near the Lac d'Amour again. 'They may think me as drowned as they please,' thought I, 'I have had quite enough of canals to last me a lifetime.'

In the Béguinage meadow at evensong little groups of painters are dotted about in the grass with spindle-legged easels which seem to possess a separate individuality, and stand rudely defying their efforts and return-ing their long, long gaze with an unfinished stare. English girls wearing flower-wreathed hats and the promise of young American manhood, give expression to their souls with a gaiety and 'camaraderie,' a sort of 'the world is our shining playground' spirit – theoretically delightful. They call to one another, and throw cigarettes and fruit and chocolates with youthful naïveté, while parties of tourists who have escaped the clutches of an old woman lying in wait for them in the shadow of the chapel door, pause thoughtfully in front of the easels to 'see and remark, and say whose?'

I was lying under a tree with the guilty consciousness of no sketch book – watching the swifts wheel and dip in the bright air, and wonder-ing if all the brown dogs resting in the grass belonged to the young painters, when two people passed me, a man and a girl, their heads bent over a book. There was something vaguely familiar in their walk. Sud-denly they looked down at me – we stared – opened our mouths. She swooped down upon me, and he took off his immaculate straw hat and placed it under his left arm.

'Katherine! How extraordinary! How incredible after all these years!' cried she. Turning to the man: 'Guy, can you believe it? – It's Katherine, in Bruges of all places in the world!'

'Why not?' said I, looking very bright and trying to remember her name.

'But, my dear, the last time we met was in New Zealand – only think of the miles!'

Of course, she was Betty Sinclair; I'd been to school with her.

'Where are you staying; have you been here long? Oh, you haven't changed a day – not a day. I'd have known you anywhere.'

She beckoned to the young man, and said, blushing as though she were ashamed of the fact, but it had to be faced, 'This is my husband.' We shook hands. He sat down and chewed a grass twig. Silence fell while Betty recovered breath and squeezed my hand.

'I didn't know you were married,' I said stupidly.

'Oh, my dear – got a baby!' said Betty. 'We live in England now. We're frightfully keen on the Suffrage,[8] you know.'

Guy removed the straw. 'Are you with us?' he asked, intensely.

I shook my head. He put the straw back again and narrowed his eyes.

'Then here's the opportunity,' said Betty. 'My dear, how long are you going to stay? We must go about together and have long talks. Guy and I aren't a honeymoon couple, you know. We love to have other people with us sometimes.'

The belfry clashed into *See the Conquering Hero Comes!*

'Unfortunately I have to go home quite soon. I've had an urgent letter.'

'How disappointing! You know Bruges is simply packed with treasures and churches and pictures. There's an outdoor concert to-night in the Grand' Place, and a competition of bell ringers to-morrow to go on for a whole week.'

'Go I must,' I said so firmly that my soul felt imperative marching orders, stimulated by the belfry.

'But the quaint streets and the Continental smells, and the lace-makers – if we could just wander about – we three – and absorb it all.' I sighed and bit my underlip.

'What's your objection to the vote?' asked Guy, watching the nuns wending their way in sweet procession among the trees.

'I always had the idea you were so frightfully keen on the future of women,' said Betty. 'Come to dinner with us to-night. Let's thrash the whole subject out. You know, after the strenuous life in London, one does seem to see things in such a different light in this old world city.'

'Oh, a very different light indeed,' I answered, shaking my head at the familiar guide-book emerging from Guy's pocket.

(1910)

New Dresses

Mrs Carsfield and her mother sat at the dining-room table putting the finishing touches to some green cashmere dresses. They were to be worn by the two Misses Carsfield at church on the following day, with apple-green sashes, and straw hats with ribbon tails. Mrs Carsfield had set her heart on it, and this being a late night for Henry, who was attending a meeting of the Political League,[1] she and the old mother had the dining-room to themselves, and could make 'a peaceful litter' as she expressed it. The red cloth was taken off the table – where stood the wedding-present sewing machine, a brown work-basket, the 'material,' and some torn fashion journals. Mrs Carsfield worked the machine, slowly, for she feared the green thread would give out, and had a sort of tired hope that it might last longer if she was careful to use a little at a time; the old woman sat in a rocking chair, her skirt turned back, and her felt-slippered feet on a hassock, tying the machine threads and stitching some narrow lace on the necks and cuffs. The gas jet flickered. Now and again the old woman glanced up at the jet and said, 'There's water in the pipe, Anne, that's what's the matter,' then was silent, to say again a moment later, 'There must be water in that pipe, Anne,' and again, with quite a burst of energy, '*Now* there is – I'm *certain* of it.'

Anne frowned at the sewing machine. 'The way mother *harps* on things – it gets frightfully on my nerves,' she thought. 'And always when there's no earthly opportunity to better a thing . . . I suppose it's old age – but most aggravating.' Aloud she said: 'Mother, I'm having a really substantial hem in this dress of Rose's – the child has got so leggy, lately. And don't put any lace on Helen's cuffs; it will make a distinction, and besides she's so careless about rubbing her hands on anything grubby.'

'Oh there's plenty,' said the old woman. 'I'll put it a little higher up.' And she wondered why Anne had such a down on Helen – Henry was just the same. They seemed to want to hurt Helen's feelings – the distinction was merely an excuse.

'Well,' said Mrs Carsfield, 'you didn't see Helen's clothes when I took them off to-night. Black from head to foot after a week. And when I compared them before her eyes with Rose's she merely shrugged, you know that habit she's got, and began stuttering. I really shall have to see Dr Malcolm about her stuttering, if only to give her a good fright. I believe it's merely an affectation she's picked up at school – that she can help it.'

'Anne, you know she's always stuttered. You did just the same when you were her age, she's highly strung.' The old woman took off her spectacles, breathed on them, and rubbed them with a corner of her sewing apron.

'Well, the last thing in the world to do her any good is to let her imagine *that*,' answered Anne, shaking out one of the green frocks, and pricking at the pleats with her needle. 'She is treated exactly like Rose, and the Boy hasn't a nerve. Did you see him when I put him on the rocking-horse to-day, for the first time? He simply gurgled with joy. He's more the image of his father every day.'

'Yes, he certainly is a thorough Carsfield,' assented the old woman, nodding her head.

'Now that's another thing about Helen,' said Anne. 'The peculiar way she treats Boy, staring at him and frightening him as she does. You remember when he was a baby how she used to take away his bottle to see what he would do? Rose is perfect with the child – but Helen . . .'

The old woman put down her work on the table. A little silence fell, and through the silence the loud ticking of the dining-room clock. She wanted to speak her mind to Anne once and for all about the way she and Henry were treating Helen, ruining the child, but the ticking noise distracted her. She could not think of the words and sat there stupidly, her brain going *tick*, *tick*, to the dining-room clock.

'How loudly that clock ticks,' was all she said.

'Oh there's mother – off the subject again – giving me no help or encouragement,' thought Anne. She glanced at the clock.

'Mother, if you've finished that frock, would you go into the kitchen and heat up some coffee, and perhaps cut a plate of ham. Henry will be in directly. I'm practically through with this second frock by myself.' She held it up for inspection. 'Aren't they charming? They ought to last the children a good two years, and then I expect they'll do for school – lengthened, and perhaps dyed.'

'I'm glad we decided on the more expensive material,' said the old woman.

Left alone in the dining-room Anne's frown deepened, and her mouth drooped – a sharp line showed from nose to chin. She breathed deeply, and pushed back her hair. There seemed to be no air in the room, she felt stuffed up, and it seemed so useless to be tiring herself out with fine sewing for Helen. One never got through with children, and never had any gratitude from them – except Rose – who was exceptional. Another sign of old age in mother was her absurd point of view about Helen, and her 'touchiness' on the subject. There was one thing, Mrs Carsfield said to herself. She was determined to keep Helen apart from Boy. He had all his father's sensitiveness to unsympathetic influences. A blessing that the girls were at school all day!

At last the dresses were finished and folded over the back of the chair. She carried the sewing machine over to the book-shelves, spread the table-cloth, and went over to the window. The blind was up, she could see the garden quite plainly: there must be a moon about. And then she caught sight of something shining on the garden seat. A book, yes, it must be a book, left there to get soaked through by the dew. She went out into the hall, put on her goloshes, gathered up her skirt, and ran into the garden. Yes, it was a book. She picked it up carefully. Damp already – and the cover bulging. She shrugged her shoulders in the way that her little daughter had caught from her. In the shadowy garden that smelled of grass and rose leaves, Anne's heart hardened. Then the gate clicked and she saw Henry striding up the front path.

'Henry!' she called.

'Hullo,' he cried, 'what on earth are you doing down there . . . Moon-gazing, Anne?' She ran forward and kissed him.

'Oh, look at this book,' she said. 'Helen's been leaving it about, again. My dear, how you smell of cigars!'

Said Henry: 'You've got to smoke a decent cigar when you're with these other chaps. Looks so bad if you don't. But come inside, Anne; you haven't got anything on. Let the book go hang! You're cold, my dear, you're shivering.' He put his arm round her shoulder. 'See the moon over there, by the chimney? Fine night. By jove! I had the fellows roaring to-night – I made a colossal joke. One of them said: "Life is a game of cards," and I, without thinking, just straight out . . .' Henry paused by the door and held up a finger. 'I said . . . well I've forgotten the exact words, but they shouted, my dear, simply shouted. No, I'll remember what I said in bed to-night; you know I always do.'

'I'll take this book into the kitchen to dry on the stove-rack,' said Anne, and she thought, as she banged the pages, 'Henry has been drinking beer again, that means indigestion to-morrow. No use mentioning Helen to-night.'

When Henry had finished the supper, he lay back in the chair, picking his teeth, and patted his knee for Anne to come and sit there.

'Hullo,' he said, jumping her up and down, 'what's the green fandangles on the chair back? What have you and mother been up to, eh?'

Said Anne, airily, casting a most careless glance at the green dresses, 'Only some frocks for the children. Remnants for Sunday.'

The old woman put the plate and cup and saucer together, then lighted a candle.

'I think I'll go to bed,' she said, cheerfully.

'Oh, dear me, how unwise of Mother,' thought Anne. 'She makes Henry suspect by going away like that, as she always does if there's any unpleasantness brewing.'

'No, don't go to bed yet, mother,' cried Henry, jovially. 'Let's have a look at the things.' She passed him over the dresses, faintly smiling. Henry rubbed them through his fingers.

'So these are the remnants, are they, Anne? Don't feel much like the Sunday trousers my mother used to make me out of an ironing blanket. How much did you pay for this a yard, Anne?'

Anne took the dresses from him, and played with a button of his waistcoat.

'Forget the exact price, darling. Mother and I rather skimped them, even though they were so cheap. What can great big men bother about clothes . . .? Was Lumley there, to-night?'

'Yes, he says their kid was a bit bandy-legged at just the same age as Boy. He told me of a new kind of chair for children that the draper has just got in – makes them sit with their legs straight. By the way, have you got this month's draper's bill?'

She had been waiting for that – had known it was coming. She slipped off his knee and yawned.

'Oh, dear me,' she said, 'I think I'll follow mother. Bed's the place for me.' She stared at Henry, vacantly. 'Bill – bill did you say, dear? Oh, I'll look it out in the morning.'

'No, Anne, hold on.' Henry got up and went over to the cupboard where the bill file was kept. 'To-morrow's no good – because it's

Sunday. I want to get that account off my chest before I turn in. Sit down there – in the rocking-chair – you needn't stand!'

She dropped into the chair, and began humming, all the while her thoughts coldly busy, and her eyes fixed on her husband's broad back as he bent over the cupboard door. He dawdled over finding the file.

'He's keeping me in suspense on purpose,' she thought. 'We can afford it – otherwise why should I do it? I know our income and our expenditure. I'm not a fool. They're a hell upon earth every month, these bills.' And she thought of her bed upstairs, yearned for it, imagining she had never felt so tired in her life.

'Here we are!' said Henry. He slammed the file on to the table.

'Draw up your chair . . .'

'Clayton: Seven yards green cashmere at five shillings a yard – thirty-five shillings.' He read the item twice – then folded the sheet over, and bent towards Anne. He was flushed and his breath smelt of beer. She knew exactly how he took things in that mood, and she raised her eyebrows and nodded.

'Do you mean to tell me,' stormed Henry, 'that lot over there cost thirty-five shillings – that stuff you've been mucking up for the children. Good God! Anybody would think you'd married a millionaire. You could buy your mother a trousseau with that money. You're making yourself a laughing-stock for the whole town. How do you think I can buy Boy a chair or anything else – if you chuck away my earnings like that? Time and again you impress upon me the impossibility of keeping Helen decent; and then you go decking her out the next moment in thirty-five shillings worth of green cashmere . . .'

On and on stormed the voice.

'He'll have calmed down in the morning, when the beer's worked off,' thought Anne, and later, as she toiled up to bed, 'When he sees how they'll last, he'll understand . . .'

A brilliant Sunday morning. Henry and Anne quite reconciled, sitting in the dining-room waiting for church time to the tune of Carsfield junior, who steadily thumped the shelf of his high-chair with a gravy spoon given him from the breakfast table by his father.

'That beggar's got muscle,' said Henry, proudly. 'I've timed him by my watch. He's kept that up for five minutes without stopping.'

'Extraordinary,' said Anne, buttoning her gloves. 'I think he's had that spoon almost long enough now, dear, don't you? I'm so afraid of him putting it into his mouth.'

'Oh, I've got an eye on him.' Henry stood over his small son. 'Go it, old man. Tell Mother boys like to kick up a row.'

Anne kept silence. At any rate it would keep his eye off the children when they came down in those cashmeres. She was still wondering if she had drummed into their minds often enough the supreme import-ance of being careful and of taking them off immediately after church before dinner, and why Helen was fidgety when she was pulled about at all, when the door opened and the old woman ushered them in, com-plete to the straw hats with ribbon tails.

She could not help thrilling, they looked so very superior – Rose carrying her prayer-book in a white case embroidered with a pink woollen cross. But she feigned indifference immediately, and the lateness of the hour. Not a word more on the subject from Henry, even with the thirty-five shillings worth walking hand in hand before him all the way to church. Anne decided that was really generous and noble of him. She looked up at him, walking with the shoulders thrown back. How fine he looked in that long black coat, with the white silk tie just showing! And the children looked worthy of him. She squeezed his hand in church, conveying by that silent pressure, 'It was for your sake I made the dresses; of course you can't understand that, but *really*, Henry.' And she fully believed it.

On their way home the Carsfield family met Doctor Malcolm, out walking with a black dog carrying his stick in its mouth. Doctor Mal-colm stopped and asked after Boy so intelligently that Henry invited him to dinner.

'Come and pick a bone with us and see Boy for yourself,' he said. And Doctor Malcolm accepted. He walked beside Henry and shouted over his shoulder, 'Helen, keep an eye on *my* boy baby, will you, and see he doesn't swallow that walking-stick. Because if he does, a tree will grow right out of his mouth or it will go to his tail and make it so stiff that a wag will knock you into kingdom come!'

'Oh, Doctor Malcolm!' laughed Helen, stooping over the dog, 'Come along, doggie, give it up, there's a good boy!'

'Helen, your dress!' warned Anne.

'Yes, indeed,' said Doctor Malcolm. 'They are looking top-notchers to-day – the two young ladies.'

'Well, it really *is* Rose's colour,' said Anne. 'Her complexion is so much more vivid than Helen's.'

Rose blushed. Doctor Malcolm's eyes twinkled, and he kept a tight rein on himself from saying she looked like a tomato in a lettuce salad.

'That child wants taking down a peg,' he decided. 'Give me Helen every time. She'll come to her own yet, and lead them just the dance they need.'

Boy was having his mid-day sleep when they arrived home, and Doctor Malcolm begged that Helen might show him round the garden. Henry, repenting already of his generosity, gladly assented, and Anne went into the kitchen to interview the servant girl.

'Mumma, let me come too and taste the gravy,' begged Rose.

'Huh!' muttered Doctor Malcolm. 'Good riddance.'

He established himself on the garden bench – put up his feet and took off his hat, to give the sun 'a chance of growing a second crop,' he told Helen.

She asked, soberly: 'Doctor Malcolm, do you really like my dress?'

'Of course I do, my lady. Don't you?'

'Oh yes, I'd like to be born and die in it, but it was such a fuss – tryings on, you know, and pullings, and "don'ts." I believe mother would kill me if it got hurt. I even knelt on my petticoat all through church because of dust on the hassock.'

'Bad as that!' asked Doctor Malcolm, rolling his eyes at Helen.

'Oh, *far* worse,' said the child, then burst into laughter and shouted, 'Hellish!' dancing over the lawn.

'Take care, they'll hear you, Helen.'

'Oh, booh! It's just dirty old cashmere – serve them right. They can't see me if they're not here to see and so it doesn't matter. It's only with them I feel funny.'

'Haven't you got to remove your finery before dinner?'

'No, because you're here.'

'O my prophetic soul!' groaned Doctor Malcolm.

Coffee was served in the garden. The servant girl brought out some cane chairs and a rug for Boy. The children were told to go away and play.

'Leave off worrying Doctor Malcolm, Helen,' said Henry. 'You mustn't be a plague to people who are not members of your own family.' Helen pouted, and dragged over to the swing for comfort. She swung high, and thought Doctor Malcolm was a most beautiful man –

and wondered if his dog had finished the plate of bones in the back yard. Decided to go and see. Slower she swung, then took a flying leap; her tight skirt caught on a nail – there was a sharp, tearing sound – quickly she glanced at the others – they had not noticed – and then at the frock – at a hole big enough to stick her hand through. She felt neither frightened nor sorry. 'I'll go and change it,' she thought.

'Helen, where are you going to?' called Anne.

'Into the house for a book.'

The old woman noticed that the child held her skirt in a peculiar way. Her petticoat string must have come untied. But she made no remark. Once in the bedroom Helen unbuttoned the frock, slipped out of it, and wondered what to do next. Hide it somewhere – she glanced all round the room – there was nowhere safe from them. Except the top of the cupboard – but even standing on a chair she could not throw so high – it fell back on top of her every time – the horrid, hateful thing. Then her eyes lighted on her school satchel hanging on the end of the bed post. Wrap it in her school pinafore – put it in the bottom of the bag with the pencil case on top. They'd never look there. She returned to the garden in the every-day dress – but forgot about the book.

'A-ah,' said Anne, smiling ironically. 'What a new leaf for Doctor Malcolm's benefit! Look, Mother, Helen has changed without being told to.'

'Come here, dear, and be done up properly.' She whispered to Helen: 'Where did you leave your dress?'

'Left it on the side of the bed. *Where* I took it off,' sang Helen.

Doctor Malcolm was talking to Henry of the advantages derived from public school education for the sons of commercial men, but he had his eye on the scene, and watching Helen, he smelt a rat – smelt a Hamelin tribe[2] of them.

Confusion and consternation reigned. One of the green cashmeres had disappeared – spirited off the face of the earth – during the time that Helen took it off and the children's tea.

'Show me the exact spot,' scolded Mrs Carsfield for the twentieth time. 'Helen, tell the truth.'

'Mumma, I *swear* I left it on the floor.'

'Well, it's no good swearing if it's not there. It can't have been stolen!'

'I did see a very funny-looking man in a white cap walking up and

down the road and staring in the windows as I came up to change.'
Sharply Anne eyed her daughter.

'Now,' she said. 'I *know* you are telling lies.'

She turned to the old woman, in her voice something of pride and
joyous satisfaction. 'You hear, Mother – this cock-and-bull story?'

When they were near the end of the bed Helen blushed and turned
away from them. And now and again she wanted to shout 'I tore it, I
tore it,' and she fancied she had said it and seen their faces, just as
sometimes in bed she dreamed she had got up and dressed. But as the
evening wore on she grew quite careless – glad only of one thing –
people had to go to sleep at night. Viciously she stared at the sun
shining through the window space and making a pattern of the curtain
on the bare nursery floor. And then she looked at Rose, painting a text
at the nursery table with a whole egg cup full of water to herself . . .

Henry visited their bedroom the last thing. She heard him come
creaking into their room and hid under the bedclothes. But Rose betrayed her.

'Helen's not asleep,' piped Rose.

Henry sat by the bedside pulling his moustache.

'If it were not Sunday, Helen, I would whip you. As it is, and I must
be at the office early to-morrow, I shall give you a sound smacking after
tea in the evening . . . Do you hear me?'

She grunted.

'You love your father and mother, don't you?'

No answer.

Rose gave Helen a dig with her foot.

'Well,' said Henry, sighing deeply, 'I suppose you love Jesus?'

'Rose has scratched my leg with her toe-nail,' answered Helen.

Henry strode out of the room and flung himself on to his own bed,
with his outdoor boots on the starched bolster, Anne noticed, but he
was too overcome for her to venture a protest. The old woman was in
the bedroom too, idly combing the hairs from Anne's brush. Henry told
them the story, and was gratified to observe Anne's tears.

'It *is* Rose's turn for her toe-nails after the bath next Saturday,' commented the old woman.

In the middle of the night Henry dug his elbow into Mrs Carsfield.

'I've got an idea,' he said. 'Malcolm's at the bottom of this.'

'No . . . how . . . why . . . where . . . bottom of what?'

'Those damned green dresses.'

'Wouldn't be surprised,' she managed to articulate, thinking, 'imagine his rage if I woke *him* up to tell him an idiotic thing like that!'

'Is Mrs Carsfield at home?' asked Doctor Malcolm.

'No, sir, she's out visiting,' answered the servant girl.

'Is Mr Carsfield anywhere about?'

'Oh, no, sir, he's never home midday.'

'Show me into the drawing-room.'

The servant girl opened the drawing-room door, cocked her eye at the doctor's bag. She wished he would leave it in the hall – even if she could only *feel* the outside without opening it . . . But the doctor kept it in his hand.

The old woman sat in the drawing-room, a roll of knitting on her lap. Her head had fallen back – her mouth was open – she was asleep and quietly snoring. She started up at the sound of the doctor's footsteps and straightened her cap.

'Oh, Doctor – you *did* take me by surprise. I was dreaming that Henry had bought Anne five little canaries. Please sit down!'

'No, thanks. I just popped in on the chance of catching you alone . . . You see this bag?'

The old woman nodded.

'Now, are you any good at opening bags?'

'Well, my husband was a great traveller and once I spent a whole night in a railway train.'

'Well, have a go at opening this one.'

The old woman knelt on the floor – her fingers trembled.

'There's nothing startling inside?' she asked.

'Well, it won't bite exactly,' said Doctor Malcolm.

The catch sprang open – the bag yawned like a toothless mouth, and she saw, folded in its depths – green cashmere – with narrow lace on the neck and sleeves.

'Fancy that!' said the old woman mildly. 'May I take it out, Doctor?' She professed neither astonishment nor pleasure – and Malcolm felt disappointed.

'Helen's dress,' he said, and bending towards her, raised his voice. 'That young spark's Sunday rig-out.'

'I'm not deaf, Doctor,' answered the old woman. 'Yes, I thought it looked like it. I told Anne only this morning it was bound to turn up somewhere.' She shook the crumpled frock, and looked it over. 'Things always do if you give them time; I've noticed that so often – it's such a blessing.'

'You know Lindsay – the postman? Gastric ulcers – called there this morning . . . Saw this brought in by Lena, who'd got it from Helen on her way to school. Said the kid fished it out of her satchel rolled in a pinafore, and said her mother had told her to give it away because it did not fit her. When I saw the tear I understood yesterday's "new leaf," as Mrs Carsfield put it. Was up to the dodge in a jiffy. Got the dress – bought some stuff at Clayton's and made my sister Bertha sew it while I had dinner. I knew what would be happening this end of the line – and I knew you'd see Helen through for the sake of getting one in at Henry.'

'How thoughtful of you, Doctor!' said the old woman. 'I'll tell Anne I found it under my dolman.'³

'Yes, that's your ticket,' said Doctor Malcolm.

'But of course Helen would have forgotten the whipping by to-morrow morning, and I'd promised her a new doll . . .' The old woman spoke regretfully.

Doctor Malcolm snapped his bag together. 'It's no good talking to the old bird,' he thought, 'she doesn't take in half I say. Don't seem to have got any forrader than doing Helen out of a doll.'⁴

(1910)

The Woman at the Store

All that day the heat was terrible. The wind blew close to the ground; it rooted among the tussock grass, slithered along the road, so that the white pumice dust swirled in our faces, settled and sifted over us and was like a dry-skin itching for growth on our bodies. The horses stumbled along, coughing and chuffing. The pack horse was sick – with a big, open sore rubbed under the belly. Now and again she stopped short, threw back her head, looked at us as though she were going to cry, and whinnied. Hundreds of larks shrilled; the sky was slate colour, and the sound of the larks reminded me of slate pencils scraping over its surface. There was nothing to be seen but wave after wave of tussock grass, patched with purple orchids and manuka bushes[1] covered with thick spider webs.

Jo rode ahead. He wore a blue galatea[2] shirt, corduroy trousers and riding boots. A white handkerchief, spotted with red – it looked as though his nose had been bleeding on it – was knotted round his throat. Wisps of white hair straggled from under his wideawake[3] – his moustache and eyebrows were called white – he slouched in the saddle, grunting. Not once that day had he sung

> 'I don't care, for don't you see,
> My wife's mother was in front of me!'

It was the first day we had been without it for a month, and now there seemed something uncanny in his silence. Jim rode beside me, white as a clown; his black eyes glittered, and he kept shooting out his tongue and moistening his lips. He was dressed in a Jaeger vest,[4] and a pair of blue duck trousers,[5] fastened round the waist with a plaited leather belt. We had hardly spoken since dawn. At noon we had lunched off fly biscuits[6] and apricots by the side of a swampy creek.

'My stomach feels like the crop of a hen,' said Jo. 'Now then, Jim, you're the bright boy of the party – where's this 'ere store you kep' on talking about. "Oh, yes," you says, "I know a fine store, with a paddock for the horses and a creek runnin' through, owned by a friend of mine who'll give yer a bottle of whisky before 'e shakes hands with yer." I'd like ter see that place – merely as a matter of curiosity – not that I'd ever doubt yer word – as yer know very well – *but . . .*'

Jim laughed. 'Don't forget there's a woman too, Jo, with blue eyes and yellow hair, who'll promise you something else before she shakes hands with you. Put that in your pipe and smoke it.'

'The heat's making you balmy,' said Jo. But he dug his knees into the horse. We shambled on. I half fell asleep, and had a sort of uneasy dream that the horses were not moving forward at all – then that I was on a rocking-horse, and my old mother was scolding me for raising such a fearful dust from the drawing-room carpet. 'You've entirely worn off the pattern of the carpet,' I heard her saying, and she gave the reins a tug. I snivelled and woke to find Jim leaning over me, maliciously smiling.

'That was a case of all but,' said he. 'I just caught you. What's up? Been bye-bye?'

'No!' I raised my head. 'Thank the Lord we're arriving somewhere.'

We were on the brow of the hill, and below us there was a whare[7] roofed with corrugated iron. It stood in a garden, rather far back from the road – a big paddock opposite, and a creek and a clump of young willow trees. A thin line of blue smoke stood up straight from the chimney of the whare; and as I looked a woman came out, followed by a child and a sheep dog – the woman carrying what appeared to me a black stick. She made gestures at us. The horses put on a final spurt, Jo took off his wideawake, shouted, threw out his chest, and began singing, 'I don't care, for don't you see . . .' The sun pushed through the pale clouds and shed a vivid light over the scene. It gleamed on the woman's yellow hair, over her flapping pinafore and the rifle she was carrying. The child hid behind her, and the yellow dog, a mangy beast, scuttled back into the whare, his tail between his legs. We drew rein and dismounted.

'Hallo,' screamed the woman. 'I thought you was three 'awks. My kid comes runnin' in ter me. "Mumma," says she, "there's three brown things comin' over the 'ill," says she. An' I comes out smart, I can tell yer. "They'll be 'awks," I says to her. Oh, the 'awks about 'ere, yer wouldn't believe.'

The 'kid' gave us the benefit of one eye from behind the woman's pinafore – then retired again.

'Where's your old man?' asked Jim.

The woman blinked rapidly, screwing up her face.

'Away shearin'. Bin away a month. I suppose yer not goin' to stop, are yer? There's a storm comin' up.'

'You bet we are,' said Jo. 'So you're on your lonely, missus?'

She stood, pleating the frills of her pinafore, and glancing from one to the other of us, like a hungry bird. I smiled at the thought of how Jim had pulled Jo's leg about her. Certainly her eyes were blue, and what hair she had was yellow, but ugly. She was a figure of fun. Looking at her, you felt there was nothing but sticks and wires under that pinafore – her front teeth were knocked out, she had red pulpy hands, and she wore on her feet a pair of dirty Bluchers.[8]

'I'll go and turn out the horses,' said Jim. 'Got any embrocation? Poi's rubbed herself to hell!'

''Arf a mo!' The woman stood silent a moment, her nostrils expanding as she breathed. Then she shouted violently. 'I'd rather you didn't stop . . . You *can't*, and there's the end of it. I don't let out that paddock any more. You'll have to go on; I ain't got nothing!'

'Well, I'm blest!' said Jo, heavily. He pulled me aside. 'Gone a bit off 'er dot,' he whispered. 'Too much alone, *you know*,' very significantly. 'Turn the sympathetic tap on 'er, she'll come round all right.'

But there was no need – she had come round by herself.

'Stop if yer like!' she muttered, shrugging her shoulders. To me – 'I'll give yer the embrocation if yer come along.'

'Right-o, I'll take it down to them.' We walked together up the garden path. It was planted on both sides with cabbages. They smelled like stale dish-water. Of flowers there were double poppies and sweet-williams. One little patch was divided off by pawa[9] shells – presumably it belonged to the child – for she ran from her mother and began to grub in it with a broken clothes-peg. The yellow dog lay across the doorstep, biting fleas; the woman kicked him away.

'Gar-r, get away, you beast . . . the place ain't tidy. I 'aven't 'ad time ter fix things to-day – been ironing. Come right in.'

It was a large room, the walls plastered with old pages of English periodicals. Queen Victoria's Jubilee[10] appeared to be the most recent number. A table with an ironing board and wash tub on it, some wooden forms, a black horsehair sofa, and some broken cane chairs pushed against the walls. The mantelpiece above the stove was draped in pink paper, further ornamented with dried grasses and ferns and a coloured print of Richard Seddon.[11] There were four doors – one, judging from the smell, let into the 'Store,' one on to the 'back yard,' through a third I saw the bedroom. Flies buzzed in circles round the ceiling, and treacle papers and bundles of dried clover were pinned to the window curtains.

I was alone in the room; she had gone into the store for the embrocation. I heard her stamping about and muttering to herself: 'I got some, now where did I put that bottle? . . . It's behind the pickles . . . no, it ain't.' I cleared a place on the table and sat there, swinging my legs. Down in the paddock I could hear Jo singing and the sound of hammer strokes as Jim drove in the tent pegs. It was sunset. There is no twilight in our New Zealand days, but a curious half-hour when everything appears grotesque – it frightens – as though the savage spirit of the country walked abroad and sneered at what it saw. Sitting alone in the hideous room I grew afraid. The woman next door was a long time finding that stuff. What was she doing in there? Once I thought I heard her bang her hands down on the counter, and once she half moaned, turning it into a cough and clearing her throat. I wanted to shout 'Buck up!' but I kept silent.

'Good Lord, what a life!' I thought. 'Imagine being here day in, day out, with that rat of a child and a mangy dog. Imagine bothering about ironing. *Mad*, of course she's mad! Wonder how long she's been here – wonder if I could get her to talk.'

At that moment she poked her head round the door.

'Wot was it yer wanted?' she asked.

'Embrocation.'

'Oh, I forgot. I got it, it was in front of the pickle jars.'

She handed me the bottle.

'My, you do look tired, you do! Shall I knock yer up a few scones for supper! There's some tongue in the store, too, and I'll cook yer a cabbage if you fancy it.'

'Right-o.' I smiled at her. 'Come down to the paddock and bring the kid for tea.'

She shook her head, pursing up her mouth.

'Oh no. I don't fancy it. I'll send the kid down with the things and a billy of milk. Shall I knock up a few extry scones to take with yer ter-morrow?'

'Thanks.'

She came and stood by the door.

'How old is the kid?'

'Six – come next Christmas. I 'ad a bit of trouble with 'er one way an' another. I 'adn't any milk till a month after she was born and she sickened like a cow.'

'She's not like you – takes after her father?' Just as the woman had shouted her refusal at us before, she shouted at me then.

'No, she don't! She's the dead spit of me. Any fool could see that. Come on in now, Else, you stop messing in the dirt.'

I met Jo climbing over the paddock fence.

'What's the old bitch got in the store?' he asked.

'Don't know – didn't look.'

'Well, of all the fools. Jim's slanging you. What have you been doing all the time?'

'She couldn't find this stuff. Oh, my shakes, you are smart!'

Jo had washed, combed his wet hair in a line across his forehead, and buttoned a coat over his shirt. He grinned.

Jim snatched the embrocation from me. I went to the end of the paddock where the willows grew and bathed in the creek. The water was clear and soft as oil. Along the edges held by the grass and rushes, white foam tumbled and bubbled. I lay in the water and looked up at the trees that were still a moment, then quivered lightly, and again were still. The air smelt of rain. I forgot about the woman and the kid until I came back to the tent. Jim lay by the fire, watching the billy boil.

I asked where Jo was, and if the kid had brought our supper.

'Pooh,' said Jim, rolling over and looking up at the sky. 'Didn't you see how Jo had been titivating? He said to me before he went up to the whare, "Dang it! she'll look better by night light – at any rate, my buck, she's female flesh!"'

'You had Jo about her looks – you had me, too.'

'No – look here. I can't make it out. It's four years since I came past this way, and I stopped here two days. The husband was a pal of mine once, down the West Coast – a fine, big chap, with a voice on him like a trombone. She'd been barmaid down the Coast – as pretty as a wax doll. The coach used to come this way then once a fortnight, that was before they opened the railway up Napier[12] way, and she had no end of a time!

Told me once in a confidential moment that she knew one hundred and twenty-five different ways of kissing!'

'Oh, go on, Jim! She isn't the same woman!'

'Course she is . . . I can't make it out. What I think is the old man's cleared out and left her: that's all my eye about shearing. Sweet life! The only people who come through now are Maoris and sundowners!'[13]

Through the dark we saw the gleam of the kid's pinafore. She trailed over to us with a basket in her hand, the milk billy in the other. I unpacked the basket, the child standing by.

'Come over here,' said Jim, snapping his fingers at her.

She went, the lamp from the inside of the tent cast a bright light over her. A mean, undersized brat, with whitish hair, and weak eyes. She stood, legs wide apart and her stomach protruding.

'What do you do all day?' asked Jim.

She scraped out one ear with her little finger, looked at the result and said, 'Draw.'

'Huh! What do you draw? Leave your ears alone!'

'Pictures.'

'What on?'

'Bits of butter paper an' a pencil of my Mumma's.'

'Boh! What a lot of words at one time!' Jim rolled his eyes at her. 'Baa-lambs and moo-cows?'

'No, everything. I'll draw all of you when you're gone, and your horses and the tent, and that one' – she pointed to me – 'with no clothes on in the creek. I looked at her where she couldn't see me from.'[14]

'Thanks very much. How ripping of you,' said Jim. 'Where's Dad?'

The kid pouted. 'I won't tell you because I don't like yer face!' She started operations on the other ear.

'Here,' I said. 'Take the basket, get along home and tell the other man supper's ready.'

'I don't want to.'

'I'll give you a box on the ear if you don't,' said Jim, savagely.

'Hie! I'll tell Mumma. I'll tell Mumma.' The kid fled.

We ate until we were full, and had arrived at the smoke stage before Jo came back, very flushed and jaunty, a whisky bottle in his hand.

''Ave a drink – you two!' he shouted, carrying off matters with a high hand. ''Ere, shove along the cups.'

'One hundred and twenty-five different ways,' I murmured to Jim.

'What's that? Oh! stow it!' said Jo. 'Why 'ave you always got your knife into me. You gas like a kid at a Sunday School beano. She wants us to go up there to-night, and have a comfortable chat. I' – he waved his hand airily – 'I got 'er round.'

'Trust you for that,' laughed Jim. 'But did she tell you where the old man's got to?'

Jo looked up. 'Shearing! You 'eard 'er, you fool!'

The woman had fixed up the room, even to a light bouquet of sweet-williams on the table. She and I sat one side of the table, Jo and Jim the other. An oil lamp was set between us, the whisky bottle and glasses, and a jug of water. The kid knelt against one of the forms, drawing on butter paper; I wondered, grimly, if she was attempting the creek episode. But Jo had been right about night time. The woman's hair was tumbled – two red spots burned in her cheeks – her eyes shone – and we knew that they were kissing feet under the table. She had changed the blue pinafore for a white calico[15] dressing jacket and a black skirt – the kid was decorated to the extent of a blue sateen[16] hair ribbon. In the stifling room, with the flies buzzing against the ceiling and dropping on to the table, we got slowly drunk.

'Now listen to me,' shouted the woman, banging her fist on the table. 'It's six years since I was married, and four miscarriages. I says to 'im, I says, what do you think I'm doin' up 'ere? If you was back at the coast, I'd 'ave you lynched for child murder. Over and over I tells 'im – you've broken my spirit and spoiled my looks, and wot for – that's wot I'm driving at.' She clutched her head with her hands and stared round at us. Speaking rapidly, 'Oh, some days – an' months of them – I 'ear them two words knockin' inside me all the time – "Wot for!" but sometimes I'll be cooking the spuds an' I lifts the lid off to give 'em a prong and I 'ears, quite suddin again, "Wot for!" Oh! I don't mean only the spuds and the kid – I mean – I mean,' she hiccoughed – 'you know what I mean, Mr Jo.'

'I know,' said Jo, scratching his head.

'Trouble with me is,' she leaned across the table, 'he left me too much alone. When the coach stopped coming, sometimes he'd go away days, sometimes he'd go away weeks, and leave me ter look after the store. Back 'e'd come – pleased as Punch. "Oh, 'allo," 'e'd say. "'Ow are you gettin' on. Come and give us a kiss." Sometimes I'd turn a bit nasty, and then 'e'd go off again, and if I took it all right, 'e'd wait till 'e could twist me round 'is finger, then 'e'd say, "Well, so long, I'm off," and do you think I could keep 'im? – not me!'

'Mumma,' bleated the kid, 'I made a picture of them on the 'ill, an' you an' me, an' the dog down below.'

'Shut your mouth!' said the woman.

A vivid flash of lightning played over the room – we heard the mutter of thunder.

'Good thing that's broke loose,' said Jo. 'I've 'ad it in me 'ead for three days.'

'Where's your old man now?' asked Jim, slowly.

The woman blubbered and dropped her head on to the table. 'Jim, 'e's gone shearin' and left me alone again,' she wailed.

''Ere, look out for the glasses,' said Jo. 'Cheer-o, 'ave another drop. No good cryin' over spilt 'usbands! You Jim, you blasted cuckoo!'

'Mr Jo,' said the woman, drying her eyes on her jacket frill, 'you're a gent, an' if I was a secret woman, I'd place any confidence in your 'ands. I don't mind if I do 'ave a glass on that.'

Every moment the lightning grew more vivid and the thunder sounded nearer. Jim and I were silent – the kid never moved from her bench. She poked her tongue out and blew on her paper as she drew.

'It's the loneliness,' said the woman, addressing Jo – he made sheep's eyes at her – 'and bein' shut up 'ere like a broody 'en.' He reached his hand across the table and held hers, and though the position looked most uncomfortable when they wanted to pass the water and whisky, their hands stuck together as though glued. I pushed back my chair and went over to the kid, who immediately sat flat down on her artistic achievements and made a face at me.

'You're not to look,' said she.

'Oh, come on, don't be nasty!' Jim came over to us, and we were just drunk enough to wheedle the kid into showing us. And those drawings of hers were extraordinary and repulsively vulgar. The creations of a lunatic with a lunatic's cleverness. There was no doubt about it, the kid's mind was diseased. While she showed them to us, she worked herself up into a mad excitement, laughing and trembling, and shooting out her arms.

'Mumma,' she yelled. 'Now I'm going to draw them what you told me I never was to – now I am.'

The woman rushed from the table and beat the child's head with the flat of her hand.

'I'll smack you with yer clothes turned up if yer dare say that again,' she bawled.

Jo was too drunk to notice, but Jim caught her by the arm. The kid did not utter a cry. She drifted over to the window and began picking flies from the treacle paper.

We returned to the table – Jim and I sitting one side, the woman and Jo, touching shoulders, the other. We listened to the thunder, saying stupidly, 'That was a near one,' 'There it goes again,' and Jo, at a heavy hit, 'Now we're off,' 'Steady on the brake,' until rain began to fall, sharp as cannon shot on the iron roof.

'You'd better doss here for the night,' said the woman.

'That's right,' assented Jo, evidently in the know about this move.

'Bring up yer things from the tent. You two can doss in the store along with the kid – she's used to sleep in there and won't mind you.'

'Oh Mumma, I never did,' interrupted the kid.

'Shut yer lies! An' Mr Jo can 'ave this room.'

It sounded a ridiculous arrangement, but it was useless to attempt to cross them, they were too far gone. While the woman sketched the plan of action, Jo sat, abnormally solemn and red, his eyes bulging, and pulling at his moustache.

'Give us a lantern,' said Jim, 'I'll go down to the paddock.' We two went together. Rain whipped in our faces, the land was light as though a bush fire was raging. We behaved like two children let loose in the thick of an adventure, laughed and shouted to each other, and came back to the whare to find the kid already bedded in the counter of the store. The woman brought us a lamp. Jo took his bundle from Jim, the door was shut.

'Good-night all,' shouted Jo.

Jim and I sat on two sacks of potatoes. For the life of us we could not stop laughing. Strings of onions and half-hams dangled from the ceiling – wherever we looked there were advertisements for 'Camp Coffee'[17] and tinned meats. We pointed at them, tried to read them aloud – overcome with laughter and hiccoughs. The kid in the counter stared at us. She threw off her blanket and scrambled to the floor, where she stood in her grey flannel night-gown, rubbing one leg against the other. We paid no attention to her.

'Wot are you laughing at?' she said, uneasily.

'You!' shouted Jim. 'The red tribe of you, my child.'

She flew into a rage and beat herself with her hands. 'I won't be laughed at, you curs – you.' He swooped down upon the child and swung her on to the counter.

'Go to sleep, Miss Smarty – or make a drawing – here's a pencil – you can use Mumma's account book.'

Through the rain we heard Jo creak over the boarding of the next room – the sound of a door being opened – then shut to.

'It's the loneliness,' whispered Jim.

'One hundred and twenty-five different ways – alas! my poor brother!'

The kid tore out a page and flung it at me.

'There you are,' she said. 'Now I done it ter spite Mumma for shutting me up 'ere with you two. I done the one she told me I never ought to. I done the one she told me she'd shoot me if I did. Don't care! Don't care!'

The kid had drawn the picture of the woman shooting at a man with a rook rifle and then digging a hole to bury him in.

She jumped off the counter and squirmed about on the floor biting her nails.

Jim and I sat till dawn with the drawing beside us. The rain ceased, the little kid fell asleep, breathing loudly. We got up, stole out of the whare, down into the paddock. White clouds floated over a pink sky – a chill wind blew; the air smelled of wet grass. Just as we swung into the saddle Jo came out of the whare – he motioned to us to ride on.

'I'll pick you up later,' he shouted.

A bend in the road, and the whole place disappeared.

(1911)

Ole Underwood

To Anne Estelle Rice[1]

Down the windy hill stalked Ole Underwood. He carried a black umbrella in one hand, in the other a red and white spotted handkerchief knotted into a lump. He wore a black peaked cap like a pilot; gold rings gleamed in his ears and his little eyes snapped like two sparks. Like two sparks they glowed in the smoulder of his bearded face. On one side of the hill grew a forest of pines from the road right down to the sea. On the other side short tufted grass and little bushes of white manuka flower. The pine-trees roared like waves in their topmost branches, their stems creaked like the timber of ships; in the windy air flew the white manuka flower. 'Ah-k!' shouted Ole Underwood, shaking his umbrella at the wind bearing down upon him, beating him, half strangling him with his black cape. 'Ah-k!' shouted the wind a hundred times as loud, and filled his mouth and nostrils with dust. Something inside Ole Underwood's breast beat like a hammer. One, two – one, two – never stopping, never changing. He couldn't do anything. It wasn't loud. No, it didn't make a noise – only a thud. One, two – one, two – like someone beating on an iron in a prison, someone in a secret place – bang – bang – bang – trying to get free. Do what he would, fumble at his coat, throw his arms about, spit, swear, he couldn't stop the noise. Stop! Stop! Stop! Stop! Ole Underwood began to shuffle and run.

Away below, the sea heaving against the stone walls, and the little town just out of its reach close packed together, the better to face the grey water. And up on the other side of the hill the prison with high red walls. Over all bulged the grey sky with black web-like clouds streaming.

Ole Underwood slackened his pace as he neared the town, and when he came to the first house he flourished his umbrella like a herald's staff and threw out his chest, his head glancing quickly from right to left. They were ugly little houses leading into the town, built of wood – two windows and a door, a stumpy verandah and a green mat of grass before. Under one verandah yellow hens huddled out of the wind. 'Shoo!' shouted Ole Underwood, and laughed to see them fly, and

47

laughed again at the woman who came to the door and shook a red, soapy fist at him. A little girl stood in another yard untwisting some rags from a clothes-line. When she saw Ole Underwood she let the clothes-prop fall and rushed screaming to the door, beating it, screaming 'Mumma – Mumma!' That started the hammer in Ole Underwood's heart. Mum-ma – Mum-ma! He saw an old face with a trembling chin and grey hair nodding out of the window as they dragged him past. Mumma – Mum-ma! He looked up at the big red prison perched on the hill and he pulled a face as if he wanted to cry.

At the corner in front of the pub some carts were pulled up, and some men sat in the porch of the pub drinking and talking. Ole Underwood wanted a drink. He slouched into the bar. It was half full of old and young men in big coats and top boots with stock whips in their hands. Behind the counter a big girl with red hair pulled the beer handles and cheeked the men. Ole Underwood sneaked to one side, like a cat. Nobody looked at him, only the men looked at each other, one or two of them nudged. The girl nodded and winked at the fellow she was serving. He took some money out of his knotted handkerchief and slipped it on to the counter. His hand shook. He didn't speak. The girl took no notice; she served everybody, went on with her talk, and then as if by accident shoved a mug towards him. A great big jar of red pinks stood on the bar counter. Ole Underwood stared at them as he drank and frowned at them. Red – red – red – red! beat the hammer. It was very warm in the bar and quiet as a pond, except for the talk and the girl. She kept on laughing. Ha! Ha! That was what the men liked to see, for she threw back her head and her great breasts lifted and shook to her laughter.

In one corner sat a stranger. He pointed at Ole Underwood. 'Cracked!' said one of the men. 'When he was a young fellow, thirty years ago, a man 'ere done in 'is woman, and 'e foun' out an' killed 'er. Got twenty years in quod up on the 'ill. Came out cracked.'

'Oo done 'er in?' asked the man.

'Dunno. 'E dunno, nor nobody. 'E was a sailor till 'e marrid 'er. Cracked!' The man spat and smeared the spittle on the floor, shrugging his shoulders. "E's 'armless enough.'

Ole Underwood heard; he did not turn, but he shot out an old claw and crushed up the red pinks. 'Uh-Uh! You ole beast! Uh! You ole swine!' screamed the girl, leaning across the counter and banging him with a tin jug. 'Get art! Get art! Don' you never come 'ere no more!' Somebody kicked him: he scuttled like a rat.

He walked past the Chinamen's shops.[2] The fruit and vegetables were all piled up against the windows. Bits of wooden cases, straw, and old newspapers were strewn over the pavement. A woman flounced out of a shop and slushed a pail of slops over his feet. He peered in at the windows, at the Chinamen sitting in little groups on old barrels playing cards. They made him smile. He looked and looked, pressing his face against the glass and sniggering. They sat still with their long pigtails bound round their heads and their faces yellow as lemons. Some of them had knives in their belts, and one old man sat by himself on the floor plaiting his long crooked toes together. The Chinamen didn't mind Ole Underwood. When they saw him they nodded. He went to the door of a shop and cautiously opened it. In rushed the wind with him, scattering the cards. 'Ya-Ya! Ya-Ya!' screamed the Chinamen, and Ole Underwood rushed off, the hammer beating quick and hard. Ya-Ya! He turned a corner out of sight. He thought he heard one of the Chinks after him, and he slipped into a timber-yard. There he lay panting . . .

Close by him, under another stack there was a heap of yellow shavings. As he watched them they moved and a little grey cat unfolded herself and came out waving her tail. She trod delicately over to Ole Underwood and rubbed against his sleeve. The hammer in Ole Underwood's heart beat madly. It pounded up into his throat, and then it seemed to half stop and beat very, very faintly. 'Kit! Kit! Kit!' That was what she used to call the little cat he brought her off the ship – 'Kit! Kit! Kit!' – and stoop down with the saucer in her hands. 'Ah! my God! my Lord!' Ole Underwood sat up and took the kitten in his arms and rocked to and fro, crushing it against his face. It was warm and soft, and it mewed faintly. He buried his eyes in its fur. My God! My Lord! He tucked the little cat in his coat and stole out of the woodyard, and slouched down towards the wharves. As he came near the sea, Ole Underwood's nostrils expanded. The mad wind smelled of tar and ropes and slime and salt. He crossed the railway line, he crept behind the wharf-sheds and along a little cinder path that threaded through a patch of rank fennel to some stone drain pipes carrying the sewage into the sea. And he stared up at the wharves and at the ships with flags flying, and suddenly the old, old lust swept over Ole Underwood. 'I will! I will! I will!' he muttered.

He tore the little cat out of his coat and swung it by its tail and flung it out to the sewer opening. The hammer beat loud and strong. He tossed his head, he was young again. He walked on to the wharves, past the wool-bales, past the loungers and the loafers to the extreme end of the wharves. The sea sucked against the wharf-poles as though it drank something from the land. One ship was loading wool. He heard a crane rattle and the shriek of a whistle. So he came to the little ship lying by herself with a bit of a plank for a gangway, and no sign of anybody – anybody at all. Ole Underwood looked once back at the town, at the prison perched like a red bird, at the black webby clouds trailing. Then he went up the gangway and on to the slippery deck. He grinned, and rolled in his walk, carrying high in his hand the red and white hand-kerchief. His ship! Mine! Mine! Mine! beat the hammer. There was a door latched open on the lee-side, labelled 'State-room.' He peered in. A man lay sleeping on a bunk – his bunk – a great big man in a seaman's coat with a long fair beard and hair on the red pillow. And looking down upon him from the wall there shone her picture – his woman's picture – smiling and smiling at the big sleeping man.

(1912)

The Little Girl

To the little girl he was a figure to be feared and avoided. Every morning before going to business he came into the nursery and gave her a perfunctory kiss, to which she responded with 'Good-bye, father.' And oh, the glad sense of relief when she heard the noise of the buggy[1] growing fainter and fainter down the long road!

In the evening, leaning over the banisters at his home-coming, she heard his loud voice in the hall. 'Bring my tea into the smoking-room . . . Hasn't the paper come yet? Have they taken it into the kitchen again? Mother, go and see if my paper's out there – and bring me my slippers.'

'Kezia,' mother would call to her, 'if you're a good girl you can come down and take off father's boots.' Slowly the girl would slip down the stairs, holding tightly to the banisters with one hand – more slowly still, across the hall, and push open the smoking-room door.

By that time he had his spectacles on and looked at her over them in a way that was terrifying to the little girl.

'Well, Kezia, get a move on and pull off these boots and take them outside. Been a good girl to-day?'

'I d-d-don't know, father.'

'You d-d-don't know? If you stutter like that mother will have to take you to the doctor.'

She never stuttered with other people – had quite given it up – but only with father, because then she was trying so hard to say the words properly.

'What's the matter? What are you looking so wretched about? Mother, I wish you would teach this child not to appear on the brink of suicide . . . Here, Kezia, carry my teacup back to the table – carefully; your hands jog like an old lady's. And try to keep your handkerchief in your pocket, *not* up your sleeve.'

'Y-y-yes, father.'

On Sundays she sat in the same pew with him in church, listening while he sang in a loud, clear voice, watching while he made little notes during the sermon with the stump of a blue pencil on the back of an envelope – his eyes narrowed to a slit – one hand beating a silent tattoo on the pew ledge. He said his prayers so loudly she was certain God heard him above the clergyman.

He was so big – his hands and his neck, especially his mouth when he yawned. Thinking about him alone in the nursery was like thinking about a giant.

On Sunday afternoons grandmother sent her down to the drawing-room, dressed in her brown velvet, to have a 'nice talk with father and mother.' But the little girl always found mother reading the *Sketch*[2] and father stretched out on the couch, his handkerchief on his face, his feet propped on one of the best sofa pillows, and so soundly sleeping that he snored.

She, perched on the piano-stool, gravely watched him until he woke and stretched, and asked the time – then looked at her.

'Don't stare so, Kezia. You look like a little brown owl.'

One day, when she was kept indoors with a cold, the grandmother told her that father's birthday was next week, and suggested she should make him a pincushion for a present out of a beautiful piece of yellow silk.

Laboriously, with a double cotton, the little girl stitched three sides. But what to fill it with? That was the question. The grandmother was out in the garden, and she wandered into mother's bedroom to look for 'scraps.' On the bed table she discovered a great many sheets of fine paper, gathered them up, shredded them into tiny pieces, and stuffed her case, then sewed up the fourth side.

That night there was a hue and cry over the house. Father's great speech for the Port Authority[3] had been lost. Rooms were ransacked – servants questioned. Finally mother came into the nursery.

'Kezia, I suppose you didn't see some papers on a table in our room?'

'Oh, yes,' she said. 'I tore them up for my s'prise.'

'*What!*' screamed mother. 'Come straight down to the dining-room this instant.'

And she was dragged down to where father was pacing to and fro, hands behind his back.

'Well?' he said sharply.

Mother explained.

He stopped and stared in a stupefied manner at the child.

'Did you do that?'

'N-n-no,' she whispered.

'Mother, go up to the nursery and fetch down the damned thing – see that the child's put to bed this instant.'

Crying too much to explain, she lay in the shadowed room watching the evening light sift through the venetian blinds and trace a sad little pattern on the floor.

Then father came into the room with a ruler in his hands.

'I am going to whip you for this,' he said.

'Oh, no, no!' she screamed, cowering down under the bedclothes.

He pulled them aside.

'Sit up,' he commanded, 'and hold out your hands. You must be taught once and for all not to touch what does not belong to you.'

'But it was for your b-b-birthday.'

Down came the ruler on her little, pink palms.

Hours later, when the grandmother had wrapped her in a shawl and rocked her in the rocking-chair the child cuddled close to her soft body.

'What did Jesus make fathers for?' she sobbed.

'Here's a clean hanky, darling, with some of my lavender water on it. Go to sleep, pet; you'll forget all about it in the morning. I tried to explain to father, but he was too upset to listen to-night.'

But the child never forgot. Next time she saw him she whipped both hands behind her back, and a red colour flew into her cheeks.

The Macdonalds lived in the next-door house. Five children there were. Looking through a hole in the vegetable garden fence the little girl saw them playing 'tag' in the evening. The father with the baby Mac on his shoulders, two little girls hanging on to his coat tails, ran round and round the flower beds, shaking with laughter. Once she saw the boys turn the hose on him – *turn the hose on him* – and he made a great grab at them, tickling them until they got hiccoughs.

Then it was she decided there were different sorts of fathers.

Suddenly, one day, mother became ill, and she and grandmother drove into town in a closed carriage.

The little girl was left alone in the house with Alice, the 'general.'[4] That was all right in the daytime, but while Alice was putting her to bed she grew suddenly afraid.

'What'll I do if I have nightmares?' she asked. 'I *often* have nightmares, and then grannie takes me into her bed – I can't stay in the dark – it all gets "whispery" . . . What'll I do if I do?'

'You just go to sleep, child,' said Alice, pulling off her socks and whacking them against the bedrail, 'and don't you holler out and wake your poor pa.'

But the same old nightmare came – the butcher with a knife and a rope who grew nearer and nearer, smiling that dreadful smile, while she could not move, could only stand still, crying out, 'Grandma, Grandma!' She woke shivering, to see father beside her bed, a candle in his hand.

'What's the matter?' he said.

'Oh, a butcher – a knife – I want grannie.' He blew out the candle, bent down and caught up the child in his arms, carrying her along the passage to the big bedroom. A newspaper was on the bed – a half-smoked cigar balanced against his reading-lamp. He pitched the paper on the floor, threw the cigar into the fireplace, then carefully tucked up the child. He lay down beside her. Half asleep still, still with the butcher's smile all about her, it seemed, she crept close to him, snuggled her head under his arm, held tightly to his pyjama jacket.

Then the dark did not matter; she lay still.

'Here, rub your feet against my legs and get them warm,' said father.

Tired out, he slept before the little girl. A funny feeling came over her. Poor father! Not so big, after all – and with no one to look after him . . . He was harder than the grandmother, but it was a nice hardness . . . And every day he had to work and was too tired to be a Mr Macdonald . . . She had torn up all his beautiful writing . . . She stirred suddenly, and sighed.

'What's the matter?' asked father. 'Another dream?'

'Oh,' said the little girl, 'my head's on your heart; I can hear it going. What a big heart you've got, father dear.'

(1912)

Millie

Millie stood leaning against the verandah until the men were out of sight. When they were far down the road Willie Cox turned round on his horse and waved. But she didn't wave back. She nodded her head a little and made a grimace. Not a bad young fellow, Willie Cox, but a bit too free and easy for her taste. Oh, my word! it was hot. Enough to fry your hair!

Millie put her handkerchief over her head and shaded her eyes with her hand. In the distance along the dusty road she could see the horses, like brown spots dancing up and down, and when she looked away from them and over the burnt paddocks she could see them still – just before her eyes, jumping like mosquitoes. It was half-past two in the afternoon. The sun hung in the faded blue sky like a burning mirror, and away beyond the paddocks the blue mountains quivered and leapt like sea.

Sid wouldn't be back until half-past ten. He had ridden over to the township with four of the boys to help hunt down the young fellow who'd murdered Mr Williamson. Such a dreadful thing! And Mrs Williamson left all alone with all those kids. Funny! she couldn't think of Mr Williamson being dead! He was such a one for a joke. Always having a lark. Willie Cox said they found him in the barn, shot bang through the head, and the young English 'johnny" who'd been on the station learning farming – disappeared. Funny! she couldn't think of anyone shooting Mr Williamson, and him so popular and all. My word! when they caught that young man! Well, you couldn't be sorry for a young fellow like that. As Sid said, if he wasn't strung up where would they all be? A man like that doesn't stop at one go. There was blood all over the barn. And Willie Cox said he was that knocked out he picked a cigarette up out of the blood and smoked it. My word! he must have been half dotty.

Millie went back into the kitchen. She put some ashes on the stove and sprinkled them with water. Languidly, the sweat pouring down her face, and dropping off her nose and chin, she cleared away the dinner, and going into the bedroom, stared at herself in the fly-specked mirror, and wiped her face and neck with a towel. She didn't know what was the matter with herself that afternoon. She could have a good cry – just for nothing – and then change her blouse and have a good cup of tea. Yes, she felt like that!

She flopped down on the side of the bed and stared at the coloured print on the wall opposite, *Garden Party at Windsor Castle*. In the foreground emerald lawns planted with immense oak trees, and in their grateful shade, a muddle of ladies and gentlemen and parasols and little tables. The background was filled with the towers of Windsor Castle, flying three Union Jacks, and in the middle of the picture the old Queen, like a tea cosy with a head on top of it. 'I wonder if it really looked like that.' Millie stared at the flowery ladies, who simpered back at her. 'I wouldn't care for that sort of thing. Too much side. What with the Queen an' one thing an' another.'

Over the packing-case dressing-table there was a large photograph of her and Sid, taken on their wedding day. Nice picture that – if you *do* like. She was sitting down in a basket chair, in her cream cashmere and satin ribbons, and Sid, standing with one hand on her shoulder, looking at her bouquet. And behind them there were some fern trees, and a waterfall, and Mount Cook² in the distance, covered with snow. She had almost forgotten her wedding day; time did pass so, and if you hadn't any one to talk things over with, they soon dropped out of your mind. 'I wunner why we never had no kids . . .' She shrugged her shoulders – gave it up. 'Well, *I've* never missed them. I wouldn't be surprised if Sid had, though. He's softer than me.'

And then she sat quiet, thinking of nothing at all, her red swollen hands rolled in her apron, her feet stuck out in front of her, her little head with the thick screw of dark hair drooped on her chest. *Tick-tick* went the kitchen clock, the ashes clinked in the grate, and the venetian blind knocked against the kitchen window. Quite suddenly Millie felt frightened. A queer trembling started inside her – in her stomach – and then spread all over to her knees and hands. 'There's somebody about.' She tiptoed to the door and peered into the kitchen. Nobody there; the verandah doors were closed, the blinds were down, and in the dusky light the white face of the clock shone, and the furniture seemed to bulge and breathe . . . and listen, too. The clock – the ashes – and the venetian – and then again – something else, like steps in the back yard. 'Go an' see what it is, Millie Evans.'

She darted to the back door, opened it, and at the same moment someone ducked behind the wood pile. 'Who's that?' she cried, in a loud, bold voice. 'Come out o' that! I seen yer. I know where y'are. I got my gun. Come out from behind of that wood stack!' She was not frightened any more. She was furiously angry. Her heart banged like a drum. 'I'll teach you to play tricks with a woman,' she yelled, and she took a gun from the kitchen corner, and dashed down the verandah steps, across the glaring yard to the other side of the wood stack. A young man lay there, on his stomach, one arm across his face. 'Get up! You're shamming!' Still holding the gun she kicked him in the shoulders. He gave no sign. 'Oh, my God, I believe he's dead.' She knelt down, seized hold of him, and turned him over on his back. He rolled like a sack. She crouched back on her haunches, staring; her lips and nostrils fluttered with horror.

He was not much more than a boy, with fair hair, and a growth of fair down on his lips and chin. His eyes were open, rolled up, showing the whites, and his face was patched with dust caked with sweat. He wore a cotton shirt and trousers, with sandshoes on his feet. One of the trousers was stuck to his leg with a patch of dark blood. 'I *can't*,' said Millie, and then, 'You've got to.' She bent over and felt his heart. 'Wait a minute,' she stammered, 'wait a minute,' and she ran into the house for brandy and a pail of water. 'What are you going to do, Millie Evans? Oh, I don't know. I never seen anyone in a dead faint before.' She knelt down, put her arm under the boy's head and poured some brandy between his lips. It spilled down both sides of his mouth. She dipped a corner of her apron in the water and wiped his face and his hair and his throat, with fingers that trembled. Under the dust and sweat his face gleamed, white as her apron, and thin, and puckered in little lines. A strange dreadful feeling gripped Millie Evans' bosom – some seed that had never flourished there, unfolded and struck deep roots and burst into painful leaf. 'Are yer coming round? Feeling all right again?' The boy breathed sharply, half choked, his eyelids quivered, and he moved his head from side to side. 'You're better,' said Millie, smoothing his hair. 'Feeling fine now again, ain't you?' The pain in her bosom half suffocated her. 'It's no good you crying, Millie Evans. You got to keep your head.' Quite suddenly he sat up and leaned against the wood pile, away from her, staring on the ground. 'There now!' cried Millie Evans, in a strange, shaking voice.

The boy turned and looked at her, still not speaking, but his eyes were so full of pain and terror that she had to shut her teeth and clench her hands to stop from crying. After a long pause he said in the little voice of a child talking in his sleep, 'I'm hungry.' His lips quivered. She scrambled to her feet and stood over him. 'You come right into the house and have a sit down meal,' she said. 'Can you walk?' 'Yes,' he whispered, and swaying he followed her across the glaring yard to the verandah. At the bottom step he paused, looking at her again. 'I'm not coming in,' he said. He sat on the verandah step in the little pool of shade that lay round the house. Millie watched him. 'When did yer last 'ave anythink to eat?' He shook his head. She cut a chunk off the greasy corned beef and a round of bread plastered with butter; but when she brought it he was standing up, glancing round him, and paid no attention to the plate of food. 'When are they coming back?' he stammered.

At that moment she knew. She stood, holding the plate, staring. He was Harrison. He was the English johnny who'd killed Mr Williamson. 'I know who you are,' she said, very slowly, 'yer can't fox me. That's who you are. I must have been blind in me two eyes not to 'ave known from the first.' He made a movement with his hands as though that was all nothing. 'When are they coming back?' And she meant to say, 'Any minute. They're on their way now.' Instead she said to the dreadful, frightened face, 'Not till 'arf past ten.' He sat down, leaning against one of the verandah poles. His face broke up into little quivers. He shut his eyes and tears streamed down his cheeks. 'Nothing but a kid. An' all them fellows after 'im. 'E don't stand any more of a chance than a kid would.' 'Try a bit of beef,' said Millie. 'It's the food you want. Something to steady your stomach.' She moved across the verandah and sat down beside him, the plate on her knees. ''Ere – try a bit.' She broke the bread and butter into little pieces, and she thought, 'They won't ketch him. Not if I can 'elp it. Men is all beasts. I don' care wot 'e's done, or wot 'e 'asn't done. See 'im through, Millie Evans. 'E's nothink but a sick kid.'

Millie lay on her back, her eyes wide open, listening. Sid turned over, hunched the quilt round his shoulders, muttered 'Good-night, ole girl.' She heard Willie Cox and the other chap drop their clothes on to the kitchen floor, and then their voices, and Willie Cox saying, 'Lie down, Gumboil. Lie down, yer little devil,' to his dog. The house dropped quiet. She lay and listened. Little pulses tapped in her body, listening, too. It was hot. She was frightened to move because of Sid. ''E must get off. 'E must. I don' care anythink about justice an' all the rot they've bin spoutin' to-night,' she thought, savagely. ''Ow are yer to know what anythink's like till yer *do* know. It's all rot.' She strained to the silence. He ought to be moving . . . Before there was a sound from outside, Willie Cox's Gumboil got up and padded sharply across the kitchen floor and sniffed at the back door. Terror started up in Millie. 'What's that dog doing? Uh! What a fool that young fellow is with a dog 'anging about. Why don't 'e lie down an' sleep.' The dog stopped, but she knew it was listening.

Suddenly, with a sound that made her cry out in horror the dog started barking and rushing to and fro. 'What's that? What's up?' Sid flung out of bed. 'It ain't nothink. It's only Gumboil. Sid, Sid!' She clutched his arm, but he shook her off. 'My Christ, there's somethink up. My God!' Sid flung into his trousers. Willie Cox opened the back door. Gumboil in a fury darted out into the yard, round the corner of the house. 'Sid, there's someone in the paddock,' roared the other chap. 'What is it – what's that?' Sid dashed out on to the front verandah. ''Ere, Millie, take the lantin. Willie, some skunk's got 'old of one of the 'orses.' The three men bolted out of the house, and at the same moment Millie saw Harrison dash across the paddock on Sid's horse and down the road. 'Millie, bring that blasted lantin.' She ran in her bare feet, her nightdress flicking her legs. They were after him in a flash. And at the sight of Harrison in the distance, and the three men hot after, a strange mad joy smothered everything else. She rushed into the road – she laughed and shrieked and danced in the dust, jigging the lantern. 'A – ah! Arter 'im, Sid! A – a – a – h! Ketch him, Willie. Go it! Go it! A – ah, Sid! Shoot 'im down. Shoot 'im!'

(1913)

Pension Séguin

The servant who opened the door was twin sister to that efficient and hideous creature bearing a soup tureen into the *First French Picture*.[1] Her round red face shone like freshly washed china. She had a pair of immense bare arms to match, and a quantity of mottled hair arranged in a sort of bow. I stammered in a ridiculous, breathless fashion, as though a pack of Russian wolves were behind me, rather than five flights of beautifully polished French stairs.

'Have you a room?' The servant girl did not know. She would ask Madame. Madame was at dinner.

'Will you come in, please?'

Through the dark hall, guarded by a large black stove that had the appearance of a headless cat with one red all-seeing eye in the middle of its stomach, I followed her into the salon.

'Please to sit down,' said the servant girl, closing the door behind her. I heard her list slippers shuffle along the corridor, the sound of another door opening – a little clamour – instantly suppressed. Silence followed.

The salon was long and narrow, with a yellow floor dotted with white mats. White muslin curtains hid the windows: the walls were white, decorated with pictures of pale ladies drifting down cypress avenues to forsaken temples, and moons rising over boundless oceans. You would have thought that all the long years of Madame's virginity had been devoted to the making of white mats – that her childish voice had lisped its numbers in crochet-work stitches. I did not dare to begin counting them. They rained upon me from every possible place, like impossible snowflakes. Even the piano stool was buttoned into one embroidered with P. F.

I had been looking for a resting place all the morning. At the start I flew up innumerable stairs as though they were major scales – the most cheerful things in the world – but after repeated failures the scales had resolved into the minor, and my heart, which was quite cast down by this time, leapt up again at these signs and tokens of virtue and sobriety. 'A woman with such sober passions,' thought I, 'is bound to be quiet and clean, with few babies and a much absent husband. Mats are not the sort of things that lend themselves in their making to cheerful singing. Mats are essentially the fruits of pious solitude. I shall certainly take a room here.' And I began to dream of unpacking my clothes in a little white room, and getting into a kimono and lying on a white bed, watching the curtains float out from the windows in the delicious autumn air that smelled of apples and honey . . . until the door opened and a tall thin woman in a lilac pinafore came in, smiling in a vague fashion.

'Madame Séguin?'

'Yes, Madame.'

I repeated the familiar story. A quiet room, removed from any church bells, or crowing cocks, or little boys' schools, or railway stations.

'There are none of such things anywhere near here,' said Madame, looking very surprised. 'I have a very beautiful room to let, and quite unexpectedly. It has been occupied by a young gentleman from Buenos Aires whose father died, unfortunately, and implored him to return home immediately. Quite natural, indeed.'

'Oh, very!' said I, hoping that the Hamlet-like apparition[2] was at rest again and would not invade my solitude to make certain of his son's obedience.

'If Madame will follow me.'

Down a dark corridor, round a corner I felt my way. I wanted to ask Madame if this was where Buenos Aires *père* appeared unto his son, but I did not dare to.

'Here – you see. Quite away from everything,' said Madame.

I have always viewed with a proper amount of respect and abhorrence those penetrating spirits who are not susceptible to appearances. What is there to believe in except appearances? I have nearly always found that they are the only things worth enjoying at all, and if ever an innocent child lays its head upon my knee and begs for the truth of the matter, I shall tell it the story of my one and only nurse, who, knowing my horror of gooseberry jam, spread a coat of apricot over the top of the jam jar. As long as I believed it apricot I was happy, and learning wisdom, I contrived to eat the apricot and leave the gooseberry behind. 'So, you see, my little innocent creature,' I shall end, 'the great thing to learn in this life is to be content with appearances, and shun the vulgarities of the grocer and philosopher.'

Bright sunlight streamed through the windows of the delightful room. There was an alcove for the bed, a writing table was placed against the window, a couch against the wall. And outside the window I looked down upon an avenue of gold and red trees and up at a range of mountains white with fresh fallen snow.

'One hundred and eighty francs a month,' murmured Madame, smiling at nothing, but seeming to imply by her manner, 'Of course this has nothing to do with the matter.' I said, 'That is too much. I cannot afford more than one hundred and fifty francs.'

'But,' explained Madame, 'the size! the alcove! And the extreme rarity of being overlooked by so many mountains.'

'Yes,' I said.

'And then the food. There are four meals a day, and breakfast in your room if you wish it.'

'Yes,' I said, more feebly.

'And my husband a Professor at the Conservatoire' – that again is so rare.'

Courage is like a disobedient dog, once it starts running away it flies all the faster for your attempts to recall it.

'One hundred and sixty,' I said.

'If you agree to take it for two months I will accept,' said Madame, very quickly. I agreed.

Marie helped to unstrap my boxes. She knelt on the floor, grinning and scratching her big red arms.

'Ah, how glad I am Madame has come,' she said. 'Now we shall have some life again. Monsieur Arthur, who lived in this room – he was a gay one. Singing all day and sometimes dancing. Many a time Mademoiselle Ambatielos would be playing and he'd dance for an hour without stopping.'

'Who is Mademoiselle Ambatielos?' I asked.

'A young lady studying at the Conservatoire,' said Marie, sniffing in a very friendly fashion. 'But she gives lessons too. *Ah, mon Dieu*, sometimes when I am dusting in her room I think her fingers will drop off. She plays all day long. But I like that – that's life, noise is. That's what I say. You'll hear her soon. Up and down she goes!' said Marie, with extreme heartiness.

'But,' I cried, loathing Marie, 'how many other people are staying here?'

Marie shrugged. 'Nobody to speak of. There's the Russian gentle-man, a priest he is, and Madame's three children – and that's all. The children are lively enough,' she said, filling the wash-stand pitcher, 'but then there's the baby – the boy! Ah, you'll know about him, poor little one, soon enough!' She was so detestable I would not ask her anything further.

I waited until she was gone, and leaned against the window sill, watching the sun deepen in the trees until they seemed full and trem-bling with gold, and wondering what was the matter with the mysterious baby.

All through the afternoon Mademoiselle Ambatielos and the piano warred with the Appassionata Sonata.[4] They shattered it to bits and re-made it to their heart's desire – they unpicked it – and tried it in various styles. They added a little touch – caught up something. Finally they decided that the only thing of importance was the loud pedal. The mysterious baby, hidden behind Heaven knows how many doors, cried with such curious persistence that I had to strain my ears, wondering if it was a baby or an engine or a far-off whistle. At dusk Marie, accom-panied by the two little girls, brought me a lamp. My appearance dis-turbed these charming children to such an extent that they rushed up and down the corridor in a frenzied state for half-an-hour afterwards, bumping themselves against the walls, and shrieking with derisive laughter.

At eight the gong sounded for supper. I was hungry. The corridor was filled with the warm, strong smell of cooked meat. 'Well,' I thought, 'at any rate, judging by the smell, the food must be good.' And feeling very frightened I entered the dining-room.

Two rows of faces turned to watch me. M. Séguin introduced me, rapped on the table with the soup spoon, and the two little girls, impu-dent and scornful, cried: '*Bon soir, Madame,*' while the baby, half washed away by his afternoon's performance, emptied his cup of milk over his head while Madame Séguin showed me my seat. In the confusion caused by this last episode, and by his being carried away by Marie, screaming and spitting with rage, I sat down next to the Russian priest and oppos-ite Mademoiselle Ambatielos. M. Séguin took a loaf of bread from a three-legged basket at his elbow and carved it against his chest. Soup was served – with vermicelli letters of the alphabet floating in it. These were last straws to the little Séguins' table manners.

'*Maman*, Yvonne's got more letters than me.'

'*Maman*, Hélène keeps taking my letters out with her spoon.'

'Children! Children! Quiet, quiet!' said Madame Séguin gently. 'No, don't do it.'

Hélène seized Yvonne's plate and pulled it towards her.

'Stop,' said M. Séguin, who was like a rat, with spectacles all misted over with soup steam. 'Hélène, leave the table. Go to Marie.' Exit Hélène, with her apron over her head.

Soup was followed by chestnuts and Brussels sprouts. All the time the Russian priest, who wore a pale blue tie with a buttoned frock coat and a moustache fierce as a Gogol novel,[1] kept up a flow of conversation with Mademoiselle Ambatielos. She looked very young. She was stout, with a high firm bust decorated with a spray of artificial roses. She never ceased touching the roses or her blouse or hair, or looking at her hands – with a smile trembling on her mouth and her blue eyes wide and staring. She seemed half intoxicated with her fresh young body.

'I saw you this morning when you didn't see me,' said the priest.

'You didn't.'

'I did.'

'He didn't, did he, Madame?'

Madame Séguin smiled, and carried away the chestnuts, bringing back a dish of pears.

'I hope you will come into the salon after dinner,' she said to me. 'We always chat a little – we are such a family party.' I smiled, wondering why pears should follow chestnuts.

'I must apologise for baby,' she went on. 'He is so nervous. But he spends his day in a room at the other end of the apartment to you. You will not be troubled. Only think of it! He passes whole days banging his little head against the floor and walls. The doctors cannot understand it at all.'

M. Séguin pushed back his chair, said grace. I followed desperately into the salon. 'I expect you have been admiring my mats,' said Madame Séguin, with more animation than she had hitherto shown. 'People always imagine they are the product of my industry. But, alas, no! They are all made by my friend, Madame Kummer, who has the pension on the first floor.'

(1913)

Violet

'I met a young virgin
Who sadly did moan . . .'

There is a very unctuous and irritating English proverb to the effect that
'Every cloud has a silver lining.' What comfort can it be to one steeped
to the eyebrows in clouds to ponder over their linings, and what an
unpleasant picture-postcard seal it sets upon one's tragedy – turning it
into a little ha'penny monstrosity with a moon in the left-hand corner
like a vainglorious threepenny bit! Nevertheless, like most unctuous and
irritating things, it is true. The lining woke me after my first night at the
Pension Séguin and showed me over the feather bolster a room bright
with sunlight as if every golden-haired baby in Heaven were pelting the
earth with buttercup posies. 'What a charming fancy!' I thought. 'How
much prettier than the proverb! It sounds like a day in the country
with Katharine Tynan.'

And I saw a little picture of myself and Katharine Tynan being
handed glasses of milk by a red-faced woman with an immensely fat
apron, while we discussed the direct truth of proverbs as opposed to
the fallacy of playful babies. But in such a case imaginary I was ranged
on the side of the proverbs. 'There's a lot of sound sense in 'em,' said
that coarse being. 'I admire the way they put their collective foot down
upon the female attempt to embroider everything. "The pitcher that
goes too often to the well gets broken." *Also gut.* Not even a loophole
for a set of verses to a broken pitcher. No possible chance of the well
being one of those symbolic founts to which all hearts in the form of
pitchers are carried. The only proverb I disapprove of,' went on this
impossible creature, pulling a spring onion from the garden bed and
chewing on it, 'is the one about a bird in the hand. I naturally prefer
birds in bushes.' 'But,' said Katharine Tynan, tender and brooding, as
she lifted a little green fly from her milk glass, 'but if you were Saint
Francis, the bird would not *mind* being in your hand. It would *prefer* the
white nest of your fingers to any bush.'

I jumped out of bed and ran over to the window and opened it wide and leaned out. Down below in the avenue a wind shook and swung the trees; the scent of leaves was on the lifting air. The houses lining the avenue were small and white. Charming, chaste-looking little houses, showing glimpses of lace and knots of ribbon, for all the world like country children in a row, about to play 'Nuts and May.' I began to imagine an adorable little creature named Yvette who lived in one and all of these houses . . . She spends her morning in a white lace boudoir cap, worked with daisies, sipping chocolate from a Sèvres cup[3] with one hand, while a faithful attendant polishes the little pink nails of the other. She spends the afternoon in her tiny white and gold boudoir, curled up, a Persian kitten on her lap, while her ardent, beautiful lover leans over the back of the sofa, kissing and kissing again that thrice fascinating dimple on her left shoulder . . . When one of the balcony windows opened, and a stout servant swaggered out with her arms full of rugs and carpet strips. With a gesture expressing fury and disgust she flung them over the railing, disappeared, re-appeared again with a long-handled cane broom and fell upon the wretched rugs and carpets. Bang! Whack! Whack! Bang! Their feeble, pitiful jigging inflamed her to ever greater effort. Clouds of dust flew up round her, and when one little rug escaped and flopped down to the avenue below, like a fish, she leaned over the balcony, shaking her fist and the broom at it.

Lured by the noise, an old gentleman came to a window opposite and cast an eye of approval upon the industrious girl and yawned in the face of the lovely day. There was an air of detachment and deliberation about the way he carefully felt over the muscles of his arms and legs, pressed his throat, coughed, and shot a jet of spittle out of the window. Nobody seemed more surprised at this last feat than he. He seemed to regard it as a small triumph in its way, buttoning his immense stomach into a white piqué[4] waistcoat with every appearance of satisfaction. Away flew my charming Yvette in a black and white check dress, an alpaca[5] apron, and a market basket over her arm.

I dressed, ate a roll and drank some tepid coffee, feeling very sobered. I thought how true it was that the world was a delightful place if it were not for the people, and how more than true it was that people were not worth troubling about, and that wise men should set their affections upon nothing smaller than cities, heavenly or otherwise, and country-sides, which are always heavenly.

With these reflections, both pious and smug, I put on my hat, groped my way along the dark passage, and ran down the five flights of stairs into the Rue St Léger.[6] There was a garden on the opposite side of the street, through which one walked to the University and the more pretentious avenues fronting the Place du Théâtre.[7] Although autumn was well advanced, not a leaf had fallen from the trees, the little shrubs and bushes were touched with pink and crimson, and against the blue sky the trees stood sheathed in gold. On stone benches nursemaids in white cloaks and stiff white caps chattered and wagged their heads like a company of cockatoos, and, up and down, in the sun, some genteel babies bowled hoops with a delicate air. What peculiar pleasure it is to wander through a strange city and amuse oneself as a child does, playing a solitary game!

'*Pardon, Madame, mais voulez-vous . . .*' and then the voice faltered and cried my name as though I had been given up for lost times without number; as though I had been drowned in foreign seas, and burnt in American hotel fires, and buried in a hundred lonely graves. 'What on *earth* are you doing here?' Before me, not a day changed, not a hairpin altered, stood Violet Burton. I was flattered beyond measure at this enthusiasm, and pressed her cold, strong hand, and said 'Extraordinary!'

'But what are you *here* for?'

'. . . Nerves.'

'Oh, impossible, I really can't believe that.'

'It is perfectly true,' I said, my enthusiasm waning. There is nothing more annoying to a woman than to be suspected of nerves of iron.

'Well, you certainly don't *look* it,' said she, scrutinising me, with that direct English frankness that makes one feel as though sitting in the glare of a window at breakfast-time.

'What are *you* here for?' I said, smiling graciously to soften the glare. At that she turned and looked across the lawns, and fidgeted with her umbrella like a provincial actress about to make a confession.

'I' – in a quiet affected voice – 'I came here to forget . . . But,' facing me again, and smiling energetically, 'don't let's talk about that. Not yet. I can't explain. Not until I know you all over again.' Very solemnly – 'Not until I am sure you are to be trusted.'

'Oh, don't trust me, Violet!' I cried. 'I'm not to be trusted. I wouldn't if I were you.' She frowned and stared.

'What a terrible thing to say. You can't be in earnest.'

'Yes, I am. There's nothing I adore talking about so much as another person's secret.' To my surprise, she came to my side and put her arm through mine.

'Thank you,' she said, gratefully. 'I think it's awfully good of you to take me into your confidence like that. Awfully. And even if it were true . . . but no, it can't be true, otherwise you wouldn't have told me. I mean it can't be psychologically true of the same nature to be frank and dishonourable at the same time. Can it? But then . . . I don't know. I suppose it is possible. Don't you find that the Russian novelists have made an upheaval of all your conclusions?' We walked, *bras dessus bras dessous*, down the sunny path.

'Let's sit down,' said Violet. 'There's a fountain quite near this bench. I often come here. You can hear it all the time.' The faint noise of the water sounded like a half-forgotten tune, half sly, half laughing.

'Isn't it wonderful!' breathed Violet. 'Like weeping in the night.'

'Oh, Violet,' said I, terrified at this turn. 'Wonderful things don't weep in the night. They sleep like tops and know nothing more till again it is day.'

She put her arm over the back of the bench and crossed her legs.

'Why do you persist in denying your emotions? Why are you ashamed of them?' she demanded.

'I'm not. But I keep them tucked away, and only produce them very occasionally, like special little pots of jam, when the people whom I love come to tea.'

'There you are again! Emotions and jam! Now, I'm absolutely different. I live on mine. Sometimes I wish I didn't – but then again I would rather suffer through them – suffer intensely, I mean; go down into the depths with them, for the sake of that wonderful upward swing on to the pinnacles of happiness.' She edged nearer to me.

'I wish I could think where I get my nature from,' she went on. 'Father and mother are absolutely different. I mean – they're quite normal – quite commonplace.' I shook my head and raised my eyebrows. 'But it is no use fighting it. It has beaten me. Absolutely – once and for all.' A pause, inadequately filled by the sly, laughing water. 'Now,' said Violet, impressively, 'you know what I meant when I said I came here to forget.'

'But I assure you I don't, Violet. How can you expect me to be so subtle? I quite understand that you don't wish to tell me until you know me better. Quite!'

She opened her eyes and her mouth.

'I *have* told you! I mean – not straight out. Not in so many words. But then – how could I? But when I told you of my emotional nature, and that I had been in the depths and swept up to the pinnacles ... surely, surely you realised that I was telling you, symbolically. What else can you have thought?'

No young girl ever performs such gymnastic feats by herself. Yet in my experience I had always imagined that the depths followed the pinnacles. I ventured to suggest so.

'They do,' said Violet, gloomily. 'You see them, if you look, before and after.'

'Like the people in Shelley's "Skylark",[8] said I.

Violet looked vague, and I repented. But I did not know how to sympathise, and I had no idea of the relative sizes.

'It was in the summer,' said Violet. 'I had been most frightfully depressed. I don't know what it was. For one thing I felt as though I could not make up my mind to anything. I felt so terribly useless – that I had no place in the scheme of things – and worst of all, nobody who understood me ... It may have been what I was reading at the time ... but I don't think ... not entirely. Still one never knows. Does one? And then I met ... Mr Farr, at a dance –'

'Oh, call him by his Christian name, Violet. You can't go on telling me about Mr Farr and you ... on the heights.'

'Why on earth not? Very well – I met – Arthur. I think I must have been mad that evening. For one thing there had been a bother about going. Mother didn't want me to, because she said there wouldn't be anybody to see me home. And I was frightfully keen. I must have had a presentiment, I think. Do you believe in presentiments? ... I don't know, we can't be certain, can we? Anyhow, I went. And *he* was there.' She turned a deep scarlet and bit her lip. Oh, I really began to like Violet Burton – to like her very much indeed.

'Go on,' I said.

'We danced together seven times and we talked the whole time. The music was very slow, – we talked of everything. You know ... about books and theatres and all that sort of thing at first, and then – about our souls.'

'... What?'

'I said – our souls. He understood me *absolutely*. And after the seventh dance . . . No, I must tell you the first thing he ever said to me. He said, "Do you believe in Pan?"[9] Quite quietly. Just like that. And then he said, "I knew you did." Wasn't that extra-or-din-ary! After the seventh dance we sat out on the landing. And . . . shall I go on?'

'Yes, go on.'

'He said, "I think I must be mad. I want to kiss you," – and – I let him.'

'Do go on.'

'I simply can't tell you what I felt like. Fancy! I'd never kissed out of the family before. I mean – of course – never a man. And then he said: "I must tell you – I am engaged."'

'Well?'

'What else is there? Of course I simply rushed upstairs and tumbled everything over in the dressing-room and found my coat and went home. And next morning I made Mother let me come here. I thought,' said Violet, 'I thought I would have died of shame.'

'Is that all?' I cried. 'You can't mean to say that's all?'

'What else could there be? What on earth did you expect? How extra-ordinary you are – staring at me like that!'

And in the long pause I heard again the little fountain, half sly, half laughing – at me, I thought, not at Violet.

(1913)

Bains Turcs

'Third storey – to the left, Madame,' said the cashier, handing me a pink ticket. 'One moment – I will ring for the elevator.' Her black satin skirt swished across the scarlet and gold hall, and she stood among the artificial palms, her white neck and powdered face topped with masses of gleaming orange hair – like an over-ripe fungus bursting from a thick, black stem. She rang and rang. 'A thousand pardons, Madame. It is disgraceful. A new attendant. He leaves this week.' With her fingers on the bell she peered into the cage as though she expected to see him, lying on the floor, like a dead bird. 'It is disgraceful.' There appeared from nowhere a tiny figure disguised in a peaked cap and dirty white cotton gloves. 'Here you are!' she scolded. 'Where have you been? What have you been doing?' For answer the figure hid its face behind one of the white cotton gloves and sneezed twice. 'Ugh! Disgusting! Take Madame to the third storey!' The midget stepped aside, bowed, entered after me and clashed the gates to. We ascended, very slowly, to an accompaniment of sneezes and prolonged, half whistling sniffs. I asked the top of the patent-leather cap: 'Have you a cold?' 'It is the air, Madame,' replied the creature, speaking through its nose with a re-strained air of great relish, 'one is never dry here. Third floor – *if* you please,' sneezing over my ten-centime tip.

I walked along a tiled corridor decorated with advertisements for lingerie and bust improvers – was allotted a tiny cabin and a blue print chemise and told to undress and find the Warm Room as soon as possible. Through the matchboard walls and from the corridor sounded cries and laughter and snatches of conversation.

'Are you ready?'

'Are you coming out now?'

'Wait till you see me!'

'Berthe – Berthe!'

'One moment! One moment! Immediately!'

I undressed quickly and carelessly, feeling like one of a troupe of little schoolgirls let loose in a swimming-bath.

The Warm Room was not large. It had terracotta painted walls with a fringe of peacocks, and a glass roof, through which one could see the sky, pale and unreal as a photographer's background screen. Some round tables strewn with shabby fashion journals, a marble basin in the centre of the room, filled with yellow lilies, and on the long, towel enveloped chairs, a number of ladies, apparently languid as the flowers . . . I lay back with a cloth over my head, and the air, smelling of jungles and circuses and damp washing made me begin to dream . . . Yes, it might have been very fascinating to have married an explorer . . . and lived in a jungle, as long as he didn't shoot anything or take anything captive. I detest performing beasts. Oh . . . those circuses at home . . . the tent in the paddock and the children swarming over the fence to stare at the waggons and at the clown making up, with his glass stuck on the waggon wheel – and the steam organ playing the 'Honeysuckle and the Bee'¹ much too fast . . . over and over. I know what this air reminds me of – a game of follow my leader among the clothes hung out to dry . . .

The door opened. Two tall blonde women in red and white check gowns came in and took the chairs opposite mine. One of them carried a box of mandarins wrapped in silver paper and the other a manicure set. They were very stout, with gay, bold faces, and quantities of exquisite whipped fair hair.

Before sitting down they glanced round the room, looked the other women up and down, turned to each other, grimaced, whispered something, and one of them said, offering the box, 'Have a mandarin?' At that they started laughing – they lay back and shook, and each time they caught sight of each other broke out afresh.

'Ah, that was too good,' cried one, wiping her eyes very carefully, just at the corners. 'You and I, coming in here, quite serious, you know, very correct – and looking round the room – and – and as a result of our *careful* inspection – I offer you a mandarin. No, it's too funny. I must remember that. It's good enough for a music hall. Have a mandarin?'

'But I cannot imagine,' said the other, 'why women look so hideous in Turkish baths – like beef-steaks in chemises. Is it the women – or is it the air? Look at that one, for instance – the skinny one, reading a book and sweating at the moustache – and those two over in the corner, discussing whether or not they ought to tell their non-existent babies

how babies come – and . . . Heavens! Look at this one coming in. Take
the box, dear. Have all the mandarins.'

The newcomer was a short stout little woman with flat, white feet,
and a black mackintosh cap over her hair. She walked up and down the
room, swinging her arms, in affected unconcern, glancing contemptu-
ously at the laughing women, and rang the bell for the attendant. It was
answered immediately by Berthe, half naked and sprinkled with soap-
suds. 'Well, what is it, Madame? I've no time . . .'

'Please bring me a hand towel,' said the Mackintosh Cap, in German.

'Pardon? I do not understand. Do you speak French?'

'*Non*,' said the Mackintosh Cap.

'Ber-the!' shrieked one of the blonde women, 'have a mandarin. Oh,
mon Dieu, I shall die of laughing.'

The Mackintosh Cap went through a pantomime of finding herself
wet and rubbing herself dry. '*Verstehen Sie?*'

'*Mais non, Madame*,' said Berthe, watching with round eyes that
snapped with laughter, and she left the Mackintosh Cap, winked at the
blonde women, came over, felt them as though they had been a pair of
prize poultry, said 'You are doing very well,' and disappeared again.

The Mackintosh Cap sat down on the edge of a chair, snatched a
fashion journal, smacked over the crackling pages and pretended to
read, while the blonde women leaned back eating the mandarins and
throwing the peelings into the lily basin. A scent of fruit, fresh and
penetrating, hung on the air. I looked round at the other women. Yes,
they were hideous, lying back, red and moist, with dull eyes and lank
hair, the only little energy they had vented in shocked prudery at the
behaviour of the two blondes. Suddenly I discovered Mackintosh Cap
staring at me over the top of her fashion journal, so intently that I took
flight and went into the hot room. But in vain! Mackintosh Cap followed after and planted herself in front of me.

'I know,' she said, confident and confiding, 'that you can speak
German. I saw it in your face just now. Wasn't that a scandal about the
attendant refusing me a towel? I shall speak to the management about
that, and I shall get my husband to write them a letter this evening.
Things always come better from a man, don't they? No,' she said, rubbing her yellowish arms, 'I've never been in such a scandalous place –
and four francs fifty to pay! Naturally, I shall not give a tip. You
wouldn't, would you? Not after that scandal about a hand towel . . . I've

a great mind to complain about those women as well. Those two that keep on laughing and eating. Do you know who they are?' She shook her head. 'They're not respectable women – you can tell at a glance. At least I can, any married woman can. They're nothing but a couple of street women. I've never been so insulted in my life. Laughing at me, mind you! The great big fat pigs like that! And I haven't sweated at all properly, just because of them. I got so angry that the sweat turned in instead of out; it does in excitement, you know, sometimes, and now instead of losing my cold I wouldn't be surprised if I brought on a fever.'

I walked round the hot room in misery pursued by the Mackintosh Cap until the two blonde women came in, and seeing her, burst into another fit of laughter. To my rage and disgust Mackintosh Cap sidled up to me, smiled meaningly, and drew down her mouth. 'I don't care,' she said, in her hideous German voice. 'I shouldn't lower myself by paying any attention to a couple of street women. If my husband knew he'd never get over it. Dreadfully particular he is. We've been married six years. We come from Pfalzburg. It's a nice town. Four children I have living, and it was really to get over the shock of the fifth that we came here. The fifth,' she whispered, padding after me, 'was born, a fine healthy child, and it never breathed! Well, after nine months, a woman can't help being disappointed, can she?'

I moved towards the vapour room. 'Are you going in there?' she said. 'I wouldn't if I were you. Those two have gone in. They may think you want to strike up an acquaintance with them. You never know women like that.' At that moment they came out, wrapping themselves in the rough gowns, and passing Mackintosh Cap like disdainful queens. 'Are you going to take your chemise off in the vapour room?' asked she. 'Don't mind me, you know. Woman is woman, and besides, if you'd rather, I won't look at you. I know – I used to be like that. I wouldn't mind betting,' she went on savagely, 'those filthy women had a good look at each other. Pooh! women like that. You can't shock them. And don't they look dreadful? Bold, and all that false hair. That manicure box one of them had was fitted up with gold. Well, I don't suppose it was real, but I think it was disgusting to bring it. One might at least cut one's nails in private, don't you think? I *cannot* see,' she said, 'what men see in such women. No, a husband and children and a home to look after, that's what a woman needs. That's what my husband says. Fancy one of these hussies peeling potatoes or choosing the meat! Are you going already?'

I flew to find Berthe, and all the time I was soaped and smacked and sprayed and thrown in a cold water tank I could not get out of my mind the ugly, wretched figure of the little German with a good husband and four children, railing against the two fresh beauties who had never peeled potatoes nor chosen the right meat. In the ante-room I saw them once again. They were dressed in blue. One was pinning on a bunch of violets, the other buttoning a pair of ivory suède gloves. In their charming feathered hats and furs they stood talking. 'Yes, there they are,' said a voice at my elbow.

And there was Mackintosh Cap, transformed, in a blue and white check blouse and crochet collar, with the little waist and large hips of the German woman and a terrible bird nest, which Pfalzburg doubtless called *Reisehut*,[2] on her head. 'How do you suppose they can afford clothes like that? The horrible, low creatures. No, they're enough to make a young girl think twice.' And as the two walked out of the ante-room, Mackintosh Cap stared after them, her sallow face all mouth and eyes, like the face of a hungry child before a forbidden table.

(1913)

Something Childish but very Natural

Whether he had forgotten what it felt like, or his head had really grown bigger since the summer before, Henry could not decide. But his straw hat hurt him: it pinched his forehead and started a dull ache in the two bones just over the temples. So he chose a corner seat in a third-class 'smoker,' took off his hat and put it in the rack with his large black cardboard portfolio and his Aunt B's Christmas-present gloves. The carriage smelt horribly of wet india-rubber and soot. There were ten minutes to spare before the train went, so Henry decided to go and have a look at the book-stall. Sunlight darted through the glass roof of the station in long beams of blue and gold; a little boy ran up and down carrying a tray of primroses; there was something about the people – about the women especially – something idle and yet eager. The most thrilling day of the year, the first real day of Spring had unclosed its warm delicious beauty even to London eyes. It had put a spangle in every colour and a new tone in every voice, and city folks walked as though they carried real live bodies under their clothes with real live hearts pumping the stiff blood through.

Henry was a great fellow for books. He did not read many nor did he possess above half-a-dozen. He looked at all in the Charing Cross Road during lunch-time and at any odd time in London; the quantity with which he was on nodding terms was amazing. By his clean neat handling of them and by his nice choice of phrase when discussing them with one or another bookseller you would have thought that he had taken his pap with a tome propped before his nurse's bosom. But you would have been quite wrong. That was only Henry's way with everything he touched or said. That afternoon it was an anthology of English poetry, and he turned over the pages until a title struck his eye – 'Something Childish but very Natural!'[1]

> Had I but two little wings,
> And were a little feathery bird,
> To you I'd fly, my dear,

76

> But thoughts like these are idle things,
> And I stay here.
>
> But in my sleep to you I fly,
> I'm always with you in my sleep,
> The world is all one's own,
> But then one wakes and where am I?
> All, all alone.
>
> Sleep stays not though a monarch bids,
> So I love to wake at break of day,
> For though my sleep be gone,
> Yet while 'tis dark one shuts one's lids,
> And so, dreams on.

He could not have done with the little poem. It was not the words so much as the whole air of it that charmed him! He might have written it lying in bed, very early in the morning, and watching the sun dance on the ceiling. 'It is *still*, like that,' thought Henry. 'I am sure he wrote it when he was half-awake some time, for it's got a smile of a dream on it.' He stared at the poem and then looked away and repeated it by heart, missed a word in the third verse and looked again, and again until he became conscious of shouting and shuffling, and he looked up to see the train moving slowly.

'God's thunder!' Henry dashed forward. A man with a flag and a whistle had his hand on a door. He clutched Henry somehow . . . Henry was inside with the door slammed, in a carriage that wasn't a 'smoker,' that had not a trace of his straw hat or the black portfolio or his Aunt B's Christmas-present gloves. Instead, in the opposite corner, close against the wall, there sat a girl. Henry did not dare to look at her, but he felt certain she was staring at him. 'She must think I'm mad,' he thought, 'dashing into a train without even a hat, and in the evening, too.' He felt so funny. He didn't know how to sit or sprawl. He put his hands in his pockets and tried to appear quite indifferent and frown at a large photo-graph of Bolton Abbey.[2] But feeling her eyes on him he gave her just the tiniest glance. Quick she looked away out of the window, and then Henry, careful of her slightest movement, went on looking. She sat pressed against the window, her cheek and shoulder half hidden by a long wave of marigold-coloured hair. One little hand in a grey cotton glove held a leather case on her lap with the initials E. M. on it. The other hand she had slipped through the window-strap, and Henry noticed a silver bangle on the wrist with a Swiss cow-bell and a silver shoe and a fish. She wore a green coat and a hat with a wreath round it. All this Henry saw while the title of the new poem persisted in his brain – 'Something Childish but very Natural.' 'I suppose she goes to some school in London,' thought Henry. 'She might be in an office. Oh, no, she is too young. Besides she'd have her hair up if she was. It isn't even down her back.' He could not keep his eyes off that beautiful waving hair. '"My eyes are like two drunken bees . . ." Now, I wonder if I read that or made it up?'

That moment the girl turned round and, catching his glance, she blushed. She bent her head to hide the red colour that flew in her cheeks, and Henry, terribly embarrassed, blushed too. 'I shall have to speak – have to – have to!' He started putting up his hand to raise the hat that wasn't there. He thought that funny; it gave him confidence.

'I'm – I'm most awfully sorry,' he said, smiling at the girl's hat. 'But I can't go on sitting in the same carriage with you and not explaining why I dashed in like that, without my hat even. I'm sure I gave you a fright, and just now I was staring at you – but that's only an awful fault of mine; I'm a terrible starer! If you'd like me to explain – how I got in here – not about the staring, of course,' – he gave a little laugh – 'I will.'

For a minute she said nothing, then in a low, shy voice – 'It doesn't matter.'

The train had flung behind the roofs and chimneys. They were swinging into the country, past little black woods and fading fields and pools of water shining under an apricot evening sky. Henry's heart began to thump and beat to the beat of the train. He couldn't leave it like that. She sat so quiet, hidden in her fallen hair. He felt that it was absolutely necessary that she should look up and understand him – understand him at least. He leant forward and clasped his hands round his knees.

'You see I'd just put all my things – a portfolio – into a third-class "smoker" and was having a look at the book-stall,' he explained.

As he told the story she raised her head. He saw her grey eyes under the shadow of her hat and her eyebrows like two gold feathers. Her lips were faintly parted. Almost unconsciously he seemed to absorb the fact that she was wearing a bunch of primroses and that her throat was white – the shape of her face wonderfully delicate against all that burning hair. 'How beautiful she is! How simply beautiful she is!' sang Henry's heart, and swelled with the words, bigger and bigger and trembling like a marvellous bubble – so that he was afraid to breathe for fear of breaking it.

'I hope there was nothing valuable in the portfolio,' said she, very grave.

'Oh, only some silly drawings that I was taking back from the office,' answered Henry, airily. 'And – I was rather glad to lose my hat. It had been hurting me all day.'

'Yes,' she said, 'it's left a mark,' and she nearly smiled.

Why on earth should those words have made Henry feel so free suddenly and so happy and so madly excited? What was happening between them? They said nothing, but to Henry their silence was alive and warm. It covered him from his head to his feet in a trembling wave. Her marvellous words, 'It's made a mark,' had in some mysterious fashion established a bond between them. They could not be utter strangers to each other if she spoke so simply and so naturally. And now she was really smiling. The smile danced in her eyes, crept over her cheeks to her lips and stayed there. He leant back. The words flew from him. – 'Isn't life wonderful!'

At that moment the train dashed into a tunnel. He heard her voice raised against the noise. She leant forward.

'I don't think so. But then I've been a fatalist for a long time now' – a pause – 'months.'

They were shattering through the dark. 'Why?' called Henry.

'Oh . . .'

Then she shrugged, and smiled and shook her head, meaning she could not speak against the noise. He nodded and leant back. They came out of the tunnel into a sprinkle of lights and houses. He waited for her to explain. But she got up and buttoned her coat and put her hands to her hat, swaying a little. 'I get out here,' she said. That seemed quite impossible to Henry.

The train slowed down and the lights outside grew brighter. She moved towards his end of the carriage.

'Look here!' he stammered. 'Shan't I see you again?' He got up, too, and leant against the rack with one hand. 'I *must* see you again.' The train was stopping.

She said breathlessly, 'I come down from London every evening.'

'You – you – you do – really?' His eagerness frightened her. He was quick to curb it. Shall we or shall we not shake hands? raced through his brain. One hand was on the door-handle, the other held the little bag. The train stopped. Without another word or glance she was gone.

Then came Saturday – a half day at the office – and Sunday between. By Monday evening Henry was quite exhausted. He was at the station far too early, with a pack of silly thoughts at his heels as it were driving him up and down. 'She didn't say she came by this train!' 'And supposing I go up and she cuts me.' 'There may be somebody with her.' 'Why do you suppose she's ever thought of you again?' 'What are you going to say if you do see her?' He even prayed, 'Lord if it be Thy will, let us meet.'

But nothing helped. White smoke floated against the roof of the station – dissolved and came again in swaying wreaths. Of a sudden, as he watched it, so delicate and so silent, moving with such mysterious grace above the crowd and the scuffle, he grew calm. He felt very tired – he only wanted to sit down and shut his eyes – she was not coming – a forlorn relief breathed in the words. And then he saw her quite near to him walking towards the train with the same little leather case in her hand. Henry waited. He knew, somehow, that she had seen him, but he did not move until she came close to him and said in her low, shy voice – 'Did you get them again?'

'Oh, yes, thank you, I got them again,' and with a funny half gesture he showed her the portfolio and the gloves. They walked side by side to the train and into an empty carriage. They sat down oppos-ite to each other, smiling timidly but not speaking, while the train moved slowly, and slowly gathered speed and smoothness. Henry spoke first.

'It's so silly,' he said, 'not knowing your name.' She put back a big piece of hair that had fallen on her shoulder, and he saw how her hand in the grey glove was shaking. Then he noticed that she was sitting very stiffly with her knees pressed together – and he was, too – both of them trying not to tremble so. She said 'My name is Edna.'

'And mine is Henry.'

In the pause they took possession of each other's names and turned them over and put them away, a shade less frightened after that.

'I want to ask you something else now,' said Henry. He looked at Edna, his head a little on one side. 'How old are you?'

'Over sixteen,' she said, 'and you?'

'I'm nearly eighteen . . .'

'Isn't it hot?' she said suddenly, and pulled off her grey gloves and put her hands to her cheeks and kept them there. Their eyes were not frightened – they looked at each other with a sort of desperate calmness. If only their bodies would not tremble so stupidly! Still half hidden by her hair, Edna said:

'Have you ever been in love before?'

'No, never! Have you?'

'Oh, never in all my life.' She shook her head. 'I never even thought it possible.'

His next words came in a rush. 'Whatever have you been doing since last Friday evening? Whatever did you do all Saturday and all Sunday and to-day?'

But she did not answer – only shook her head and smiled and said, 'No, you tell *me*.'

'I?' cried Henry – and then he found he couldn't tell her either. He couldn't climb back to those mountains of days, and he had to shake his head, too.

'But it's been agony,' he said, smiling brilliantly – 'agony.' At that she took away her hands and started laughing, and Henry joined her. They laughed until they were tired.

'It's so – so extraordinary,' she said. 'So suddenly, you know, and I feel as if I'd known you for years.'

'So do I . . .' said Henry. 'I believe it must be the Spring. I believe I've swallowed a butterfly – and it's fanning its wings just here.' He put his hand on his heart.

'And the really extraordinary thing is,' said Edna, 'that I had made up my mind that I didn't care for – men at all. I mean all the girls at College –'

'Were you at College?'

She nodded. 'A training college, learning to be a secretary.' She sounded scornful.

'I'm in an office,' said Henry. 'An architect's office – such a funny little place up one hundred and thirty stairs. We ought to be building nests instead of houses, I always think.'

'Do you like it?'

'No, of course I don't. I don't want to do anything, do you?'

'No, I hate it . . . And,' she said, 'my mother is a Hungarian – I believe that makes me hate it even more.'

That seemed to Henry quite natural. 'It would,' he said.

'Mother and I are exactly alike. I haven't a thing in common with my father; he's just . . . a little man in the City – but mother has got wild blood in her and she's given it to me. She hates our life just as much as I do.' She paused and frowned. 'All the same, we don't get on a bit together – that's funny – isn't it? But I'm absolutely alone at home.'

Henry was listening – in a way he was listening, but there was something else he wanted to ask her. He said, very shyly, 'Would you – would you take off your hat?'

She looked startled. 'Take off my hat?'

'Yes – it's your hair. I'd give anything to see your hair properly.'

She protested. 'It isn't really . . .'

'Oh, it *is*,' cried Henry, and then, as she took off the hat and gave her head a little toss, 'Oh, Edna! it's the loveliest thing in the world.'

'Do you like it?' she said, smiling and very pleased. She pulled it round her shoulders like a cape of gold. 'People generally laugh at it. It's such an absurd colour.' But Henry would not believe that. She leaned her elbows on her knees and cupped her chin in her hands. 'That's how I often sit when I'm angry and then I feel it burning me up . . . Silly?'

'No, no, not a bit,' said Henry. 'I knew you did. It's your sort of weapon against all the dull horrid things.'

'However did you know that? Yes, that's just it. But however did you know?'

'Just knew,' smiled Henry. 'My God!' he cried, 'what fools people are! All the little pollies³ that you know and that I know. Just look at you and me. Here we are – that's all there is to be said. I know about you and you know about me – we've just found each other – quite simply – just by being natural. That's all life is – something childish and very natural. Isn't it?'

'Yes – yes,' she said eagerly. 'That's what I've always thought.'

'It's people that make things so – silly. As long as you can keep away from them you're safe and you're happy.'

'Oh, I've thought that for a long time.'

'Then you're just like me,' said Henry. The wonder of that was so great that he almost wanted to cry. Instead he said very solemnly: 'I believe we're the only two people alive who think as we do. In fact, I'm sure of it. Nobody understands me. I feel as though I were living in a world of strange beings – do you?'

'Always.'

'We'll be in that loathsome tunnel again in a minute,' said Henry. 'Edna! can I – just touch your hair?'

She drew back quickly. 'Oh, no, please don't,' and as they were going into the dark she moved a little away from him.

'Edna! I've bought the tickets. The man at the concert hall didn't seem at all surprised that I had the money. Meet me outside the gallery doors at three, and wear that cream blouse and the corals – will you? I love you. I don't like sending these letters to the shop. I always feel those people with "Letters received" in their window keep a kettle in their back parlour that would steam open an elephant's ear of an envelope. But it really doesn't matter, does it, darling? Can you get away on Sunday? Pretend you are going to spend the day with one of the girls from the office, and let's meet at some little place and walk or find a field where we can watch the daisies uncurling. I do love you, Edna. But Sundays without you are simply impossible. Don't get run over before Saturday, and don't eat anything out of a tin or drink anything from a public fountain. That's all, darling.'

'My dearest, yes, I'll be there on Saturday – and I've arranged about Sunday, too. That is one great blessing. I'm quite free at home. I have just come in from the garden. It's such a lovely evening. Oh, Henry, I could sit and cry, I love you so to-night. Silly – isn't it? I either feel so happy I can hardly stop laughing or else so sad I can hardly stop crying and both for the same reason. But we are so young to have found each other, aren't we? I am sending you a violet. It is quite warm. I wish you were here now, just for a minute even. Good-night, darling. I am, Edna.'

'Safe,' said Edna, 'safe! And excellent places, aren't they, Henry?'

She stood up to take off her coat and Henry made a movement to help her. 'No – no – it's off.' She tucked it under the seat. She sat down beside him. 'Oh, Henry, what have you got there? Flowers?'

'Only two tiny little roses.' He laid them in her lap.

'Did you get my letter all right?' asked Edna, unpinning the paper.

'Yes,' he said, 'and the violet is growing beautifully. You should see my room. I planted a little piece of it in every corner and one on my pillow and one in the pocket of my pyjama jacket.'

She shook her hair at him. 'Henry, give me the programme.'

'Here it is – you can read it with me. I'll hold it for you.'

'No, let me have it.'

'Well, then, I'll read it for you.'

'No, you can have it after.'

'Edna,' he whispered.

'Oh, please don't,' she pleaded. 'Not here – the people.'

Why did he want to touch her so much and why did she mind? Whenever he was with her he wanted to hold her hand or take her arm when they walked together, or lean against her – not hard – just lean lightly so that his shoulder should touch her shoulder – and she wouldn't even have that. All the time that he was away from her he was hungry, he craved the nearness of her. There seemed to be comfort and warmth breathing from Edna that he needed to keep him calm. Yes, that was it. He couldn't get calm with her because she wouldn't let him touch her. But she loved him. He knew that. Why did she feel so curiously about it? Every time he tried to or even asked for her hand she shrank back and looked at him with pleading frightened eyes as though he wanted to hurt her. They could say anything to each other. And there wasn't any question of their belonging to each other. And yet he couldn't touch her. Why, he couldn't even help her off with her coat. Her voice dropped into his thoughts.

'Henry!' He leaned to listen, setting his lips. 'I want to explain something to you. I will – I will – I promise – after the concert.'

'All right.' He was still hurt.

'You're not sad, are you?' she said.

He shook his head.

'Yes, you are, Henry.'

'No, really not.' He looked at the roses lying in her hands.

'Well, are you happy?'

'Yes. Here comes the orchestra.'

It was twilight when they came out of the hall. A blue net of light hung over the streets and houses, and pink clouds floated in a pale sky. As they walked away from the hall Henry felt they were very little and alone. For the first time since he had known Edna his heart was heavy.

'Henry!' She stopped suddenly and stared at him. 'Henry, I'm not coming to the station with you. Don't – don't wait for me. Please, please leave me.'

'My God!' cried Henry, and started, 'what's the matter – Edna – darling – Edna, what have I done?'

'Oh, nothing – go away,' and she turned and ran across the street into a square and leaned up against the square railings – and hid her face in her hands.

'Edna – Edna – my little love – you're crying. Edna, my baby girl!'

She leaned her arms along the railings and sobbed distractedly.

'Edna – stop – it's all my fault. I'm a fool – I'm a thundering idiot. I've spoiled your afternoon. I've tortured you with my idiotic mad bloody clumsiness. That's it. Isn't it, Edna? For God's sake.'

'Oh,' she sobbed, 'I do hate hurting you so. Every time you ask me to let – let you hold my hand or – or kiss me I could kill myself for not doing it – for not letting you. I don't know why I don't even.' She said wildly. 'It's not that I'm frightened of you – it's not that – it's only a feeling, Henry, that I can't understand myself even. Give me your hand-kerchief, darling.' He pulled it from his pocket. 'All through the concert I've been haunted by this, and every time we meet I know it's bound to come up. Somehow I feel if once we did that – you know – held each other's hands and kissed it would be all changed – and I feel we wouldn't be free like we are – we'd be doing something secret. We wouldn't be children any more ... silly, isn't it? I'd feel awkward with you, Henry, and I'd feel shy, and I do so feel that just because you and I are you and I, we don't need that sort of thing.' She turned and looked at him, pressing her hands to her cheeks in the way he knew so well, and behind her as in a dream he saw the sky and half a white moon and the trees of the square with their unbroken buds. He kept twisting, twisting up in his hands the concert programme. 'Henry! You do understand me – don't you?'

'Yes, I think I do. But you're not going to be frightened any more, are you?' He tried to smile. 'We'll forget, Edna. I'll never mention it again. We'll bury the bogy in this square – now – you and I – won't we?'

'But,' she said, searching his face – 'will it make you love me less?'

'Oh, no,' he said. 'Nothing could – nothing on earth could do that.'

London became their play-ground. On Saturday afternoons they ex-plored. They found their own shops where they bought cigarettes and sweets for Edna – and their own tea-shop with their own table – their own streets – and one night when Edna was supposed to be at a lecture at the Polytechnic they found their own village. It was the name that made them go there. 'There's white geese in that name,' said Henry, telling it to Edna. 'And a river and little low houses with old men sitting outside them – old sea captains with wooden legs winding up their watches, and there are little shops with lamps in the windows.'

It was too late for them to see the geese or the old men, but the river was there and the houses and even the shops with lamps. In one a woman sat working a sewing-machine on the counter. They heard the whirring hum and they saw her big shadow filling the shop. 'Too full for a single customer,' said Henry. 'It is a perfect place.'

The houses were small and covered with creepers and ivy. Some of them had worn wooden steps leading up to the doors. You had to go down a little flight of steps to enter some of the others; and just across the road – to be seen from every window – was the river, with a walk beside it and some high poplar trees.

'This is the place for us to live in,' said Henry. 'There's a house to let, too. I wonder if it would wait if we asked it. I'm sure it would.'

'Yes, I would like to live there,' said Edna. They crossed the road and she leaned against the trunk of a tree and looked up at the empty house, with a dreamy smile.

'There is a little garden at the back, dear,' said Henry, 'a lawn with one tree on it and some daisy bushes round the wall. At night the stars shine in the tree like tiny candles. And inside there are two rooms downstairs and a big room with folding doors upstairs and above that an attic. And there are eight stairs to the kitchen – very dark, Edna. You are rather frightened of them, you know. "Henry, dear, would you mind bringing the lamp? I just want to make sure that Euphemia has raked out the fire before we go to bed."'

'Yes,' said Edna. 'Our bedroom is at the very top – that room with the two square windows. When it is quiet we can hear the river flowing and the sound of the poplar trees far, far away, rustling and flowing in our dreams, darling.'

'You're not cold – are you?' he said, suddenly.

'No – no, only happy.'

'The room with the folding doors is yours.' Henry laughed. 'It's a mixture – it isn't a room at all. It's full of your toys and there's a big blue chair in it where you sit curled up in front of the fire with the flames in your curls – because though we're married you refuse to put your hair up and only tuck it inside your coat for the church service. And there's a rug on the floor for me to lie on, because I'm so lazy. Euphemia – that's our servant – only comes in the day. After she's gone we go down to the kitchen and sit on the table and eat an apple, or perhaps we make some tea, just for the sake of hearing the kettle sing. That's not joking. If you listen to a kettle right through it's like an early morning in Spring.'

'Yes, I know,' she said. 'All the different kinds of birds.'

A little cat came through the railings of the empty house and into the road. Edna called it and bent down and held out her hands – 'Kitty! Kitty!' The little cat ran to her and rubbed against her knees.

'If we're going for a walk just take the cat and put it inside the front door,' said Henry, still pretending. 'I've got the key.'

They walked across the road and Edna stood stroking the cat in her arms while Henry went up the steps and pretended to open the door.

He came down again quickly. 'Let's go away at once. It's going to turn into a dream.'

The night was dark and warm. They did not want to go home. 'What I feel so certain of is,' said Henry, 'that we ought to be living there, now. We oughtn't to wait for things. What's age? You're as old as you'll ever be and so am I. You know,' he said, 'I have a feeling often and often that it's dangerous to wait for things – that if you wait for things they only go further and further away.'

'But, Henry, – money! You see we haven't any money.'

'Oh, well, – perhaps if I disguised myself as an old man we could get a job as caretakers in some large house – that would be rather fun. I'd make up a terrific history of the house if anyone came to look over it and you could dress up and be the ghost moaning and wringing your hands in the deserted picture gallery, to frighten them off. Don't you ever feel that money is more or less accidental – that if one really wants things it's either there or it doesn't matter?'

She did not answer that – she looked up at the sky and said, 'Oh dear, I don't want to go home.'

'Exactly – that's the whole trouble – and we oughtn't to go home. We ought to be going back to the house and find an odd saucer to give the cat the dregs of the milk-jug in. I'm not really laughing – I'm not even happy. I'm lonely for you, Edna – I would give anything to lie down and cry' . . . and he added limply, 'with my head in your lap and your darling cheek in my hair.'

'But, Henry,' she said, coming closer, 'you have faith, haven't you? I mean you are absolutely certain that we shall have a house like that and everything we want – aren't you?'

'Not enough – that's not enough. I want to be sitting on those very stairs and taking off these very boots this very minute. Don't you? Is faith enough for you?'

'If only we weren't so young . . .' she said miserably. 'And yet,' she sighed, 'I'm sure I don't feel very young – I feel twenty at least.'

Henry lay on his back in the little wood. When he moved the dead leaves rustled beneath him, and above his head the new leaves quivered like fountains of green water steeped in sunlight. Somewhere out of sight Edna was gathering primroses. He had been so full of dreams that morning that he could not keep pace with her delight in the flowers. 'Yes, love, you go and come back for me. I'm too lazy.' She had thrown off her hat and knelt down beside him, and by and by her voice and her footsteps had grown fainter. Now the wood was silent except for the leaves, but he knew that she was not far away and he moved so that the tips of his fingers touched her pink jacket. Ever since waking he had felt so strangely that he was not really awake at all, but just dreaming. The time before, Edna was a dream and now he and she were dreaming together and somewhere in some dark place another dream waited for him. 'No, that can't be true because I can't ever imagine the world without us. I feel that we two together mean something that's got to be there just as naturally as trees or birds or clouds.' He tried to remember what it had felt like without Edna, but he could not get back to those days. They were hidden by her; Edna, with the marigold hair and strange, dreamy smile filled him up to the brim. He breathed her; he ate and drank her. He walked about with a shining ring of Edna keeping the world away or touching whatever it lighted on with its own beauty. 'Long after you have stopped laughing,' he told her, 'I can hear your laugh running up and down my veins – and yet – are we a dream?' And suddenly he saw himself and Edna as two very small children walking through the streets, looking through windows, buying things and playing with them, talking to each other, smiling – he saw even their gestures and the way they stood, so often, quite still, face to face – and then he rolled over and pressed his face in the leaves – faint with longing. He wanted to kiss Edna, and to put his arms round her and press her to him and feel her cheek hot against his kiss and kiss her until he'd no breath left and so stifle the dream.

'No, I can't go on being hungry like this,' said Henry, and jumped up and began to run in the direction she had gone. She had wandered a long way. Down in a green hollow he saw her kneeling, and when she saw him she waved and said – 'Oh, Henry – such beauties! I've never seen such beauties. Come and look.' By the time he had reached her he would have cut off his hand rather than spoil her happiness. How strange Edna was that day! All the time she talked to Henry her eyes laughed; they were sweet and mocking. Two little spots of colour like strawberries glowed on her cheeks and 'I wish I could feel tired,' she kept saying. 'I want to walk over the whole world until I die. Henry – come along. Walk faster – Henry! If I start flying suddenly, you'll promise to catch hold of my feet, won't you? Otherwise I'll never come down.' And 'Oh,' she cried, 'I am so happy. I'm so frightfully happy!' They came to a weird place, covered with heather. It was early afternoon and the sun streamed down upon the purple.

'Let's rest here a little,' said Edna, and she waded into the heather and lay down. 'Oh, Henry, it's so lovely. I can't see anything except the little bells and the sky.'

Henry knelt down by her and took some primroses out of her basket and made a long chain to go round her throat. 'I could almost fall asleep,' said Edna. She crept over to his knees and lay hidden in her hair just beside him. 'It's like being under the sea, isn't it, dearest, so sweet and so still?'

'Yes,' said Henry, in a strange husky voice. 'Now I'll make you one of violets.' But Edna sat up. 'Let's go in,' she said.

They came back to the road and walked a long way. Edna said, 'No, I couldn't walk over the world – I'm tired now.' She trailed on the grass edge of the road. 'You and I are tired, Henry! How much further is it?'

'I don't know – not very far,' said Henry, peering into the distance. Then they walked in silence.

'Oh,' she said at last, 'it really is too far, Henry, I'm tired and I'm hungry. Carry my silly basket of primroses.' He took them without looking at her.

At last they came to a village and a cottage with a notice 'Teas Provided.'

'This is the place,' said Henry. 'I've often been here. You sit on the little bench and I'll go and order the tea.' She sat down on the bench, in the pretty garden all white and yellow with spring flowers. A woman came to the door and leaned against it watching them eat. Henry was very nice to her, but Edna did not say a word. 'You haven't been here for a long spell,' said the woman.

'No – the garden's looking wonderful.'

'Fair,' said she. 'Is the young lady your sister?' Henry nodded Yes, and took some jam.

'There's a likeness,' said the woman. She came down into the garden and picked a head of white jonquils and handed it to Edna. 'I suppose you don't happen to know anyone who wants a cottage,' said she. 'My sister's taken ill and she left me hers. I want to let it.'

'For a long time?' asked Henry, politely.

'Oh,' said the woman vaguely, 'that depends.'

Said Henry, 'Well – I might know of somebody – could we go and look at it?'

'Yes, it's just a step down the road, the little one with the apple trees in front – I'll fetch you the key.'

While she was away Henry turned to Edna and said, 'Will you come?' She nodded.

They walked down the road and in through the gate and up the grassy path between the pink and white trees. It was a tiny place – two rooms downstairs and two rooms upstairs. Edna leaned out of the top window, and Henry stood at the doorway. 'Do you like it?' he asked.

'Yes,' she called, and then made a place for him at the window. 'Come and look. It's so sweet.'

He came and leant out of the window. Below them were the apple trees tossing in a faint wind that blew a long piece of Edna's hair across his eyes. They did not move. It was evening – the pale green sky was sprinkled with stars. 'Look!' she said – 'stars, Henry.'

'There will be a moon in two T''s,' said Henry.

She did not seem to move and yet she was leaning against Henry's shoulder; he put his arm round her – 'Are all those trees down there – apple?' she asked in a shaky voice.

'No, darling,' said Henry. 'Some of them are full of angels and some

of them are full of sugar almonds – but evening light is awfully decep-
tive.' She sighed. 'Henry – we mustn't stay here any longer.'

He let her go and she stood up in the dusky room and touched her
hair. 'What has been the matter with you all day?' she said – and then did
not wait for an answer but ran to him and put her arms round his neck,
and pressed his head into the hollow of her shoulder. 'Oh,' she breathed,
'I do love you. Hold me, Henry.' He put his arms round her, and she
leaned against him and looked into his eyes. 'Hasn't it been terrible, all
to-day?' said Edna. 'I knew what was the matter and I've tried every way
I could to tell you that I wanted you to kiss me – that I'd quite got over
the feeling.'

'You're perfect, perfect, perfect,' said Henry.

'The thing is,' said Henry, 'how am I going to wait until evening?' He
took his watch out of his pocket, went into the cottage and popped it
into a china jar on the mantelpiece. He'd looked at it seven times in one
hour, and now he couldn't remember what time it was. Well, he'd look
once again. Half-past four. Her train arrived at seven. He'd have to start
for the station at half-past six. Two hours more to wait. He went
through the cottage again – downstairs and upstairs. 'It looks lovely,' he
said. He went into the garden and picked a round bunch of white pinks
and put them in a vase on the little table by Edna's bed. 'I don't believe
this,' thought Henry. 'I don't believe this for a minute. It's too much.
She'll be here in two hours and we'll walk home, and then I'll take that
white jug off the kitchen table and go across to Mrs Biddie's and get the
milk, and then come back, and when I come back she'll have lighted
the lamp in the kitchen and I'll look through the window and see her
moving about in the pool of lamplight. And then we shall have supper,
and after supper (Bags I washing up!) I shall put some wood on the fire
and we'll sit on the hearth-rug and watch it burning. There won't be a
sound except the wood and perhaps the wind will creep round the
house once . . . And then we shall change our candles and she will go up
first with her shadow on the wall beside her, and she will call out, Good-
night, Henry – and I shall answer – Good-night, Edna. And then I shall
dash upstairs and jump into bed and watch the tiny bar of light from her
room brush my door, and the moment it disappears will shut my eyes
and sleep until morning. Then we'll have all to-morrow and to-morrow
and to-morrow night. Is she thinking all this, too? Edna, come quickly!

> Had I two little wings,
> And were a little feathery bird,
> To you I'd fly, my dear –

No, no, dearest . . . Because the waiting is a sort of Heaven, too, darling. If you can understand that. Did you ever know a cottage could stand on tip-toe? This one is doing it now.'

He was downstairs and sat on the doorstep with his hands clasped round his knees. That night when they found the village – and Edna said, 'Haven't you faith, Henry?' 'I hadn't then. Now I have,' he said, 'I feel just like God.'

He leaned his head against the lintel. He could hardly keep his eyes open, not that he was sleepy, but . . . for some reason . . . and a long time passed.

Henry thought he saw a big white moth flying down the road. It perched on the gate. No, it wasn't a moth. It was a little girl in a pinafore. What a nice little girl, and he smiled in his sleep, and she smiled, too, and turned in her toes as she walked. 'But she can't be living here,' thought Henry. 'Because this is ours. Here she comes.'

When she was quite close to him she took her hand from under her pinafore and gave him a telegram and smiled and went away. There's a funny present! thought Henry, staring at it. 'Perhaps it's only a make-believe one, and it's got one of those snakes inside it that fly up at you.' He laughed gently in the dream and opened it very carefully. 'It's just a folded paper.' He took it out and spread it open.

The garden became full of shadows – they span a web of darkness over the cottage and the trees and Henry and the telegram. But Henry did not move.

(1914)

An Indiscreet Journey

She is like St Anne. Yes, the concierge is the image of St Anne, with that black cloth over her head, the wisps of grey hair hanging, and the tiny smoking lamp in her hand. Really very beautiful, I thought, smiling at St Anne, who said severely: 'Six o'clock. You have only just got time. There is a bowl of milk on the writing table.' I jumped out of my pyjamas and into a basin of cold water like any English lady in any French novel. The concierge, persuaded that I was on my way to prison cells and death by bayonets, opened the shutters and the cold clear light came through. A little steamer hooted on the river; a cart with two horses at a gallop flung past. The rapid swirling water; the tall black trees on the far side, grouped together like negroes conversing. Sinister, very, I thought, as I buttoned on my age-old Burberry.[1] (That Burberry was very significant. It did not belong to me. I had borrowed it from a friend. My eye lighted upon it hanging in her little dark hall. The very thing! The perfect and adequate disguise – an old Burberry. Lions have been faced in a Burberry. Ladies have been rescued from open boats in mountainous seas wrapped in nothing else. An old Burberry seems to me the sign and the token of the undisputed venerable traveller, I decided, leaving my purple peg-top[2] with the real seal collar and cuffs in exchange.)

'You will never get there,' said the concierge, watching me turn up the collar. 'Never! Never!' I ran down the echoing stairs – strange they sounded, like a piano flicked by a sleepy housemaid – and on to the Quai. 'Why so fast, *ma mignonne?*' said a lovely little boy in coloured socks, dancing in front of the electric lotus buds that curve over the entrance to the Métro. Alas! there was not even time to blow him a kiss. When I arrived at the big station I had only four minutes to spare, and the platform entrance was crowded and packed with soldiers, their yellow papers in one hand and big untidy bundles. The Commissaire of Police stood on one side, a Nameless Official on the other. Will he let me pass? Will he? He was an old man with a fat swollen face covered with big warts. Horn-rimmed spectacles squatted on his nose.

Trembling, I made an effort. I conjured up my sweetest early-morning smile and handed it with the papers. But the delicate thing fluttered against the horn spectacles and fell. Nevertheless, he let me pass, and I ran, ran in and out among the soldiers and up the high steps into the yellow-painted carriage.

'Does one go direct to X?' I asked the collector who dug at my ticket with a pair of forceps and handed it back again. 'No, Mademoiselle, you must change at X.Y.Z.'

'At —?'

'X.Y.Z.'

Again I had not heard. 'At what time do we arrive there if you please?'

'One o'clock.' But that was no good to me. I hadn't a watch. Oh, well – later.

Ah! the train had begun to move. The train was on my side. It swung out of the station, and soon we were passing the vegetable gardens, passing the tall blind houses to let, passing the servants beating carpets. Up already and walking in the fields, rosy from the rivers and the red-fringed pools, the sun lighted upon the swinging train and stroked my muff and told me to take off that Burberry. I was not alone in the carriage. An old woman sat opposite, her skirt turned back over her knees, a bonnet of black lace on her head. In her fat hands, adorned with a wedding and two mourning rings, she held a letter. Slowly, slowly she sipped a sentence, and then looked up and out of the window, her lips trembling a little, and then another sentence, and again the old face turned to the light, tasting it . . . Two soldiers leaned out of the window, their heads nearly touching – one of them was whistling, the other had his coat fastened with some rusty safety-pins. And now there were soldiers everywhere working on the railway line, leaning against trucks or standing hands on hips, eyes fixed on the train as though they expected at least one camera at every window. And now we were passing big wooden sheds like rigged-up dancing halls or seaside pavilions, each flying a flag. In and out of them walked the Red Cross men; the wounded sat against the walls sunning themselves. At all the bridges, the crossings, the stations, a *petit soldat*, all boots and bayonet. Forlorn and desolate he looked, – like a little comic picture waiting for the joke to be written underneath. Is there really such a thing as war? Are all these laughing voices really going to the war? These dark woods lighted so mysteriously by the white stems of the birch and the ash – these watery fields with the big birds flying over – these rivers green and blue in the light – have battles been fought in places like these?

What beautiful cemeteries we are passing! They flash gay in the sun. They seem to be full of cornflowers and poppies and daisies. How can there be so many flowers at this time of the year? But they are not flowers at all. They are bunches of ribbons tied on to the soldiers' graves.

I glanced up and caught the old woman's eye. She smiled and folded the letter. 'It is from my son – the first we have had since October. I am taking it to my daughter-in-law.'

'. . .?'

'Yes, very good,' said the old woman, shaking down her skirt and putting her arm through the handle of her basket. 'He wants me to send him some handkerchieves and a piece of stout string.'

What is the name of the station where I have to change? Perhaps I shall never know. I got up and leaned my arms across the window rail, my feet crossed. One cheek burned as in infancy on the way to the sea-side. When the war is over I shall have a barge and drift along these rivers with a white cat and a pot of mignonette to bear me company.

Down the side of the hill filed the troops, winking red and blue in the light. Far away, but plainly to be seen, some more flew by on bicycles. But really, *ma France adorée*, this uniform is ridiculous. Your soldiers are stamped upon your bosom like bright irreverent transfers.

The train slowed down, stopped . . . Everybody was getting out except me. A big boy, his sabots[3] tied to his back with a piece of string, the inside of his tin wine cup stained a lovely impossible pink, looked very friendly. Does one change here perhaps for X? Another whose képi had come out of a wet paper cracker swung my suitcase to earth. What darlings soldiers are! '*Merci bien, Monsieur, vous êtes tout à fait aimable . . .*' 'Not this way,' said a bayonet. 'Nor this,' said another. So I followed the crowd. 'Your passport, Mademoiselle . . .' '*We, Sir Edward Grey . . .*'[4] I ran through the muddy square and into the buffet.

A green room with a stove jutting out and tables on each side. On the counter, beautiful with coloured bottles, a woman leans, her breasts in her folded arms. Through an open door I can see a kitchen, and the cook in a white coat breaking eggs into a bowl and tossing the shells into a corner. The blue and red coats of the men who are eating hang upon the walls. Their short swords and belts are piled upon chairs.

Heavens! what a noise. The sunny air seemed all broken up and trembling with it. A little boy, very pale, swung from table to table, taking the orders, and poured me out a glass of purple coffee. *Ssssh*, came from the eggs. They were in a pan. The woman rushed from behind the counter and began to help the boy. *Toute de suite, tout' suite!* she chirruped to the loud impatient voices. There came a clatter of plates and the pop-pop of corks being drawn.

Suddenly in the doorway I saw someone with a pail of fish – brown speckled fish, like the fish one sees in a glass case, swimming through forests of beautiful pressed sea-weed. He was an old man in a tattered jacket, standing humbly, waiting for someone to attend to him. A thin beard fell over his chest, his eyes under the tufted eyebrows were bent on the pail he carried. He looked as though he had escaped from some holy picture, and was entreating the soldiers' pardon for being there at all . . .

But what could I have done? I could not arrive at X with two fishes hanging on a straw; and I am sure it is a penal offence in France to throw fish out of railway-carriage windows, I thought, miserably climbing into a smaller, shabbier train. Perhaps I might have taken them to – *ah, mon Dieu* – I had forgotten the name of my uncle and aunt again! Buffard, Buffon – what was it? Again I read the unfamiliar letter in the familiar handwriting.

My dear niece,

Now that the weather is more settled, your uncle and I would be charmed if you would pay us a little visit. Telegraph me when you are coming. I shall meet you outside the station if I am free. Otherwise our good friend, Madame Grinçon, who lives in the little toll-house by the bridge, *juste en face de la gare*, will conduct you to our home. *Je vous embrasse bien tendrement*,   JULIE BOIFFARD.

A visiting card was enclosed: *M. Paul Boiffard*.

Boiffard – of course that was the name. *Ma tante Julie et mon oncle Paul* – suddenly they were there with me, more real, more solid than any relations I had ever known. I saw *tante Julie* bridling, with the soup-tureen in her hands, and *oncle Paul* sitting at the table, with a red and white napkin tied round his neck. Boiffard – Boiffard – I must remember the name. Supposing the Commissaire Militaire should ask me who the relations were I was going to and I muddled the name – Oh, how fatal! Buffard – no, Boiffard. And then for the first time, folding Aunt

Julie's letter, I saw scrawled in a corner of the empty back page: *Venez vite, vite.* Strange impulsive woman! My heart began to beat . . .

'Ah, we are not far off now,' said the lady opposite. 'You are going to X, Mademoiselle?'

'*Oui, Madame.*'

'I also . . . You have been there before?'

'No, Madame. This is the first time.'

'Really, it is a strange time for a visit.'

I smiled faintly, and tried to keep my eyes off her hat. She was quite an ordinary little woman, but she wore a black velvet toque, with an incredibly surprised looking sea-gull camped on the very top of it. Its round eyes, fixed on me so inquiringly, were almost too much to bear. I had a dreadful impulse to shoo it away, or to lean forward and inform her of its presence . . .

'*Excusez-moi, Madame*, but perhaps you have not remarked there is an *espèce de* sea-gull *couché sur votre chapeau.*'

Could the bird be there on purpose? I must not laugh . . . I must not laugh. Had she ever looked at herself in a glass with that bird on her head?

'It is very difficult to get into X at present, to pass the station,' she said, and she shook her head with the sea-gull at me. 'Ah, such an affair. One must sign one's name and state one's business.'

'Really, is it as bad as all that?'

'But naturally. You see the whole place is in the hands of the military, and' – she shrugged – 'they have to be strict. Many people do not get beyond the station at all. They arrive. They are put in the waiting-room, and there they remain.'

Did I or did I not detect in her voice a strange, insulting relish?

'I suppose such strictness is absolutely necessary,' I said coldly, stroking my muff.

'Necessary,' she cried. 'I should think so. Why, *Mademoiselle*, you cannot imagine what it would be like otherwise! You know what women are like about soldiers' – she raised a final hand – 'mad, completely mad. But –' and she gave a little laugh of triumph – 'they could not get into X. *Mon Dieu*, no! There is no question about that.'

'I don't suppose they even try,' said I.

'Don't you?' said the sea-gull.

Madame said nothing for a moment. 'Of course the authorities are very hard on the men. It means instant imprisonment, and then – off to the firing-line without a word.'

'What are *you* going to X for?' said the sea-gull. 'What on earth are *you* doing here?'

'Are you making a long stay in X, *Mademoiselle*?'

She had won, she had won. I was terrified. A lamp-post swam past the train with the fatal name upon it. I could hardly breathe – the train had stopped. I smiled gaily at Madame and danced down the steps to the platform . . .

It was a hot little room completely furnished with two colonels seated at two tables. They were large grey-whiskered men with a touch of burnt red on their cheeks. Sumptuous and omnipotent they looked. One smoked what ladies love to call a heavy Egyptian cigarette, with a long creamy ash, the other toyed with a gilded pen. Their heads rolled on their tight collars, like big over-ripe fruits. I had a terrible feeling, as I handed my passport and ticket, that a soldier would step forward and tell me to kneel. I would have knelt without question.

'What's this?' said God I, querulously. He did not like my passport at all. The very sight of it seemed to annoy him. He waved a dissenting hand at it, with a '*Non, je ne peux pas manger ça*' air.

'But it won't do. It won't do at all, you know. Look, – read for yourself,' and he glanced with extreme distaste at my photograph, and then with even greater distaste his pebble eyes looked at me.

'Of course the photograph is deplorable,' I said, scarcely breathing with terror, 'but it has been viséd and viséd.'

He raised his big bulk and went over to God II.

'Courage!' I said to my muff and held it firmly, 'Courage!'

God II held up a finger to me, and I produced Aunt Julie's letter and her card. But he did not seem to feel the slightest interest in her. He stamped my passport idly, scribbled a word on my ticket, and I was on the platform again.

'That way – you pass out that way.'

Terribly pale, with a faint smile on his lips, his hand at salute, stood the little corporal. I gave no sign, I am sure I gave no sign. He stepped behind me.

'And then follow me as though you do not see me,' I heard him half whisper, half sing.

How fast he went, through the slippery mud towards a bridge. He had a postman's bag on his back, a paper parcel and the *Matin* in his hand. We seemed to dodge through a maze of policemen, and I could not keep up at all with the little corporal who began to whistle. From the toll-house 'our good friend, Madame Grinçon,' her hands wrapped in a shawl, watched our coming, and against the toll-house there leaned a tiny faded cab. *Montez vite, vite!* said the little corporal, hurling my suitcase, the postman's bag, the paper parcel and the *Matin* on to the floor.

'A-ie! A-ie! Do not be so mad. Do not ride yourself. You will be seen,' wailed 'our good friend, Madame Grinçon.'

'Ah, je m'en f . . .' said the little corporal.

The driver jerked into activity. He lashed the bony horse and away we flew, both doors, which were the complete sides of the cab, flapping and banging

'Bon jour, mon amie.'

'Bon jour, mon ami.'

And then we swooped down and clutched at the banging doors. They would not keep shut. They were fools of doors.

'Lean back, let me do it!' I cried. 'Policemen are as thick as violets everywhere.'

At the barracks the horse reared up and stopped. A crowd of laughing faces blotted the window.

'Prends ça, mon vieux,' said the little corporal, handing the paper parcel.

'It's all right,' called someone.

We waved, we were off again. By a river, down a strange white street, with little houses on either side, gay in the late sunlight.

'Jump out as soon as he stops again. The door will be open. Run straight inside. I will follow. The man is already paid. I know you will like the house. It is quite white, and the room is white, too, and the people are –'

'White as snow.'

We looked at each other. We began to laugh. 'Now,' said the little corporal.

Out I flew and in at the door. There stood, presumably, my aunt Julie. There in the background hovered, I supposed, my uncle Paul.

'Bon jour, Madame!' 'Bon jour, Monsieur!'

'It is all right, you are safe,' said my aunt Julie. Heavens, how I loved her! And she opened the door of the white room and shut it upon us. Down went the suitcase, the postman's bag, the *Matin*. I threw my passport up into the air, and the little corporal caught it.

What an extraordinary thing. We had been there to lunch and to dinner each day; but now in the dusk and alone I could not find it. I clop-clopped in my borrowed *sabots* through the greasy mud, right to the end of the village, and there was not a sign of it. I could not even remember what it looked like, or if there was a name painted on the outside, or any bottles or tables showing at the window. Already the village houses were sealed for the night behind big wooden shutters. Strange and mysterious they looked in the ragged drifting light and thin rain, like a company of beggars perched on the hill-side, their bosoms full of rich unlawful gold. There was nobody about but the soldiers. A group of wounded stood under a lamp-post, petting a mangy, shivering dog. Up the street came four big boys singing:

Dodo, mon homme, fais vit' dodo . . .'

and swung off down the hill to their sheds behind the railway station. They seemed to take the last breath of the day with them. I began to walk slowly back.

'It must have been one of these houses. I remember it stood far back from the road – and there were no steps, not even a porch – one seemed to walk right through the window.' And then quite suddenly the waiting-boy came out of just such a place. He saw me and grinned cheerfully, and began to whistle through his teeth.

'Bon soir, mon petit.'

'Bon soir, Madame.' And he followed me up the café to our special table, right at the far end by the window, and marked by a bunch of violets that I had left in a glass there yesterday.

'You are two?' asked the waiting-boy, flicking the table with a red and white cloth. His long swinging steps echoed over the bare floor. He disappeared into the kitchen and came back to light the lamp that hung from the ceiling under a spreading shade, like a haymaker's hat. Warm light shone on the empty place that was really a barn, set out with dilapidated tables and chairs. Into the middle of the room a black stove jutted. At one side of it there was a table with a row of bottles on it, behind which Madame sat and took the money and made entries in a red book. Opposite her desk a door led into the kitchen. The walls were covered with a creamy paper patterned all over with green and swollen trees – hundreds and hundreds of trees reared their mushroom heads to the ceiling. I began to wonder who had chosen the paper and why. Did Madame think it was beautiful, or that it was a gay and lovely thing to eat one's dinner at all seasons in the middle of a forest . . . On either side of the clock there hung a picture: one, a young gentleman in black tights wooing a pear-shaped lady in yellow over the back of a garden seat, *Premier Rencontre*; two, the black and yellow in amorous confusion, *Triomphe d'Amour*.

The clock ticked to a soothing lilt, *C'est ça, c'est ça*. In the kitchen the waiting-boy was washing up. I heard the ghostly chatter of the dishes.

And years passed. Perhaps the war is long since over – there is no village outside at all – the streets are quiet under the grass. I have an idea this is the sort of thing one will do on the very last day of all – sit in an empty café and listen to a clock ticking until—

Madame came through the kitchen door, nodded to me and took her seat behind the table, her plump hands folded on the red book. *Ping* went the door. A handful of soldiers came in, took off their coats and began to play cards, chaffing and poking fun at the pretty waiting-boy, who threw up his little round head, rubbed his thick fringe out of his eyes and cheeked them back in his broken voice. Sometimes his voice boomed up from his throat, deep and harsh, and then in the middle of a sentence it broke and scattered in a funny squeaking. He seemed to enjoy it himself. You would not have been surprised if he had walked into the kitchen on his hands and brought back your dinner turning a catherine-wheel.

Ping went the door again. Two more men came in. They sat at the table nearest Madame, and she leaned to them with a bird-like movement, her head on one side. Oh, they had a grievance! The Lieutenant was a fool – nosing about – springing out at them – and they'd only been sewing on buttons. Yes, that was all – sewing on buttons, and up comes this young spark. 'Now then, what are you up to?' They mimicked the idiotic voice. Madame drew down her mouth, nodding sympathy. The waiting-boy served them with glasses. He took a bottle of some orange-coloured stuff and put it on the table-edge. A shout from the card-players made him turn sharply, and crash! over went the bottle, spilling on the table, the floor – smash! to tinkling atoms. An amazed silence. Through it the drip-drip of the wine from the table on to the floor. It looked very strange dropping so slowly, as though the table were crying. Then there came a roar from the card-players. 'You'll catch it, my lad! That's the style! Now you've done it! . . . *Sept, huit, neuf.*' They started playing again. The waiting-boy never said a word. He stood, his head bent, his hands spread out, and then he knelt and gathered up the glass, piece by piece, and soaked the wine up with a cloth. Only when Madame cried cheerfully, 'You wait until *he* finds out,' did he raise his head.

'He can't say anything, if I pay for it,' he muttered, his face jerking, and he marched off into the kitchen with the soaking cloth.

'*Il pleure de colère*,' said Madame delightedly, patting her hair with her plump hands.

The café slowly filled. It grew very warm. Blue smoke mounted from the tables and hung about the haymaker's hat in misty wreaths. There was a suffocating smell of onion soup and boots and damp cloth. In the din the door sounded again. It opened to let in a weed of a fellow, who stood with his back against it, one hand shading his eyes.

'Hullo! you've got the bandage off?'

'How does it feel, *mon vieux*?'

'Let's have a look at them.'

But he made no reply. He shrugged and walked unsteadily to a table, sat down and leant against the wall. Slowly his hand fell. In his white face his eyes showed, pink as a rabbit's. They brimmed and spilled, brimmed and spilled. He dragged a white cloth out of his pocket and wiped them.

'It's the smoke,' said someone. 'It's the smoke tickles them up for you.'

His comrades watched him a bit, watched his eyes fill again, again brim over. The water ran down his face, off his chin on to the table. He rubbed the place with his coat-sleeve, and then, as though forgetful, went on rubbing, rubbing with his hand across the table, staring in front of him. And then he started shaking his head to the movement of his hand. He gave a loud strange groan and dragged out the cloth again.

'*Huit, neuf, dix*,' said the card-players.

'*P'tit*, some more bread.'

'Two coffees.'

'*Un Picon!*'[6]

The waiting-boy, quite recovered, but with scarlet cheeks, ran to and fro. A tremendous quarrel flared up among the card-players, raged for two minutes, and died in flickering laughter. 'Ooof!' groaned the man with the eyes, rocking and mopping. But nobody paid any attention to him except Madame. She made a little grimace at her two soldiers.

'*Mais vous savez, c'est un peu dégoûtant, ça,*' she said severely.

'*Ah, oui, Madame,*' answered the soldiers, watching her bent head and pretty hands, as she arranged for the hundredth time a frill of lace on her lifted bosom.

'*V'là Monsieur!*' cawed the waiting-boy over his shoulder to me. For some silly reason I pretended not to hear, and I leaned over the table smelling the violets, until the little corporal's hand closed over mine.

'Shall we have *un peu de charcuterie* to begin with?' he asked tenderly.

'In England,' said the blue-eyed soldier, 'you drink whisky with your meals. *N'est-ce pas, Mademoiselle?* A little glass of whisky neat before eating. Whisky and soda with your *bifteks*, and after, more whisky with hot water and lemon.'

'Is it true, that?' asked his great friend who sat opposite, a big red-faced chap with a black beard and large moist eyes and hair that looked as though it had been cut with a sewing-machine.

'Well, not quite true,' said I.

'*Si, si,*' cried the blue-eyed soldier. 'I ought to know. I'm in business. English travellers come to my place, and it's always the same thing.'

'Bah, I can't stand whisky,' said the little corporal. 'It's too disgusting the morning after. Do you remember, *ma fille*, the whisky in that little bar at Montmartre?'

'*Souvenir tendre,*' sighed Blackbeard, putting two fingers in the breast of his coat and letting his head fall. He was very drunk.

'But I know something that you've never tasted,' said the blue-eyed soldier pointing a finger at me; 'something really good.' *Cluck* he went with his tongue. '*É-pat-ant!* And the curious thing is that you'd hardly know it from whisky except that it's' – he felt with his hand for the word – 'finer, sweeter perhaps, not so sharp, and it leaves you feeling gay as a rabbit next morning.'

'What is it called?'

'Mirabelle!'[7] He rolled the word round his mouth, under his tongue. 'Ah-ha, that's the stuff.'

'I could eat another mushroom,' said Blackbeard. 'I would like another mushroom very much. I am sure I could eat another mushroom if Mademoiselle gave it to me out of her hand.'

'You ought to try it,' said the blue-eyed soldier, leaning both hands on the table and speaking so seriously that I began to wonder how much more sober he was than Blackbeard. 'You ought to try it, and to-night. I would like you to tell me if you don't think it's like whisky.'

'Perhaps they've got it here,' said the little corporal, and he called the waiting-boy. '*P'tit!*'

'*Non, monsieur,*' said the boy, who never stopped smiling. He served us with dessert plates painted with blue parrots and horned beetles.

'What is the name for this in English?' said Blackbeard, pointing. I told him 'Parrot.'

'Ah, *mon Dieu!* . . . Pair-rot . . .' He put his arms round his plate. 'I love you, *ma petite* pair-rot. You are sweet, you are blonde, you are English. You do not know the difference between whisky and mirabelle.'

The little corporal and I looked at each other, laughing. He squeezed up his eyes when he laughed, so that you saw nothing but the long curly lashes.

'Well, I know a place where they do keep it,' said the blue-eyed soldier. '*Café des Amis.* We'll go there – I'll pay – I'll pay for the whole lot of us.' His gesture embraced thousands of pounds.

But with a loud whirring noise the clock on the wall struck half-past eight; and no soldier is allowed in a café after eight o'clock at night.

'It is fast,' said the blue-eyed soldier. The little corporal's watch said the same. So did the immense turnip that Blackbeard produced, and carefully deposited on the head of one of the horned beetles.

'Ah, well, we'll take the risk,' said the blue-eyed soldier, and he thrust his arms into his immense cardboard coat. 'It's worth it,' he said. 'It's worth it. You just wait.'

Outside, stars shone between wispy clouds, and the moon fluttered like a candle flame over a pointed spire. The shadows of the dark plume-like trees waved on the white houses. Not a soul to be seen. No sound to be heard but the *Hsh! Hsh!* of a far-away train, like a big beast shuffling in its sleep.

'You are cold,' whispered the little corporal. 'You are cold, *ma fille.*'

'No, really not.'

'But you are trembling.'

'Yes, but I'm not cold.'

'What are the women like in England?' asked Blackbeard. 'After the war is over I shall go to England. I shall find a little English woman and marry her – and her pair-rot.' He gave a loud choking laugh.

'Fool!' said the blue-eyed soldier, shaking him; and he leant over to me. 'It is only after the second glass that you really taste it,' he whispered. 'The second little glass and then – ah! – then you know.'

Café des Amis gleamed in the moonlight. We glanced quickly up and down the road. We ran up the four wooden steps, and opened the ringing glass door into a low room lighted with a hanging lamp, where about ten people were dining. They were seated on two benches at a narrow table.

'Soldiers!' screamed a woman, leaping up from behind a white soup-tureen – a scrag of a woman in a black shawl. 'Soldiers! At this hour! Look at that clock, look at it.' And she pointed to the clock with the dripping ladle.

'It's fast,' said the blue-eyed soldier. 'It's fast, madame. And don't make so much noise, I beg of you. We will drink and we will go.'

'Will you?' she cried, running round the table and planting herself in front of us. 'That's just what you won't do. Coming into an honest woman's house this hour of the night – making a scene – getting the police after you. Ah, no! Ah, no! It's a disgrace, that's what it is.'

'Sh!' said the little corporal, holding up his hand. Dead silence. In the silence we heard steps passing.

'The police,' whispered Blackbeard, winking at a pretty girl with rings in her ears, who smiled back at him, saucy. 'Sh!'

The faces lifted, listening. 'How beautiful they are!' I thought. 'They are like a family party having supper in the New Testament . . .' The steps died away.

'Serve you very well right if you had been caught,' scolded the angry woman. 'I'm sorry on your account that the police didn't come. You deserve it – you deserve it.'

'A little glass of mirabelle and we will go,' persisted the blue-eyed soldier.

Still scolding and muttering she took four glasses from the cupboard and a big bottle. 'But you're not going to drink in here. Don't you believe it.' The little corporal ran into the kitchen. 'Not there! Not there! Idiot!' she cried. 'Can't you see there's a window there, and a wall opposite where the police come every evening to . . .'

'Sh!' Another scare.

'You are mad and you will end in prison, – all four of you,' said the woman. She flounced out of the room. We tiptoed after her into a dark smelling scullery, full of pans of greasy water, of salad leaves and meat-bones.

'There now,' she said, putting down the glasses. 'Drink and go!'

'Ah, at last!' The blue-eyed soldier's happy voice trickled through the dark. 'What do you think? Isn't it just as I said? Hasn't it got a taste of excellent – *ex-cellent* whisky?'

(1915)

Spring Pictures

It is raining. Big soft drops splash on the people's hands and cheeks; immense warm drops like melted stars. 'Here are roses! Here are lilies! Here are violets!' caws the old hag in the gutter. But the lilies, bunched together in a frill of green, look more like faded cauliflowers. Up and down she drags the creaking barrow. A bad, sickly smell comes from it. Nobody wants to buy. You must walk in the middle of the road, for there is no room on the pavement. Every single shop brims over; every shop shows a tattered frill of soiled lace and dirty ribbon to charm and entice you. There are tables set out with toy cannons and soldiers and Zeppelins[1] and photograph frames complete with ogling beauties. There are immense baskets of yellow straw hats piled up like pyramids of pastry, and strings of coloured boots and shoes so small that nobody could wear them. One shop is full of little squares of mackintosh, blue ones for girls and pink ones for boys with *Bébé* printed in the middle of each . . .

'Here are lilies! Here are roses! Here are pretty violets!' warbles the old hag, bumping into another barrow. But this barrow is still. It is heaped with lettuces. Its owner, a fat old woman, sprawls across, fast asleep, her nose in the lettuce roots . . . Who is ever going to buy anything here . . .? The sellers are women. They sit on little canvas stools, dreamy and vacant looking. Now and again one of them gets up and takes a feather duster, like a smoky torch, and flicks it over a thing or two and then sits down again. Even the old man in tangerine spectacles with a balloon of a belly, who turns the revolving stand of 'comic' postcards round and round cannot decide . . .

Suddenly, from the empty shop at the corner a piano strikes up, and a violin and flute join in. The windows of the shop are scrawled over – *New Songs. First Floor. Entrance Free*. But the windows of the first floor being open, nobody bothers to go up. They hang about grinning as the harsh voices float out into the warm rainy air. At the doorway there stands a lean man in a pair of burst carpet slippers. He has stuck a feather through the broken rim of his hat; with what an air he wears it!

The feather is magnificent. It is gold epaulettes, frogged coat, white kid gloves, gilded cane. He swaggers under it and the voice rolls off his chest, rich and ample.

'Come up! Come up! Here are the new songs! Each singer is an artiste of European reputation. The orchestra is famous and second to none. You can stay as long as you like. It is the chance of a lifetime, and once missed never to return!' But nobody moves. Why should they? They know all about those girls – those famous artistes. One is dressed in cream cashmere and one in blue. Both have dark crimped hair and a pink rose pinned over the ear ... They know all about the pianist's button boots – the left foot – the pedal foot – burst over the bunion on his big toe. The violinist's bitten nails, the long, far too long cuffs of the flute player – all these things are as old as the new songs.

For a long time the music goes on and the proud voice thunders. Then somebody calls down the stairs and the showman, still with his grand air, disappears. The voices cease. The piano, the violin and the flute dribble into quiet. Only the lace curtain gives a wavy sign of life from the first floor.

It is raining still; it is getting dusky ... Here are roses! Here are lilies! Who will buy my violets? ...

Hope! You misery – you sentimental, faded female! Break your last string and have done with it. I shall go mad with your endless thrumming; my heart throbs to it and every little pulse beats in time. It is morning. I lie in the empty bed – the huge bed big as a field and as cold and unsheltered. Through the shutters the sunlight comes up from the river and flows over the ceiling in trembling waves. I hear from outside a hammer tapping, and far below in the house a door swings open and shuts. Is this my room? Are those my clothes folded over an armchair? Under the pillow, sign and symbol of a lonely woman, ticks my watch. The bell jangles. Ah! At last! I leap out of bed and run to the door. Play faster – faster – Hope!

'Your milk, Mademoiselle,' says the concierge, gazing at me severely.

'Ah, thank you,' I cry, gaily swinging the milk bottle. 'No letters for me?'

'Nothing, Mademoiselle.'

'But the postman – he has called already?'

'A long half-hour ago, Mademoiselle.'

Shut the door. Stand in the little passage a moment. Listen – listen for her hated twanging. Coax her – court her – implore her to play just once that charming little thing for one string only. In vain.

Across the river, on the narrow stone path that fringes the bank, a woman is walking. She came down the steps from the Quay, walking slowly, one hand on her hip. It is a beautiful evening; the sky is the colour of lilac and the river of violet leaves. There are big bright trees along the path full of trembling light, and the boats, dancing up and down, send heavy curls of foam rippling almost to her feet. Now she has stopped. Now she has turned suddenly. She is leaning up against a tree, her hands over her face; she is crying. And now she is walking up and down wringing her hands. Again she leans against the tree, her back against it, her head raised and her hands clasped as though she leaned against someone dear. Round her shoulders she wears a little grey shawl; she covers her face with the ends of it and rocks to and fro.

But one cannot cry for ever, so at last she becomes serious and quiet, patting her hair into place, smoothing her apron. She walks a step or two. No, too soon, too soon! Again her arms fly up – she runs back – again she is blotted against the tall tree. Squares of gold light show in the houses; the street lamps gleam through the new leaves; yellow fans of light follow the dancing boats. For a moment she is a blur against the tree, white, grey and black, melting into the stones and the shadows. And then she is gone.

(1915)

Late at Night

(*Virginia is seated by the fire. Her outdoor things are thrown on a chair; her boots are faintly steaming in the fender.*)

Virginia (*laying the letter down*): I don't like this letter at all – not at all. I wonder if he means it to be so snubbing – or if it's just his way. (*Reads*). 'Many thanks for the socks. As I have had five pairs sent me lately, I am sure you will be pleased to hear I gave yours to a friend in my company.' No; it can't be my fancy. He must have meant it; it is a dreadful snub.

Oh, I wish I hadn't sent him that letter telling him to take care of himself. I'd give anything to have that letter back. I wrote it on a Sunday evening, too – that was so fatal. I never ought to write letters on Sunday evenings – I always let myself go so. I can't think why Sunday evenings always have such a funny effect on me. I simply yearn to have someone to write to – or to love. Yes, that's it; they make me feel sad and full of love. Funny, isn't it!

I must start going to church again; it's fatal sitting in front of the fire and thinking. There are the hymns, too; one can let oneself go so safely in the hymns. (*She croons*) 'And then for those our Dearest and our Best' – (*but her eye lights on the next sentence in the letter*). 'It was most kind of you, to have knitted them yourself.' Really! Really, that is too much! Men are abominably arrogant! He actually imagines that I knitted them myself. Why, I hardly know him; I've only spoken to him a few times. Why on earth should I knit him socks? He must think I am far gone to throw myself at his head like that. For it certainly is throwing oneself at a man's head to knit him socks – if he's almost a stranger. Buying him an odd pair is a different matter altogether. No; I shan't write to him again – that's definite. And, besides, what would be the use? I might get really keen on him and he'd never care a straw for me. Men don't.

I wonder why it is that after a certain point I always seem to repel people. Funny, isn't it! They like me at first; they think me uncommon, or original; but then immediately I want to show them – even give them a hint – that I like them, they seem to get frightened and begin to disappear. I suppose I shall get embittered about it later on. Perhaps they know somehow that I've got so much to give. Perhaps it's that that frightens them. Oh, I feel I've got such boundless, boundless love to give to somebody – I would care for somebody so utterly and so completely – watch over them – keep everything horrible away – and make them feel that if ever they wanted anything done I lived to do it. If only I felt that somebody wanted me, that I was of use to somebody, I should become a different person. Yes; that is the secret of life for me – to feel loved, to feel wanted, to know that somebody leaned on me for everything absolutely – for ever. And I am strong, and far, far richer than most women. I am sure that most women don't have this tremendous yearning to – express themselves. I suppose that's it – to come into flower, almost. I'm all folded and shut away in the dark, and nobody cares. I suppose that is why I feel this tremendous tenderness for plants and sick animals and birds – it's one way of getting rid of this wealth, this burden of love. And then, of course, they are so helpless – that's another thing. But I have a feeling that if a man were really in love with you he'd be just as helpless, too. Yes, I am sure that men are very helpless . . .

I don't know why, I feel inclined to cry to-night. Certainly not because of this letter; it isn't half important enough. But I keep wondering if things will ever change or if I shall go on like this until I am old – just wanting and wanting. I'm not as young as I was even now. I've got lines, and my skin isn't a bit what it used to be. I never was really pretty, not in the ordinary way, but I did have lovely skin and lovely hair – and I walked well. I only caught sight of myself in a glass to-day – stooping and shuffling along . . . I looked dowdy and elderly. Well, no; perhaps not quite as bad as that; I always exaggerate about myself. But I'm faddy about things now – that's a sign of age, I'm sure. The wind – I can't bear being blown about in the wind now; and I hate having wet feet. I never used to care about those things – I used almost to revel in them – they made me feel so *one* with Nature in a way. But now I get cross and I want to cry and I yearn for something to make me forget. I suppose that's why women take to drink. Funny, isn't it!

The fire is going out. I'll burn this letter. What's it to me? Pooh! I don't care. What is it to me? The five other women can send him socks! And I don't suppose he was a bit what I imagined. I can just hear him saying, 'It was most kind of you, to have knitted them yourself.' He has a fascinating voice. I think it was his voice that attracted me to him – and his hands; they looked so strong – they were such man's hands. Oh, well, don't sentimentalise over it; burn it! . . . No, I can't now – the fire's gone out. I'll go to bed. I wonder if he really meant to be snubbing. Oh, I am tired. Often when I go to bed now I want to pull the clothes over my head – and just cry. Funny, isn't it!

(1917)

Two Tuppenny Ones, Please

Lady. Yes, there is, dear; there's plenty of room. If the lady next to me would move her seat and sit opposite . . . Would you mind? So that my friend may sit next to me . . . Thank you so much! Yes, dear, both the cars on war work; I'm getting quite used to 'buses. Of course, if we go to the theatre, I 'phone Cynthia. She's still got one car. Her chauffeur's been called up . . . Ages ago . . . Killed by now, I think. I can't quite remember. I don't like her new man at all. I don't mind taking any reasonable risk, but he's so obstinate – he charges everything he sees. Heaven alone knows what would happen if he rushed into something that wouldn't swerve aside. But the poor creature's got a withered arm, and something the matter with one of his feet, I believe she told me. I suppose that's what makes him so careless. I mean – well! . . . Don't you know! . . .

Friend. . . .?

Lady. Yes, she's sold it. My dear, it was far too small. There were only ten bedrooms, you know. There were only ten bedrooms in that house. Extraordinary! One wouldn't believe it from the outside – would one? And with the governesses and the nurses – and so on. All the men-servants had to sleep out . . . You know what that means.

Friend. . . .!!

Conductor. Fares, please. Pass your fares along.

Lady. How much is it? Tuppence, isn't it? Two tuppenny ones, please. Don't bother – I've got some coppers, somewhere or other.

Friend. . . .!

Lady. No, it's all right. I've got some – if only I can find them.

Conductor. Parse your fares, please.

Friend. . . .!

Lady. Really? So I did. I remember now. Yes, I paid coming. Very well, I'll let you, just this once. War time, my dear.

Conductor. 'Ow far do you want ter go?

Lady. To the Boltons.

Conductor. Another 'a'penny each.

Lady. No – oh, no! I only paid tuppence coming. Are you quite sure?

Conductor (*savagely*). Read it on the board for yourself.

Lady. Oh, very well. Here's another penny. (*To friend*): Isn't it extra-ordinary how disobliging these men are? After all, he's paid to do his job. But they are nearly all alike. I've heard these motor 'buses affect the spine after a time. I suppose that's it . . . You've heard about Teddie – haven't you?'

Friend. . . .

Lady. He's got his . . . He's got his . . . Now what is it? Whatever can it be? How ridiculous of me!

Friend. . . .?

Lady. Oh, no! He's been a Major for ages.

Friend. . . .?

Lady. Colonel? Oh, no, my dear, it's something much higher than that. Not his company – he's had his company a long time. Not his battalion . . .

Friend. . . .?

Lady. Regiment! Yes, I believe it is his regiment. But what I was going to say is he's been made a . . . Oh, how silly I am! What's higher than a Brigadier-General?[1] Yes, I believe that's it. Chief of Staff. Of course, Mrs T's frightfully gratified.

Friend. . . .[2]

Lady. Oh, my dear, everybody goes over the top nowadays. Whatever his position may be. And Teddie is such a sport, I really don't see how . . . Too dreadful – isn't it!

Friend. . . .?

Lady. Didn't you know? She's at the War Office, and doing very well. I believe she got a rise the other day. She's something to do with notify-ing the deaths, or finding the missing. I don't know exactly what it is. At any rate, she says it is too depressing for words, and she has to read the most heart-rending letters from parents, and so on. Happily, they're a very cheery little group in her room – all officers' wives, and they make their own tea, and get cakes in turn from Stewart's.[3] She has one after-noon a week off, when she shops or has her hair waved. Last time she and I went to see Yvette's Spring Show.[4]

Friend. . . .?

Lady. No, not really. I'm getting frightfully sick of these coat-frocks, aren't you? I mean, as I was saying to her, what is the use of paying an

enormous price for having one made by Yvette, when you can't really
tell the difference, in the long run, between it and one of those cheap
ready-made ones. Of course, one has the satisfaction for oneself of
knowing that the material is good, and so on – but it looks nothing. No;
I advised her to get a good coat and skirt. For, after all, a good coat and
skirt always tells. Doesn't it?

Friend. . . .!

Lady. Yes, I didn't tell her that – but that's what I had in mind. She's
much too fat for those coat-frocks. She goes out far too much at the
hips. I half ordered a rather lovely indefinite blue one for myself,
trimmed with the new lobster red . . . I've lost my good Kate, you know.

Friend. . . .!

Lady. Yes, isn't it annoying! Just when I got her more or less trained.
But she went off her head, like they all do nowadays, and decided that
she wanted to go into munitions. I told her when she gave notice that
she would go on the strict understanding that if she got a job (which I
think is highly improbable), she was not to come back and disturb the
other servants.

Conductor (*savagely*). Another penny each, if you're going on.

Lady. Oh, we're there. How extraordinary! I never should have
noticed . . .

Friend. . . .?

Lady. Tuesday? Bridge on Tuesday? No, dear, I'm afraid I can't
manage Tuesday. I trot out the wounded every Tuesday you know. I let
cook take them to the Zoo, or some place like that – don't you know.
Wednesday – I'm perfectly free on Wednesday.

Conductor. It'll be Wednesday before you get off the 'bus if you don't
'urry up.

Lady. That's quite enough, my man.

Friend. . . .!!

(1917)

The Black Cap

(A lady and her husband are seated at breakfast. He is quite calm, reading the newspaper and eating; but she is strangely excited, dressed for travelling, and only pretending to eat.)

She. Oh, if you should want your flannel shirts, they are on the right-hand bottom shelf of the linen press.[1]

He (at a board meeting of the Meat Export Company). No.

She. You didn't hear what I said. I said if you should want your flannel shirts, they are on the right-hand bottom shelf of the linen press.

He (positively). I quite agree!

She. It does seem rather extraordinary that on the very morning that I am going away you cannot leave the newspaper alone for five minutes.

He (mildly). My dear woman, I don't want you to go. In fact, I have asked you not to go. I can't for the life of me see . . .

She. You know perfectly well that I am only going because I absolutely must. I've been putting it off and putting it off, and the dentist said last time . . .

He. Good! Good! Don't let's go over the ground again. We've thrashed it out pretty thoroughly, haven't we?

Servant. Cab's here, m'm.

She. Please put my luggage in.

Servant. Very good, m'm.

(She gives a tremendous sigh.)

He. You haven't got too much time if you want to catch that train.

She. I know. I'm going. *(In a changed tone.)* Darling, don't let us part like this. It makes me feel so wretched. Why is it that you always seem to take a positive delight in spoiling my enjoyment?

He. I don't think going to the dentist is so positively enjoyable.

She. Oh, you know that's not what I mean. You're only saying that to hurt me. You know you are begging the question.

He (laughing). And you are losing your train. You'll be back on Thursday evening, won't you?

She (in a low, desperate voice). Yes, on Thursday evening. Good-bye, then. (*Comes over to him, and takes his head in her hands.*) Is there anything really the matter? Do at least look at me. Don't you – care – at – all?

He. My darling girl! This is like an exit on the cinema.

She (letting her hands fall). Very well. Good-bye. (*Gives a quick tragic glance round the dining-room and goes.*)

(*On the way to the station.*)

She. How strange life is! I didn't think I should feel like this at all. All the glamour seems to have gone, somehow. Oh, I'd give anything for the cab to turn round and go back. The most curious thing is that I feel if he really had made me believe he loved me it would have been much easier to have left him. But that's absurd. How strong the hay smells. It's going to be a very hot day. I shall never see these fields again. Never! never! But in another way I am glad that it happened like this; it puts me so finally, absolutely in the right for ever! He doesn't want a woman at all. A woman has no meaning for him. He's not the type of man to care deeply for anybody except himself. I've become the person who re-members to take the links out of his shirts before they go to the wash – that is all! And that's not enough for me. I'm young – I'm too proud. I'm not the type of woman to vegetate in the country and rave over 'our' own lettuces . . .

What you have been trying to do, ever since you married me is to make me submit, to turn me into your shadow, to rely on me so utterly that you'd only to glance up to find the right time printed on me some-how, as if I were a clock. You have never been curious about me; you never wanted to explore my soul. No; you wanted me to settle down to your peaceful existence. Oh! how your blindness has outraged me – how I hate you for it! I am glad – thankful – thankful to have left you! I'm not a green girl; I am not conceited, but I do know my powers. It's not for nothing that I've always longed for riches and passion and freedom, and felt that they were mine by right. (*She leans against the buttoned back of the cab and murmurs.*) 'You are a Queen. Let mine be the joy of giving you your kingdom.' (*She smiles at her little royal hands.*) I wish my heart didn't beat so hard. It really hurts me. It tires me so and excites me so. It's like someone in a dreadful hurry beating against a door . . . This cab is only crawling along; we shall never be at the station at this rate. Hurry! Hurry! My love, I am coming as quickly as ever I can. Yes, I am suffering just like you. It's dreadful, isn't it unbearable – this last half-hour without each other . . . Oh, God! the horse has begun to walk again. Why doesn't he beat the great strong brute of a thing . . . Our wonderful life! We shall travel all over the world together. The whole world shall be ours because of our love. Oh, be patient! I am coming as fast as I possibly can . . . Ah, now it's downhill; now we really are going faster. (*An old man attempts to cross the road.*) Get out of my way, you old fool! He deserves to be run over . . . Dearest – dearest; I am nearly there. Only be patient!

(*At the station.*)

Put it in a first-class smoker . . . There's plenty of time after all. A full ten minutes before the train goes. No wonder he's not here. I mustn't appear to be looking for him. But I must say I'm disappointed. I never dreamed of being the first to arrive. I thought he would have been here and engaged a carriage and bought papers and flowers . . . How curious! I absolutely saw in my mind a paper of pink carnations . . . He knows how fond I am of carnations. But pink ones are not my favourites. I prefer dark red or pale yellow. He really will be late if he doesn't come now. The guard has begun to shut the doors. Whatever can have happened? Something dreadful. Perhaps at the last moment he has shot himself . . . I could not bear the thought of ruining your life . . . But you are not ruining my life. Ah, where are you? I shall have to get into the carriage . . . Who is this? That's not him! It can't be – yes, it is. What on earth has he got on his head? A black cap. But how awful! He's utterly changed. What can he be wearing a black cap for? I wouldn't have known him. How absurd he looks coming towards me, smiling, in that appalling cap!

He. My darling, I shall never forgive myself. But the most absurd, tragic-comic thing happened. (*They get into the carriage.*) I lost my hat. It simply disappeared. I had half the hotel looking for it. Not a sign! So finally, in despair, I had to borrow this from another man who was staying there. (*The train moves off.*) You're not angry. (*Tries to take her in his arms.*)

She. Don't! We're not even out of the station yet.

He (*ardently*). Great God! What do I care if the whole world were to see us? (*Tries to take her in his arms.*) My wonder! My joy!

She. Please don't! I hate being kissed in trains.

He (*profoundly hurt*). Oh, very well. You *are* angry. It's serious. You can't get over the fact that I was late. But if you only knew the agony I suffered . . .

She. How can you think I could be so small-minded? I am not angry at all.

He. Then why won't you let me kiss you?

She (*laughing hysterically*). You look so different somehow – almost a stranger.

He (*jumps up and looks at himself in the glass anxiously*, and *fatuously, she decides*). But it's all right, isn't it?

She. Oh, quite all right; perfectly all right. Oh, oh, oh! (*She begins to laugh and cry with rage.*)

(*They arrive*).

She (*while he gets a cab*). I must get over this. It's an obsession. It's incredible that anything should change a man so. I must tell him. Surely it's quite simple to say: Don't you think now that you are in the city you had better buy yourself a hat? But that will make him realise how frightful the cap has been. And the extraordinary thing is that he doesn't realise it himself. I mean if he has looked at himself in the glass, and doesn't think that cap too ridiculous, how different our points of view must be . . . How deeply different! I mean, if I had seen him in the street I would have said I could not possibly love a man who wore a cap like that. I couldn't even have got to know him. He isn't my style at all. (*She looks round.*) Everybody is smiling at it. Well, I don't wonder! The way it makes his ears stick out, and the way it makes him have no back to his head at all.

He. The cab is ready, my darling. (*They get in.*)

He (*tries to take her hand*). The miracle that we two should be driving together, so simply, like this.

(*She arranges her veil.*)

He (*tries to take her hand, very ardent*). I'll engage one room, my love.

She. Oh, no! Of course you must take two.

He. But don't you think it would be wiser not to create suspicion?

She. I must have my own room. (*To herself.*) You can hang your cap *behind your own door!* (*She begins to laugh hysterically.*)

He. Ah! thank God! My queen is her happy self again!

(*At the hotel.*)

Manager. Yes, Sir, I quite understand. I think I've got the very thing for you, Sir. Kindly step this way. (*He takes them into a small sitting-room, with a bedroom leading out of it.*) This would suit you nicely, wouldn't it? And if you liked, we could make you up a bed on the sofa.

He. Oh, admirable! Admirable!

(*The Manager goes.*)

She (*furious*). But I told you I wanted a room to myself. What a trick to play upon me! I told you I did not want to share a room. How dare you treat me like this? (*She mimics.*) Admirable! Admirable! I shall never forgive you for that!

He (*overcome*). Oh, God, what is happening! I don't understand – I'm in the dark. Why have you suddenly, on this day of days, ceased to love me? What have I done? Tell me!

She (*sinks on the sofa*). I'm very tired. If you do love me, please leave me alone. I – I only want to be alone for a little.

He (*tenderly*). Very well. I shall try to understand. I do begin to understand. I'll go out for half-an-hour, and then, my love, you may feel calmer. (*He looks round, distracted.*)

She. What is it?

He. My heart – you are sitting on my cap. (*She gives a positive scream and moves into the bedroom. He goes. She waits a moment, and then puts down her veil, and takes up her suitcase.*)

(*In the taxi.*)

She. Yes, Waterloo. (*She leans back.*) Ah, I've escaped – I've escaped! I shall just be in time to catch the afternoon train home. Oh, it's like a dream – I'll be home before supper. I'll tell him that the city was too hot or the dentist away. What does it matter? I've a right to my own home . . . It will be wonderful driving up from the station; the fields will smell so delicious. There is cold fowl for supper left over from yesterday, and orange jelly . . . I have been mad, but now I am sane again. Oh, my husband!

(1917)

A Suburban Fairy Tale

Mr and Mrs B. sat at breakfast in the cosy red dining-room of their 'snug little crib just under half-an-hour's run from the City.'

There was a good fire in the grate – for the dining-room was the living-room as well – the two windows overlooking the cold empty garden patch were closed, and the air smelled agreeably of bacon and eggs, toast and coffee. Now that this rationing business[1] was really over Mr B. made a point of a thoroughly good tuck-in before facing the very real perils of the day. He didn't mind who knew it – he was a true Englishman about his breakfast – he had to have it; he'd cave in without it, and if you told him that these Continental chaps could get through half the morning's work he did on a roll and a cup of coffee – you simply didn't know what you were talking about.

Mr B. was a stout youngish man who hadn't been able – worse luck – to chuck his job and join the army; he'd tried for four years to get another chap to take his place but it was no go. He sat at the head of the table reading the *Daily Mail*. Mrs B. was a youngish plump little body, rather like a pigeon. She sat opposite, preening herself behind the coffee set and keeping an eye of warning love on little B. who perched between them, swathed in a napkin and tapping the top of a soft-boiled egg.

Alas! Little B. was not at all the child that such parents had every right to expect. He was no fat little trot, no dumpling, no firm little pudding. He was under-sized for his age, with legs like macaroni, tiny claws, soft, soft hair that felt like mouse fur, and big wide-open eyes. For some strange reason everything in life seemed the wrong size for Little B. – too big and too violent. Everything knocked him over, took the wind out of his feeble sails and left him gasping and frightened. Mr and Mrs B. were quite powerless to prevent this; they could only pick him up after the mischief was done – and try to set him going again. And Mrs B. loved him as only weak children are loved – and when Mr B. thought what a marvellous little chap he was too – thought of the spunk of the little man, he – well he – by George – he . . .

'Why aren't there two kinds of eggs?' said Little B. 'Why aren't there little eggs for children and big eggs like what this one is for grown-ups?'

'Scotch hares,' said Mr B. 'Fine Scotch hares for 5s. 3d. How about getting one, old girl?'

'It would be a nice change, wouldn't it?' said Mrs B. 'Jugged.'

And they looked across at each other and there floated between them the Scotch hare in its rich gravy with stuffing balls and a white pot of red-currant jelly accompanying it.

'We might have had it for the week-end,' said Mrs B. 'But the butcher has promised me a nice little sirloin and it seems a pity' . . . Yes, it did and yet . . . Dear me, it was very difficult to decide. The hare would have been such a change – on the other hand, could you beat a really nice little sirloin?

'There's hare soup, too,' said Mr B. drumming his fingers on the table. 'Best soup in the world!'

'O-Oh!' cried Little B. so suddenly and sharply that it gave them quite a start – 'Look at the whole lot of sparrows flown on to our lawn' – he waved his spoon. 'Look at them,' he cried. 'Look!' And while he spoke, even though the windows were closed, they heard a loud shrill cheeping and chirping from the garden.

'Get on with your breakfast like a good boy, do,' said his mother, and his father said, 'You stick to the egg, old man, and look sharp about it.'

'But look at them – look at them all hopping,' he cried. 'They don't keep still not for a minute. Do you think they're hungry, father?'

Cheek-a-cheep-cheep-cheek! cried the sparrows.

'Best postpone it perhaps till next week,' said Mr B., 'and trust to luck they're still to be had then.'

'Yes, perhaps that would be wiser,' said Mrs B.

Mr B. picked another plum out of his paper.

'Have you bought any of those controlled dates yet?'

'I managed to get two pounds yesterday,' said Mrs B.

'Well a date pudding's a good thing,' said Mr B. And they looked across at each other and there floated between them a dark round pudding covered with creamy sauce. 'It would be a nice change, wouldn't it?' said Mrs B.

Outside on the grey frozen grass the funny eager sparrows hopped and fluttered. They were never for a moment still. They cried, flapped their ungainly wings. Little B., his egg finished, got down, took his bread and marmalade to eat at the window.

'Do let us give them some crumbs,' he said. 'Do open the window, father, and throw them something. Father, *please*!'

'Oh, don't nag, child,' said Mrs B., and his father said – 'Can't go opening windows, old man. You'd get your head bitten off.'

'But they're hungry,' cried Little B., and the sparrows' little voices were like ringing of little knives being sharpened. *Cheek-a-cheep-cheep-cheek!* they cried.

Little B. dropped his bread and marmalade inside the china flower pot in front of the window. He slipped behind the thick curtains to see better, and Mr and Mrs B. went on reading about what you could get now without coupons – no more ration books after May – a glut of cheese – a glut of it – whole cheeses revolved in the air between them like celestial bodies.

Suddenly as Little B. watched the sparrows on the grey frozen grass, they grew, they changed, still flapping and squeaking. They turned into tiny little boys, in brown coats, dancing, jigging outside, up and down outside the window squeaking, 'Want something to eat, want something to eat!' Little B. held with both hands to the curtain. 'Father,' he whispered, 'Father! They're not sparrows. They're little boys. Listen, Father!' But Mr and Mrs B. would not hear. He tried again. 'Mother,' he whispered. 'Look at the little boys. They're not sparrows, Mother!' But nobody noticed his nonsense.

'All this talk about famine,' cried Mr B., 'all a Fake, all a Blind.'

With white shining faces, their arms flapping in the big coats, the little boys danced. 'Want something to eat – want something to eat.'

'Father,' muttered Little B. 'Listen, Father! Mother, listen, please!'

'Really!' said Mrs B. 'The noise those birds are making! I've never heard such a thing.'

'Fetch me my shoes, old man,' said Mr B.

Cheek-a-cheep-cheep-cheek! said the sparrows.

Now where had that child got to? 'Come and finish your nice cocoa, my pet,' said Mrs B.

Mr B. lifted the heavy cloth and whispered, 'Come on, Rover,' but no little dog was there.

'He's behind the curtain,' said Mrs B.

'He never went out of the room,' said Mr B.

Mrs B. went over to the window, and Mr B. followed. And they looked out. There on the grey frozen grass, with a white white face, the little boy's thin arms flapping like wings, in front of them all, the smallest, tiniest was Little B. Mr and Mrs B. heard his voice above all the voices, 'Want something to eat, want something to eat.'

Somehow, somehow, they opened the window. 'You shall! All of you. Come in *at once*. Old man! Little man!'

But it was too late. The little boys were changed into sparrows again, and away they flew – out of sight – out of call.

(1917)

Carnation

On those hot days Eve – curious Eve – always carried a flower. She snuffed it and snuffed it, twirled it in her fingers, laid it against her cheek, held it to her lips, tickled Katie's neck with it, and ended, finally, by pulling it to pieces and eating it, petal by petal.

'Roses are delicious, my dear Katie,' she would say, standing in the dim cloak room, with a strange decoration of flowery hats on the hat pegs behind her – 'but carnations are simply divine! They taste like – like – ah well!' And away her little thin laugh flew, fluttering among those huge, strange flower heads on the wall behind her. (But how cruel her little thin laugh was! It had a long sharp beak and claws and two bead eyes, thought fanciful Katie.)

To-day it was a carnation. She brought a carnation to the French class, a deep, deep red one, that looked as though it had been dipped in wine and left in the dark to dry. She held it on the desk before her, half shut her eyes and smiled.

'Isn't it a darling?' said she. But –

'*Un peu de silence, s'il vous plaît,*' came from M. Hugo. Oh, bother! It was too hot! Frightfully hot! Grilling simply!

The two square windows of the French Room were open at the bottom and the dark blinds drawn half way down. Although no air came in, the blind cord swung out and back and the blind lifted. But really there was not a breath from the dazzle outside.

Even the girls, in the dusky room, in their pale blouses, with stiff butterfly-bow hair ribbons perched on their hair, seemed to give off a warm, weak light, and M. Hugo's white waistcoat gleamed like the belly of a shark.

Some of the girls were very red in the face and some were white. Vera Holland had pinned up her black curls *à la japonaise* with a penholder and a pink pencil; she looked charming. Francie Owen pushed her sleeves nearly up to the shoulders, and then she inked the little blue vein in her elbow, shut her arm together, and then looked to see the mark it made; she had a passion for inking herself; she always had a face drawn on her thumb nail, with black, forked hair. Sylvia Mann took off her collar and tie, took them off simply, and laid them on the desk beside her, as calm as if she were going to wash her hair in her bedroom at home. She *had* a nerve! Jennie Edwards tore a leaf out of her notebook and wrote 'Shall we ask old Hugo-Wugo to give us a thrippenny vanilla on the way home!!!' and passed it across to Connie Baker, who turned absolutely purple and nearly burst out crying. All of them lolled and gaped, staring at the round clock, which seemed to have grown paler, too; the hands scarcely crawled.

'*Un peu de silence, s'il vous plaît*,' came from M. Hugo. He held up a puffy hand. 'Ladies, as it is so 'ot we will take no more notes to-day, but I will read you,' and he paused and smiled a broad, gentle smile, 'a little French poetry.'

'Go – od God!' moaned Francie Owen.

M. Hugo's smile deepened. 'Well, Mees Owen, you need not attend. You can paint yourself. You can 'ave my red ink as well as your black one.'

How well they knew the little blue book with red edges that he tugged out of his coat-tail pocket! It had a green silk marker embroidered in forget-me-nots. They often giggled at it when he handed the book round. Poor old Hugo-Wugo! He adored reading poetry. He would begin, softly and calmly, and then gradually his voice would swell and vibrate and gather itself together, then it would be pleading and imploring and entreating, and then rising, rising triumphant, until it burst into light, as it were, and then – gradually again, it ebbed, it grew soft and warm and calm and died down into nothingness.

The great difficulty was, of course, if you felt at all feeble, not to get the most awful fit of the giggles. Not because it was funny, really, but because it made you feel uncomfortable, queer, silly, and somehow ashamed for old Hugo-Wugo. But – oh dear – if he was going to inflict it on them in this heat . . .!

'Courage, my pet,' said Eve, kissing the languid carnation.

He began, and most of the girls fell forward, over the desks, their heads on their arms, dead at the first shot. Only Eve and Katie sat upright and still. Katie did not know enough French to understand, but Eve sat listening, her eyebrows raised, her eyes half veiled, and a smile that was like the shadow of her cruel little laugh, like the wing shadows of that cruel little laugh fluttering over her lips. She made a warm, white cup of her fingers – the carnation inside. Oh, the scent! It floated across to Katie. It was too much. Katie turned away to the dazzling light outside the window.

Down below, she knew, there was a cobbled courtyard with stable buildings round it. That was why the French Room always smelled faintly of ammonia. It wasn't unpleasant; it was even part of the French language for Katie – something sharp and vivid and – and – biting!

Now she could hear a man clatter over the cobbles and the jing-jang of the pails he carried. And now *Hoo-hor-her! Hoo-hor-her!* as he worked the pump, and a great gush of water followed. Now he was flinging the water over something, over the wheels of a carriage, perhaps. And she saw the wheel, propped up, clear of the ground, spinning round, flashing scarlet and black, with great drops glancing off it. And all the while he worked the man kept up a high bold whistling, that skimmed over the noise of the water as a bird skims over the sea. He went away – he came back again leading a cluttering horse.

Hoo-hor-her! Hoo-hor-her! came from the pump. Now he dashed the water over the horse's legs and then swooped down and began brushing.

She *saw* him simply – in a faded shirt, his sleeves rolled up, his chest bare, all splashed with water – and as he whistled, loud and free, and as he moved, swooping and bending, Hugo-Wugo's voice began to warm, to deepen, to gather together, to swing, to rise – somehow or other to keep time with the man outside (Oh, the scent of Eve's carnation!) until they became one great rushing, rising, triumphant thing, bursting into light, and then –

The whole room broke into pieces.

'Thank you, ladies,' cried M. Hugo, bobbing at his high desk, over the wreckage.

And 'Keep it, dearest,' said Eve. '*Souvenir tendre,*' and she popped the carnation down the front of Katie's blouse.

(1917)

See-Saw

Spring. As the people leave the road for the grass their eyes become fixed and dreamy like the eyes of people wading in the warm sea. There are no daisies yet, but the sweet smell of the grass rises, rises in tiny waves the deeper they go. The trees are in full leaf. As far as one can see there are fans, hoops, tall rich plumes of various green. A light wind shakes them, blowing them together, blowing them free again; in the blue sky floats a cluster of tiny white clouds like a brood of ducklings. The people wander over the grass – the old ones inclined to puff and waddle after their long winter snooze; the young ones suddenly linking hands and making for that screen of trees in the hollow or the shelter of that clump of dark gorse tipped with yellow – walking very fast, almost running, as though they had heard some lovely little creature caught in the thicket crying to them to be saved.

On the top of a small green mound there is a very favourite bench. It has a young chestnut growing beside it, shaped like a mushroom. Below the earth has crumbled, fallen away, leaving three or four clayey hollows – caves – caverns – and in one of them two little people had set up house with a minute pickaxe, an empty match box, a blunted nail and a shovel for furniture. He had red hair cut in a deep fringe, light blue eyes, a faded pink smock and brown button shoes. Her flowery curls were caught up with a yellow ribbon and she wore two dresses – her this week's underneath and her last week's on top. This gave her rather a bulky air.

'If you don't get me no sticks for my fire,' said she, 'there won't be no dinner.' She wrinkled her nose and looked at him severely. 'You seem to forget I've got a fire to make.' He took it very easy, balancing on his toes – 'Well – where's I to find any sticks?'

'Oh,' said she – flinging up her hands – 'anywhere of course –' And then she whispered just loud enough for him to hear, 'they needn't be real ones – *you* know.'

'Ooh,' he breathed. And then he shouted in a loud distinct tone: 'Well I'll just go an' get a few sticks.'

He came back in a moment with an armful.

'Is that a whole pennorth?' said she, holding out her skirts for them.

'Well,' said he, 'I don't know, because I had them give to me by a man that was moving.'

'Perhaps they're bits of what was broke,' said she. 'When we moved, two of the pictures was broken and my Daddy lit the fire with them, and my Mummy said – she said –' a tiny pause – 'soldier's manners!'

'What's that?' said he.

'Good *gracious*!' She made great eyes at him. 'Don't you *know*?'

'No,' said he. 'What does it mean?'

She screwed up a bit of her skirt, scrunched it, then looked away – 'Oh, don't bother me, child,' said she.

He didn't care. He took the pickaxe and hacked a little piece out of the kitchen floor.

'Got a newspaper?'

He plucked one out of the air and handed it to her. *Ziz, ziz, ziz!* She tore it into three pieces – knelt down and laid the sticks over. 'Matches, please.' The real box was a triumph, and the blunted nails. But funny – *Zip, zip, zip*, it wouldn't light. They looked at each other in consternation.

'Try the other side,' said she. *Zip.* 'Ah! that's better.' There was a great glow – and they sat down on the floor and began to make the pie.

To the bench beside the chestnut came two fat old babies and plumped themselves down. She wore a bonnet trimmed with lilac and tied with lilac velvet strings; a black satin coat and a lace tie – and each of her hands, squeezed into black kid gloves, showed a morsel of purplish flesh. The skin of his swollen old face was tight and glazed – and he sat down clasping his huge soft belly as though careful not to jolt or alarm it.

'Very hot,' said he, and he gave a low, strange trumpeting cry with which she was evidently familiar, for she gave no sign. She looked into the lovely distance and quivered:

'Nellie cut her finger last night.'

'Oh, did she?' said the old snorter. Then – 'How did she do that?'

'At dinner,' was the reply, 'with a knife.'

They both looked ahead of them – panting – then, 'Badly?'

The weak worn old voice, the old voice that reminded one somehow of a piece of faintly smelling dark lace, said, 'Not very badly.'

Again he gave that low strange cry. He took off his hat, wiped the rim and put it on again.

The voice beside him said with a spiteful touch: 'I think it was carelessness' – and he replied, blowing out his cheeks: 'Bound to be!'

But then a little bird flew on to a branch of the young chestnut above them – and shook over the old heads a great jet of song.

He took off his hat, heaved himself up, and beat in its direction in the tree. Away it flew.

'Don't want bird muck falling on us,' said he, lowering his belly carefully – carefully again.

The fire was made.

'Put your hand in the oven,' said she, 'an' see if it's hot.'

He put his hand in, but drew it out again with a squeak, and danced up and down. 'It's ever so hot,' said he.

This seemed to please her very much. She too got up and went over to him, and touched him with a finger.

'Do you like playing with me?' And he said, in his small solid way, 'Yes, I do.' At that she flung away from him and cried, 'I'll never be done if you keep on bothering me with these questions.'

As she poked the fire he said: 'Our dog's had kittens.'

'Kittens!' She sat back on her heels – 'Can a dog have kittens?'

'Of course they can,' said he. 'Little ones, you know.'

'But cats have kittens,' cried she. 'Dogs don't, dogs have –' she stopped, stared – looked for the word – couldn't find it – it was gone. 'They have –'

'*Kittens*,' cried he. 'Our dog's been an' had two.'

She stamped her foot at him. She was pink with exasperation. 'It's *not* kittens,' she wailed, 'it's –'

'It is – it is – it is –' he shouted, waving the shovel.

She threw her top dress over her head, and began to cry. 'It's not – it's – it's . . .'

Suddenly, without a moment's warning, he lifted his pinafore and made water.

At the sound she emerged.

'Look what you've been an' done,' said she, too appalled to cry any more. 'You've put out my fire.'

'Ah, never mind. Let's move. You can take the pickaxe and the match box.'

They moved to the next cave. 'It's much nicer here,' said he.

'Off you go,' said she, 'and get me some sticks for my fire.'

The two old babies above began to rumble, and obedient to the sign they got up without a word and waddled away.

(1917)

This Flower

'But I tell you, my lord fool, out of this nettle danger, we pluck this flower, safety.'[1]

As she lay there, looking up at the ceiling, she had her moment – yes, she had her moment! And it was not connected with anything she had thought or felt before, not even with those words the doctor had scarcely ceased speaking. It was single, glowing, perfect; it was like – a pearl, too flawless to match with another . . . Could she describe what happened? Impossible. It was as though, even if she had not been conscious (and she certainly had not been conscious all the time) that she was fighting against the stream of life – the stream of life indeed! – she had suddenly ceased to struggle. Oh, more than that! She had yielded, yielded absolutely, down to every minutest pulse and nerve, and she had fallen into the bright bosom of the stream and it had borne her . . . She was part of her room – part of the great bouquet of southern anemones, of the white net curtains that blew in stiff against the light breeze, of the mirrors, the white silky rugs; she was part of the high, shaking, quivering clamour, broken with little bells and crying voices that went streaming by outside, – part of the leaves and the light.

Over. She sat up. The doctor had reappeared. This strange little figure with his stethoscope still strung round his neck – for she had asked him to examine her heart – squeezing and kneading his freshly washed hands, had told her . . .

It was the first time she had ever seen him. Roy, unable, of course, to miss the smallest dramatic opportunity, had obtained his rather shady Bloomsbury[2] address from the man in whom he always confided everything, who, although he'd never met her, knew 'all about them.'

'My darling,' Roy had said, 'we'd better have an absolutely unknown man just in case it's – well, what we don't either of us want it to be. One can't be too careful in affairs of this sort. Doctors *do* talk. It's all damned rot to say they don't.' Then, 'Not that I care a straw who on earth knows. Not that I wouldn't – if you'd have me – blazon it on the skies, or take the front page of the *Daily Mirror* and have our two names on it, in a heart, you know – pierced by an arrow.'

Nevertheless, of course, his love of mystery and intrigue, his passion for 'keeping our secret beautifully' (his phrase!) had won the day, and off he'd gone in a taxi to fetch this rather sodden-looking little man.

She heard her untroubled voice saying, 'Do you mind not mentioning anything of this to Mr King?[3] If you'd tell him that I'm a little run down and that my heart wants a rest. For I've been complaining about my heart.'

Roy had been really *too* right about the kind of man the doctor was. He gave her a strange, quick, leering look, and taking off the stethoscope with shaking fingers he folded it into his bag that looked somehow like a broken old canvas shoe.

'Don't you worry, my dear,' he said huskily. 'I'll see you through.'

Odious little toad to have asked a favour of! She sprang to her feet, and picking up her purple cloth jacket, went over to the mirror. There was a soft knock at the door, and Roy – he really did look pale, smiling his half-smile – came in and asked the doctor what he had to say.

'Well,' said the doctor, taking up his hat, holding it against his chest and beating a tattoo on it, 'all I've got to say is that Mrs – h'm – Madam wants a bit of a rest. She's a bit run down. Her heart's a bit strained. Nothing else wrong.'

In the street a barrel-organ struck up something gay, laughing, mocking, gushing, with little trills, shakes, jumbles of notes.

> That's *all* I got to say, to say,
> That's all I got to say,

it mocked. It sounded so near she wouldn't have been surprised if the doctor were turning the handle.

She saw Roy's smile deepen; his eyes took fire. He gave a little 'Ah!' of relief and happiness. And just for one moment he allowed himself to gaze at her without caring a jot whether the doctor saw or not, drinking her up with that gaze she knew so well, as she stood tying the pale ribbons of her camisole and drawing on the little purple cloth jacket.[4] He jerked back to the doctor, 'She shall go away. She shall go away to the sea at once,' said he, and then, terribly anxious, 'What about her food?' At that, buttoning her jacket in the long mirror, she couldn't help laughing at him.

'That's all very well,' he protested, laughing back delightedly at her and at the doctor. 'But if I didn't manage her food, doctor, she'd never eat anything but caviare sandwiches and – and white grapes. About wine – oughtn't she to have wine?'

Wine would do her no harm.

'Champagne,' pleaded Roy. How he was enjoying himself!

'Oh, as much champagne as she likes,' said the doctor, 'and a brandy and soda with her lunch if she fancies it.'

Roy loved that; it tickled him immensely.

'Do you hear that?' he asked solemnly, blinking and sucking in his cheeks to keep from laughing. 'Do you fancy a brandy and soda?'

And, in the distance, faint and exhausted, the barrel-organ:

> A brandy and so-da,
> A brandy and soda, please!
> A brandy and soda, please!

The doctor seemed to hear that, too. He shook hands with her and Roy went with him into the passage to settle his fee.

She heard the front door close and then – rapid, rapid steps along the passage. This time he simply burst into her room, and she was in his arms, crushed up small while he kissed her with warm quick kisses,' murmuring between them, 'My darling, my beauty, my delight. You're mine, you're safe.' And then three soft groans. 'Oh! Oh! Oh! the relief!' Still keeping his arms round her he leant his head against her shoulder as though exhausted. 'If you knew how frightened I've been,' he murmured. 'I thought we were in for it this time. I really did. And it would have been so – fatal – so fatal!'

(1919)

The Wrong House

'Two purl – two plain – woolinfrontoftheneedle – and knit two to-gether.' Like an old song, like a song that she had sung so often that only to breathe was to sing it, she murmured the knitting pattern. Another vest was nearly finished for the mission parcel.

'It's your vests, Mrs Bean, that are so acceptable. Look at these poor little mites without a shred!' And the churchwoman showed her a photograph of repulsive little black objects with bellies shaped like lemons . . .

'Two purl – two plain.' Down dropped the knitting on to her lap; she gave a great long sigh, stared in front of her for a moment and then picked the knitting up and began again. What did she think about when she sighed like that? Nothing. It was a habit. She was always sighing. On the stairs, particularly, as she went up and down, she stopped, holding her dress up with one hand, the other hand on the banister, staring at the steps – sighing.

'Woolinfrontoftheneedle . . .' She sat at the dining-room window facing the street. It was a bitter autumn day; the wind ran in the street like a thin dog; the houses opposite looked as though they had been cut out with a pair of ugly steel scissors and pasted on to the grey paper sky. There was not a soul to be seen.

'Knit two together!' The clock struck three. Only three? It seemed dusk already; dusk came floating into the room, heavy, powdery dusk settling on the furniture, filming over the mirror. Now the kitchen clock struck three – two minutes late – for *this* was the clock to go by and *not* the kitchen clock. She was alone in the house. Dollicas was out shop-ping; she had been gone since a quarter to two. Really, she got slower and slower! What did she *do* with the time? One cannot spend more than a certain time buying a chicken . . . And oh, that habit of hers of dropping the stove-rings when she made up the fire! And she set her lips, as she had set her lips for the past thirty-five years, at that habit of Dollicas'.

There came a faint noise from the street, a noise of horses' hooves.

She leaned further out to see. Good gracious! It was a funeral. First the glass coach, rolling along briskly with the gleaming, varnished coffin inside (but no wreaths), with three men in front and two standing at the back, then some carriages, some with black horses, some with brown. The dust came bowling up the road, half hiding the procession. She scanned the houses opposite to see which had the blinds down. What horrible looking men, too! laughing and joking. One leaned over to one side and blew his nose with his black glove – horrible! She gathered up the knitting, hiding her hands in it. Dollicas surely would have known . . . There, they were passing . . . It was the other end . . .

What was this? What was happening? What could it mean? Help, God! Her old heart leaped like a fish and then fell as the glass coach drew up outside her door, as the outside men scrambled down from the front, swung off the back, and the tallest of them, with a glance of surprise at the windows, came quickly, stealthily, up the garden path.

'No!' she groaned. But yes, the blow fell, and for the moment it struck her down. She gasped, a great cold shiver went through her, and stayed in her hands and knees. She saw the man withdraw a step and again – that puzzled glance at the blinds – then –

'No!' she groaned, and stumbling, catching hold of things, she managed to get to the door before the blow fell again. She opened it, her chin trembled, her teeth clacked; somehow or other she brought out, 'The wrong house!'

Oh! he was shocked. As she stepped back she saw behind him the black hats clustered at the gate. 'The wrong 'ouse!' he muttered. She could only nod. She was shutting the door again when he fished out of the tail of his coat a black, brass-bound notebook and swiftly opened it. 'No. 20 Shuttleworth Crescent?'

'S – street! Crescent round the corner.' Her hand lifted to point, but shook and fell.

He was taking off his hat as she shut the door and leaned against it, whimpering in the dusky hall, 'Go away! Go away!'

Clockety-clock-clock. Cluk! Cluk! Clockety-clock-cluk! sounded from outside, and then a faint *Cluk! Cluk!* and then silence. They were gone. They were out of sight. But still she stayed leaning against the door, staring into the hall, staring at the hall-stand that was like a great lobster with hat-pegs for feelers. But she thought of nothing; she did not even think of what had happened. It was as if she had fallen into a cave whose walls were darkness . . .

She came to herself with a deep inward shock, hearing the gate bang and quick, short steps crunching the gravel; it was Dollicas hurrying round to the back door. Dollicas must not find her there; and wavering, wavering like a candle-flame, back she went into the dining-room to her seat by the window.

Dollicas was in the kitchen. *Klang!* went one of the iron rings into the fender. Then her voice, 'I'm just putting on the tea-kettle'm.' Since they had been alone she had got into the way of shouting from one room to another. The old woman coughed to steady herself. 'Please bring in the lamp,' she cried.

'The lamp!' Dollicas came across the passage and stood in the door-way. 'Why, it's only just on four 'm.'

'Never mind,' said Mrs Bean dully. 'Bring it in!' And a moment later the elderly maid appeared, carrying the gentle lamp in both hands. Her broad soft face had the look it always had when she carried anything, as though she walked in her sleep. She set it down on the table, lowered the wick, raised it, and then lowered it again. Then she straightened up and looked across at her mistress.

'Why, 'm, whatever's that you're treading on?'

It was the mission vest.

'T't! T't!' As Dollicas picked it up she thought, 'The old lady has been asleep. She's not awake yet.' Indeed the old lady looked glazed and dazed, and when she took up the knitting she drew out a needle of stitches and began to unwind what she had done.

'Don't forget the mace,' she said. Her voice sounded thin and dry. She was thinking of the chicken for that night's supper. And Dollicas under-stood and answered, 'It's a lovely young bird!' as she pulled down the blind before going back to her kitchen . . .

(1919)

Sixpence

Children are unaccountable little creatures. Why should a small boy like Dicky, good as gold as a rule, sensitive, affectionate, obedient, and marvellously sensible for his age, have moods when, without the slightest warning, he suddenly went 'mad dog,' as his sisters called it, and there was no doing anything with him?

'Dicky, come here! Come here, sir, at once! Do you hear your mother calling you? Dicky!'

But Dicky wouldn't come. Oh, he heard right enough. A clear, ringing little laugh was his only reply. And away he flew; hiding, running through the uncut hay on the lawn, dashing past the woodshed, making a rush for the kitchen garden, and there dodging, peering at his mother from behind the mossy apple trunks, and leaping up and down like a wild Indian.

It had begun at tea-time. While Dicky's mother and Mrs Spears, who was spending the afternoon with her, were quietly sitting over their sewing in the drawing-room, this, according to the servant girl, was what had happened at the children's tea. They were eating their first bread and butter as nicely and quietly as you please, and the servant girl had just poured out the milk and water, when Dicky had suddenly seized the bread plate, put it upside down on his head, and clutched the bread knife.

'Look at me!' he shouted.

His startled sisters looked, and before the servant girl could get there, the bread plate wobbled, slid, flew to the floor, and broke into shivers. At this awful point the little girls lifted up their voices and shrieked their loudest.

'Mother, come and look what he's done!'

'Dicky's broke a great big plate!'

'Come and stop him, mother!'

You can imagine how mother came flying. But she was too late. Dicky had leapt out of his chair, run through the French windows on to the verandah, and, well – there she stood – popping her thimble on and off, helpless. What could she do? She couldn't chase after the child. She couldn't stalk Dicky among the apples and damsons. That would be too undignified. It was more than annoying, it was exasperating. Especially as Mrs Spears, Mrs Spears of all people, whose two boys were so exemplary, was waiting for her in the drawing-room.

'Very well, Dicky,' she cried, 'I shall have to think of some way of punishing you.'

'I don't care,' sounded the high little voice, and again there came that ringing laugh. The child was quite beside himself . . .

'Oh, Mrs Spears, I don't know how to apologise for leaving you by yourself like this.'

'It's quite all right, Mrs Bendall,' said Mrs Spears, in her soft, sugary voice, and raising her eyebrows in the way she had. She seemed to smile to herself as she stroked the gathers. 'These little things will happen from time to time. I only hope it was nothing serious.'

'It was Dicky,' said Mrs Bendall, looking rather helplessly for her only fine needle. And she explained the whole affair to Mrs Spears. 'And the worst of it is, I don't know how to cure him. Nothing when he's in that mood seems to have the slightest effect on him.'

Mrs Spears opened her pale eyes. 'Not even a whipping?' said she.

But Mrs Bendall, threading her needle, pursed up her lips. 'We never have whipped the children,' she said. 'The girls never seem to have needed it. And Dicky is such a baby, and the only boy. Somehow . . .'

'Oh, my dear,' said Mrs Spears, and she laid her sewing down. 'I don't wonder Dicky has these little outbreaks. You don't mind my saying so? But I'm sure you make a great mistake in trying to bring up children without whipping them. Nothing really takes its place. And I speak from experience, my dear. I used to try gentler measures' – Mrs Spears drew in her breath with a little hissing sound – 'soaping the boys' tongues, for instance, with yellow soap, or making them stand on the table for the whole of Saturday afternoon. But no, believe me,' said Mrs Spears, 'there is nothing, there is nothing like handing them over to their father.'

Mrs Bendall in her heart of hearts was dreadfully shocked to hear of that yellow soap. But Mrs Spears seemed to take it so much for granted, that she did too.

'Their father,' she said. 'Then you don't whip them yourself?'

'Never.' Mrs Spears seemed quite shocked at the idea. 'I don't think it's the mother's place to whip the children. It's the duty of the father. And, besides, he impresses them so much more.'

'Yes, I can imagine that,' said Mrs Bendall, faintly.

'Now my two boys,' Mrs Spears smiled kindly, encouragingly, at Mrs Bendall, 'would behave just like Dicky if they were not afraid to. As it is . . .'

'Oh, your boys are perfect little models,' cried Mrs Bendall.

They were. Quieter, better-behaved little boys, in the presence of grown-ups, could not be found. In fact, Mrs Spears' callers often made the remark that you never would have known that there was a child in the house. There wasn't – very often.

In the front hall, under a large picture of fat, cheery old monks fishing by the riverside, there was a thick, dark horsewhip that had belonged to Mr Spears' father. And for some reason the boys preferred to play out of sight of this, behind the dog-kennel or in the tool-house, or round about the dustbin.

'It's such a mistake,' sighed Mrs Spears; breathing softly, as she folded her work, 'to be weak with children when they are little. It's such a sad mistake, and one so easy to make. It's so unfair to the child. That is what one has to remember. Now Dicky's little escapade this afternoon seemed to me as though he'd done it on purpose. It was the child's way of showing you that he needed a whipping.'

'Do you really think so?' Mrs Bendall was a weak little thing, and this impressed her very much.

'I do; I feel sure of it. And a sharp reminder now and then,' cried Mrs Spears in quite a professional manner, 'administered by the father, will save you so much trouble in the future. Believe me, my dear.' She put her dry, cold hand over Mrs Bendall's.

'I shall speak to Edward the moment he comes in,' said Dicky's mother firmly.

The children had gone to bed before the garden gate banged, and Dicky's father staggered up the steep concrete steps carrying his bicycle. It had been a bad day at the office. He was hot, dusty, tired out.

But by this time Mrs Bendall had become quite excited over the new plan, and she opened the door to him herself.

'Oh, Edward, I'm so thankful you have come home,' she cried.

'Why, what's happened?' Edward lowered the bicycle and took off his hat. A red angry pucker showed where the brim had pressed. 'What's up?'

'Come – come into the drawing-room,' said Mrs Bendall, speaking very fast. 'I simply can't tell you how naughty Dicky has been. You have no idea – you can't have at the office all day – how a child of that age can behave. He's been simply dreadful. I have no control over him – none. I've tried everything, Edward, but it's all no use. The only thing to do,' she finished breathlessly, 'is to whip him – is for you to whip him, Edward.'

In the corner of the drawing-room there was a what-not,¹ and on the top shelf stood a brown china bear with a painted tongue. It seemed in the shadow to be grinning at Dicky's father, to be saying, 'Hooray, this is what you've come home to!'

'But why on earth should I start whipping him?' said Edward, staring at the bear. 'We've never done it before.'

'Because,' said his wife, 'don't you see, it's the only thing to do. I can't control the child . . .' Her words flew from her lips. They beat round him, beat round his tired head. 'We can't possibly afford a nurse. The servant girl has more than enough to do. And his naughtiness is beyond words. You don't understand, Edward; you can't, you're at the office all day.'

The bear poked out his tongue. The scolding voice went on. Edward sank into a chair.

'What am I to beat him with?' he said weakly.

'Your slipper, of course,' said his wife. And she knelt down to untie his dusty shoes.

'Oh, Edward,' she wailed, 'you've still got your cycling clips on in the drawing-room. No, really –'

'Here, that's enough,' Edward nearly pushed her away. 'Give me that slipper.' He went up the stairs. He felt like a man in a dark net. And now he wanted to beat Dicky. Yes, damn it, he wanted to beat something. My God, what a life! The dust was still in his hot eyes, his arms felt heavy.

He pushed open the door of Dicky's slip of a room. Dicky was standing in the middle of the floor in his night-shirt. At the sight of him Edward's heart gave a warm throb of rage.

'Well, Dicky, you know what I've come for,' said Edward.

Dicky made no reply.

'I've come to give you a whipping.'

No answer.

'Lift up your nightshirt.'

At that Dicky looked up. He flushed a deep pink. 'Must I?' he whispered.

'Come on, now. Be quick about it,' said Edward, and, grasping the slipper, he gave Dicky three hard slaps.

'There, that'll teach you to behave properly to your mother.'

Dicky stood there, hanging his head.

'Look sharp and get into bed,' said his father.

Still he did not move. But a shaking voice said, 'I've not done my teeth yet, Daddy.'

'Eh, what's that?'

Dicky looked up. His lips were quivering, but his eyes were dry. He hadn't made a sound or shed a tear. Only he swallowed and said, huskily, 'I haven't done my teeth, Daddy.'

But at the sight of that little face Edward turned, and, not knowing what he was doing, he bolted from the room, down the stairs, and out into the garden. Good God! What had he done? He strode along and hid in the shadow of the pear tree by the hedge. Whipped Dicky – whipped his little man with a slipper – and what the devil for? He didn't even know. Suddenly he barged into his room – and there was the little chap in his nightshirt. Dicky's father groaned and held on to the hedge. And he didn't cry. Never a tear. If only he'd cried or got angry. But that 'Daddy'! And again he heard the quivering whisper. Forgiving like that without a word. But he'd never forgive himself – never. Coward! Fool! Brute! And suddenly he remembered the time when Dicky had fallen off his knee and sprained his wrist while they were playing together. He hadn't cried then, either. And that was the little hero he had just whipped.

Something's got to be done about this, thought Edward. He strode back to the house, up the stairs, into Dicky's room. The little boy was lying in bed. In the half light his dark head, with the square fringe, showed plain against the pale pillow. He was lying quite still, and even now he wasn't crying. Edward shut the door and leaned against it. What he wanted to do was to kneel down by Dicky's bed and cry himself and beg to be forgiven. But, of course, one can't do that sort of thing. He felt awkward, and his heart was wrung.

'Not asleep yet, Dicky?' he said lightly.

'No, Daddy.'

Edward came over and sat on his boy's bed, and Dicky looked at him through his long lashes.

'Nothing the matter, little chap, is there?' said Edward, half whispering.

'No-o, Daddy,' came from Dicky.

Edward put out his hand, and carefully he took Dicky's hot little paw.

'You – you mustn't think any more of what happened just now, little man,' he said huskily. 'See? That's all over now. That's forgotten. That's never going to happen again. See?'

'Yes, Daddy.'

'So the thing to do now is to buck up, little chap,' said Edward, 'and to smile.' And he tried himself an extraordinary trembling apology for a smile. 'To forget all about it – to – eh? Little man . . . Old boy . . .'

Dicky lay as before. This was terrible. Dicky's father sprang up and went over to the window. It was nearly dark in the garden. The servant girl had run out, and she was snatching, twitching some white clothes off the bushes and piling them over her arm. But in the boundless sky the evening star shone, and a big gum tree, black against the pale glow, moved its long leaves softly. All this he saw, while he felt in his trouser pocket for his money. Bringing it out, he chose a new sixpence and went back to Dicky.

'Here you are, little chap. Buy yourself something,' said Edward softly, laying the sixpence on Dicky's pillow.

But could even that – could even a whole sixpence – blot out what had been?

(1921)

Poison

The post was very late. When we came back from our walk after lunch it still had not arrived.

'*Pas encore, Madame,*' sang Annette, scurrying back to her cooking.

We carried our parcels into the dining-room. The table was laid. As always, the sight of the table laid for two – for two people only – and yet so finished, so perfect, there was no possible room for a third, gave me a queer, quick thrill as though I'd been struck by that silver lightning that quivered over the white cloth, the brilliant glasses, the shallow bowl of freesias.

'Blow the old postman! Whatever can have happened to him?' said Beatrice. 'Put those things down, dearest.'

'Where would you like them . . .?'

She raised her head; she smiled her sweet, teasing smile.

'Anywhere – Silly.'

But I knew only too well that there was no such place for her, and I would have stood holding the squat liqueur bottle and the sweets for months, for years, rather than risk giving another tiny shock to her exquisite sense of order.

'Here – I'll take them.' She plumped them down on the table with her long gloves and a basket of figs. 'The Luncheon Table. Short story by – by –' She took my arm. 'Let's go on to the terrace –' and I felt her shiver. '*Ça sent,*' she said faintly, '*de la cuisine . . .*'

I had noticed lately – we had been living in the south for two months – that when she wished to speak of food, or the climate, or, playfully, of her love for me, she always dropped into French.

We perched on the balustrade under the awning. Beatrice leaned over gazing down – down to the white road with its guard of cactus spears. The beauty of her ear, just her ear, the marvel of it was so great that I could have turned from regarding it to all that sweep of glittering sea below and stammered: 'You know – her ear! She has ears that are simply the most . . .'

She was dressed in white, with pearls round her throat and lilies-of-the-valley tucked into her belt. On the third finger of her left hand she wore one pearl ring – no wedding-ring.

'Why should I, *mon ami*? Why should we pretend? Who could possibly care?'

And of course I agreed, though privately, in the depths of my heart, I would have given my soul to have stood beside her in a large, yes, a large, fashionable church, crammed with people, with old reverend clergymen, with *The Voice that breathed o'er Eden*,[1] with palms and the smell of scent, knowing there was a red carpet and confetti outside, and somewhere, a wedding-cake and champagne and a satin shoe to throw after the carriage – if I could have slipped our wedding-ring on to her finger.

Not because I cared for such horrible shows, but because I felt it might possibly perhaps lessen this ghastly feeling of absolute freedom, *her* absolute freedom, of course.

Oh, God! What torture happiness was – what anguish! I looked up at the villa, at the windows of our room hidden so mysteriously behind the green straw blinds. Was it possible that she ever came moving through the green light and smiling that secret smile, that languid, brilliant smile that was just for me? She put her arm round my neck; the other hand softly, terribly, brushed back my hair.

'Who are you?' Who was she? She was – Woman.

. . . On the first warm evening in Spring, when lights shone like pearls through the lilac air and voices murmured in the fresh-flowering gardens, it was she who sang in the tall house with the tulle curtains. As one drove in the moonlight through the foreign city hers was the shadow that fell across the quivering gold of the shutters. When the lamp was lighted, in the new-born stillness her steps passed your door. And she looked out into the autumn twilight, pale in her furs, as the automobile swept by . . .

In fact, to put it shortly, I was twenty-four at the time. And when she lay on her back, with the pearls slipped under her chin, and sighed 'I'm thirsty, dearest. *Donne-moi un orange*,' I would gladly, willingly, have dived for an orange into the jaws of a crocodile – if crocodiles ate oranges.

> 'Had I two little feathery wings
> And were a little feathery bird . . .'

sang Beatrice.

I seized her hand. 'You wouldn't fly away?'

'Not far. Not further than the bottom of the road.'

'Why on earth there?'

She quoted: 'He cometh not, she said . . .''

'Who? The silly old postman? But you're not expecting a letter.'

'No, but it's maddening all the same. Ah!' Suddenly she laughed and leaned against me. 'There he is – look – like a blue beetle.'

And we pressed our cheeks together and watched the blue beetle beginning to climb.

'Dearest,' breathed Beatrice. And the word seemed to linger in the air, to throb in the air like the note of a violin.

'What is it?'

'I don't know,' she laughed softly. 'A wave of – a wave of affection, I suppose.'

I put my arm round her. 'Then you wouldn't fly away?'

And she said rapidly and softly: 'No! No! Not for worlds. Not really. I love this place. I've loved being here. I could stay here for years, I believe. I've never been so happy as I have these last two months, and you've been so perfect to me, dearest, in every way.'

This was such bliss – it was so extraordinary, so unprecedented, to hear her talk like this that I had to try to laugh it off.

'Don't! You sound as if you were saying good-bye.'

'Oh, nonsense, nonsense. You mustn't say such things even in fun!' She slid her little hand under my white jacket and clutched my shoulder. 'You've been happy, haven't you?'

'Happy? Happy? Oh, God – if you knew what I feel at this moment . . . Happy! My Wonder! My Joy!'

I dropped off the balustrade and embraced her, lifting her in my arms. And while I held her lifted I pressed my face in her breast and muttered: 'You *are* mine?' And for the first time in all the desperate months I'd known her, even counting the last month of – surely – Heaven – I believed her absolutely when she answered:

'Yes, I am yours.'

The creak of the gate and the postman's steps on the gravel drew us apart. I was dizzy for the moment. I simply stood there, smiling, I felt, rather stupidly. Beatrice walked over to the cane chairs.

'You go – go for the letters,' said she.

I – well – I almost reeled away. But I was too late. Annette came running. '*Pas de lettres*,' said she.

My reckless smile in reply as she handed me the paper must have surprised her. I was wild with joy. I threw the paper up into the air and sang out:

'No letters, darling!' as I came over to where the beloved woman was lying in the long chair.

For a moment she did not reply. Then she said slowly as she tore off the newspaper wrapper: 'The world forgetting, *by* the world forgot.'[4]

There are times when a cigarette is just the very one thing that will carry you over the moment. It is more than a confederate, even; it is a secret, perfect little friend who knows all about it and understands absolutely. While you smoke you look down at it – smile or frown, as the occasion demands; you inhale deeply and expel the smoke in a slow fan. This was one of those moments. I walked over to the magnolia and breathed my fill of it. Then I came back and leaned over her shoulder. But quickly she tossed the paper away on to the stone.

'There's nothing in it,' said she. 'Nothing. There's only some poison trial. Either some man did or didn't murder his wife, and twenty thousand people have sat in court every day and two million words have been wired all over the world after each proceeding.'

'Silly world!' said I, flinging into another chair. I wanted to forget the paper, to return, but cautiously, of course, to that moment before the postman came. But when she answered I knew from her voice the moment was over for now. Never mind. I was content to wait – five hundred years, if need be – now that I knew.

'Not so very silly,' said Beatrice. 'After all it isn't only morbid curiosity on the part of the twenty thousand.'

'What is it, darling?' Heavens knows I didn't care.

'Guilt!' she cried. 'Guilt! Didn't you realise that? They're fascinated like sick people are fascinated by anything – any scrap of news about their own case. The man in the dock may be innocent enough, but the people in court are nearly all of them poisoners. Haven't you ever thought' – she was pale with excitement – 'of the amount of poisoning that goes on? It's the exception to find married people who don't poison each other – married people and lovers. Oh,' she cried, 'the number of cups of tea, glasses of wine, cups of coffee that are just tainted. The number I've had myself, and drunk, either knowing or not knowing – and risked it. The only reason why so many couples' – she laughed – '*survive*, is because the one is frightened of giving the other the fatal dose. That dose takes nerve! But it's bound to come sooner or later. There's no going back once the first little dose has been given. It's the beginning of the end, really – don't you agree? Don't you see what I mean?'

She didn't wait for me to answer. She unpinned the lilies-of-the-valley and lay back, drawing them across her eyes.

'Both my husbands poisoned me,' said Beatrice. 'My first husband gave me a huge dose almost immediately, but my second was really an artist in his way. Just a tiny pinch, now and again, cleverly disguised – Oh, so cleverly! – until one morning I woke up and in every single particle of me, to the ends of my fingers and toes, there was a tiny grain. I was just in time . . .'

I hated to hear her mention her husbands so calmly, especially to-day. It hurt. I was going to speak, but suddenly she cried mournfully:

'Why! Why should it have happened to me? What have I done? Why have I been all my life singled out by . . . It's a conspiracy.'

I tried to tell her it was because she was too perfect for this horrible world – too exquisite, too fine. It frightened people. I made a little joke.

'But I – I haven't tried to poison you.'

Beatrice gave a queer small laugh and bit the end of a lily stem.

'You!' said she. 'You wouldn't hurt a fly!'

Strange. That hurt, though. Most horribly.

Just then Annette ran out with our *apéritifs*. Beatrice leaned forward and took a glass from the tray and handed it to me. I noticed the gleam of the pearl on what I called her pearl finger. How could I be hurt at what she said?

'And you,' I said, taking the glass, 'you've never poisoned anybody.'

That gave me an idea; I tried to explain.

'You – you do just the opposite. What is the name for one like you who, instead of poisoning people, fills them – everybody, the postman, the man who drives us, our boatman, the flower-seller, me – with new life, with something of her own radiance, her beauty, her –'

Dreamily she smiled; dreamily she looked at me.

'What are you thinking of – my lovely darling?'

'I was wondering,' she said, 'whether, after lunch, you'd go down to the post-office and ask for the afternoon letters. Would you mind, dearest? Not that I'm expecting one – but – I just thought, perhaps – it's silly not to have the letters if they're there. Isn't it? Silly to wait till

to-morrow.' She twirled the stem of the glass in her fingers. Her beautiful head was bent. But I lifted my glass and drank, sipped rather – sipped
slowly, deliberately, looking at that dark head and thinking of – postmen
and blue beetles and farewells that were not farewells and . . .

Good God! Was it fancy? No, it wasn't fancy. The drink tasted chill,
bitter, *queer*.

(1921)

Notes

References to TS are to Antony Alpers' edition of *The Stories of Katherine Mansfield* (Oxford University Press, 1984), and to LM to Ida Baker, *Katherine Mansfield: The Memories of LM* [Ida Baker] (Michael Joseph, 1971).

TITLE PAGE

The quotation on the title page is adapted from a passage in William Gerhardi, *Anton Chehov: A Critical Study* (Cobden Sanderson, 1923, p. 19). The actual passage in Gerhardi reads: '"Why are thy songs so short?" a bird was once asked. "Is it because thou art short of breath?" "I have many songs, and I should like to sing them all."' Gerhardi comments that 'this fragment from Daudet is jotted down in one of Chehov's note-books.' Presumably Murry chose it for its aptness to Mansfield's situation (she died at the age of thirty-four after years of illness), but it also memorializes Mansfield's interest in both Gerhardi (whose first novel she had recommended for publication) and Chehov. Gerhardi acknowledges Middleton Murry's book of essays, *Countries of the Mind* (Collins, 1922), in the prefatory notes to *Anton Chehov* (p. 9). Chehov was a central inspiration for Mansfield, and Murry may well have been thinking, when he included this quotation, of a comment in Mansfield's journal for 1917: 'Tchehov makes me feel that this longing to write stories of such uneven length is quite justified' (*The Journal of Katherine Mansfield*, John Middleton Murry, ed., Constable, 1954, p. 124). Mansfield may also have identified with Chehov's death from tuberculosis. Her story, 'The-Child-Who-Was-Tired', is a loose translation of Chehov's 'Sleepyhead' and provoked charges of plagiarism against her after her death. See the appendix to Claire Tomalin, *Katherine Mansfield: A Secret Life* (Viking, 1987), for a full account of this.

DEDICATION

To H. M. Tomlinson: Henry Major Tomlinson (1873–1958) was literary editor of the *Nation* from 1917 to 1923. He also worked as a war correspondent, prompting Katherine Mansfield to comment, when she saw him during a 1920 visit to the building which housed the offices of both the *Athenaeum*, then edited by Murry, and the *Nation*: 'poor silly old men with pins in their coat lapels, Tomlinson harking back to the mud in Flanders' (quoted in Antony Alpers,

The Life of Katherine Mansfield, Oxford University Press, 1982, p. 314, from an unpublished letter to Violet Schiff, probably written mid-May 1920). However, this disparaging attitude did not prevent Mansfield from enjoying Tomlinson's *Nation* column, 'A World of Books', and she mentioned him in her will. Murry presumably dedicated this volume of his wife's stories to Tomlinson in recognition of her affection for him and, perhaps more significantly, to acknowledge his own close friendship with Tomlinson.

INTRODUCTORY NOTE

This Introductory Note by John Middleton Murry, Mansfield's husband and editor of the volume, appeared unsigned in the first edition of *Something Childish and Other Stories* (1924), was reprinted in the Constable *The Collected Stories of Katherine Mansfield* (1945), signed 'J. M. M.', and then omitted from subsequent Penguin reprints of the Constable edition. The dates that appear after each story are Murry's and refer to the dates on which the stories were written rather than published. If his dates are to be trusted, then the stories are indeed published in the order in which they were written but, in some cases, extant manuscripts and Ida Baker's evidence contradict Murry's dating (e.g. Murry dates 'Carnation' 1917, but both the holograph manuscript and a letter to Ida Baker of 3 June 1918 suggest that the story was not completed until 27 May 1918). See notes on individual stories for further details on dating.

THE TIREDNESS OF ROSABEL

This story remained unpublished during Mansfield's lifetime. After her death Murry published it in *Collier's*, NY, vol. 73, no. 6, 9 February 1924, pp. 14, 36, with illustrations by Clara Elsene Peck, before using it as the opening story of *Something Childish*. A typescript, corrected in pencil in Mansfield's hand and signed 'K. Mansfield, 1908', exists in the Newberry Library, Chicago.

Antony Alpers (TS, p. 546) assumes that this story was written in Wellington early in 1908, before Mansfield's departure for England in July, while she was waiting to hear whether or not there was a vacancy for her in Beauchamp Lodge, a hostel for music students on Warwick Crescent in Paddington overlooking the Grand Canal at Little Venice. This might explain the reference to Venice in the third paragraph and the comparison of Westbourne Grove, which is nowhere near the canal, to the Grand Canal. However, there is no Richmond Road near Westbourne Grove and, if Mansfield was trying to imagine what her life would be like as a single woman living in a hostel in London, she made no attempt to check out the geography: no bus would go via Westbourne Grove to reach Beauchamp Lodge. Ida Baker (LM, p. 42) dates the writing of the story to the autumn of 1908, when Katherine was in love with Garnet Trowell and left

Beauchamp Lodge to live briefly with the Trowell family in Carlton Hill. If she is right, then the story may reflect Mansfield's sexual awakening with Trowell and what L. M. describes as a 'time of happiness' (LM, p. 42). L. M.'s dating seems more logical than Alpers'. The story would then reflect both Mansfield's experiences at the hostel, relocated in a fictional road, and her experience of romantic love with Garnet Trowell.

1. *Lyons*: Lyons Cornerhouses were established in 1894. They served a wide range of cheap food in a chain of restaurants and teashops. There was a Lyons teashop in Oxford Street, which Murry and Mansfield used to frequent.

2. *Atlas 'bus*: The first motor bus in London was licensed in 1897.

3. *Anna Lombard*: The popular novel by Victoria Cross (pseudonym Vivian Cory) was first published in 1901 and went into many reprints, including a popular Shilling Edition in 1908.

4. *Sapolio*: A cleaning agent.

5. *Heinz's Tomato Sauce*: The American Food Company, F.&J. Heinz, was founded in 1876, and the '57 varieties' slogan devised in 1896. The firm was known for its innovative and effective marketing strategies: in 1900 it was the first firm to use an electric sign to advertise its products in Manhattan.

6. *Lamplough's Pyretic Saline*: Sometimes known as 'effervescing pyretic salts', pyretic saline was a cure for fever.

7. *electric staircase like the one at Earl's Court*: The District Line was extended to Earl's Court in the early years of the century, and electrification of trains and stations (which originally transported passengers using hydraulic lifts) proceeded from the 1890s onwards. Antony Alpers (TS, p. 546) is puzzled by this detail since, according to him, Earl's Court station had no electric escalator until 1911.

8. *motor-cap*: A fur cap with ear-flaps.

9. *electric brougham*: Broughams, originally horse-drawn vehicles, were closed carriages with two or four wheels, designed to carry two or four people.

10. *the Carlton*: The Carlton Hotel, Haymarket, opened in 1899. César Ritz had the interiors decorated in the style of the Paris Ritz, with a magnificent Palm Court, and hired Escoffier as the main chef. The hotel closed in 1939, was bombed during the war and was demolished in 1957–8.

11. *Gerard's*: Gerard's Florists was located at 178 Regent Street, in one of the smartest and most expensive areas of London.

12. *the 'Cottage'*: This teashop has not been located.

13. *white tulle*: A fine silk net, used in ladies' dresses, veils and hats.

14. *Court Circular*: No magazine of this title ever existed, but the *Court Circle*, an illustrated review of the court and fashionable society, appeared weekly from May 1882 onwards.

15. *St George's, Hanover Square*: This church was built in 1720–5 and was famous for society weddings. Lady Hamilton was married there in 1791, Shelley in 1814, Disraeli in 1839 and Asquith in 1894.

16. *'honeycomb' quilt*: A kind of woven fabric, very popular for making quilts and towels, in which the warp and weft threads form ridges and indentations, producing a ridge-like effect similar to candlewick.

HOW PEARL BUTTON WAS KIDNAPPED

This story was originally published in *Rhythm*, no. 8 (vol. 2, no. 4), September 1912, pp. 136–9, signed 'Lili Heron' and illustrated with a woodcut by Henri Gaudier-Brzeska. Murry then reprinted it in *Woman's Home Companion*, Springfield, Ohio, and New York, vol. 51, no. 2, February 1924, pp. 14–15, with illustrations by W. Emerton Heitland, before using it again in *Something Childish*, where he dates it 1910. Some of the details seem to draw on Mansfield's 1907 camping trip in the North Island of New Zealand (see Introduction), and Ian A. Gordon suggests that in her depiction of Pearl's warm welcome by the Maori, Mansfield was remembering her own experiences with a Maori family in Te Whaiti (see *The Urewera Notebook*, Ian A. Gordon, ed., Oxford University Press, 1978, pp. 28–9, 64).

1. *a big flax basket*: Traditionally, the Maori use large baskets of plaited fern for food storage etc. Mansfield was presented with a Maori basket ('kit' or 'kete') in Te Whaiti (see *The Urewera Notebook*, p. 62).

2. *a green ornament*: On her trip Mansfield saw many Maori women wearing traditional greenstone pendants, or 'tiki'. For example, describing 'a young Maori girl': 'Round her neck is a piece of twisted flax and around a long piece of greenstone – is suspended from it [sic]' (*The Urewera Notebook*, p. 84).

3. *two pieces of black hair down to her feet*: At Waipunga 'a Maori girl – with her hair in two long braids, sat at the doorstep – shelling peas' (*The Urewera Notebook*, p. 43).

THE JOURNEY TO BRUGES

This story was first published in *New Age*, vol. 9, no. 17, 24 August 1911, pp. 401–2. Murry (who did not know her at this point in her life) dates it 1910, but Alpers (TS, p. 549, and Antony Alpers, *The Life of Katherine Mansfield*, Oxford University Press, 1982, p. 127) maintains that it was written in 1911, after Mansfield, ill with 'pleurisy or bronchitis' (LM, p. 66), travelled alone to Belgium to recuperate. After some time in Bruges she went to Geneva, where a worried L.M., who had been away in Rhodesia, eventually found her. Mansfield's trip had evidently not been an easy one. L.M. writes: 'when I eventually reached the address ..., Katherine's first anxious question was: "Have you brought any money with you?" The poor child had barely £1 left' (LM, p. 66). L.M., as usual, managed to raise some funds. Mansfield returned to London in September 1911. It seems most likely, in spite of Murry's dating, that the story was written in Belgium or Geneva in summer 1911 and posted back to Orage in London for publication in *New Age* before Mansfield's return. It bears a remarkable similarity to Virginia Woolf's story 'An Unwritten Novel', about a train journey, which was probably written in 1920 and published in the *London Mercury* in July of that year.

1. *homoeopathic*: Very small, like the doses in homoeopathic medicine.
2. *dicky*: An over-jacket or outer garment.
3. *The Snark's Summer Annual*: The Snark annuals were small pamphlets, usually containing a short story and a number of comic cartoons by Stan Wood ('The Snark').
4. *fifteen bob*: 'Bob' is slang for shilling.
5. *Athenaeum*: This weekly literary periodical was established in 1828. In 1919 Murry was appointed its editor, with a brief to give it a new post-war image and increase its flagging sales. It was eventually incorporated into the *Nation* in 1921.
6. *camphor*: Used in the preparation of mothballs.
7. *Rembrandt*: Rembrandt (1606–69) is famous for his portraits. The ivory tint and delicacy of many of his paintings are perhaps what Mansfield had in mind when she wrote this.
8. *Anatole France*: French novelist, critic and man of letters (1844–1924). His series of satirical sketches of provincial life in *L'Histoire Contemporaine* (1896–1901) are perhaps what Mansfield is thinking of here.
9. *cinematograph*: Now more usually abbreviated to 'cinema'.
10. *Grand' Place*: The town centre of Bruges is the Markt, or 'Grand' Place', dominated by the famous thirteenth-century belfry and with many beautiful seventeenth-century buildings.

A TRUTHFUL ADVENTURE

This is the second of two stories that derive from Mansfield's trip to Bruges in the summer of 1911 (see notes to 'The Journey to Bruges'). It was originally published, as 'Being a Truthful Adventure', in *New Age*, vol. 9, no. 19, 7 September 1911, pp. 450–2, two issues after 'The Journey to Bruges'. Again, Murry dates the story 1910, probably wrongly. The meeting with an old schoolfriend may be an ironic reference to L.M.'s apparently unexpected appearance in Geneva, a visit of which L.M. commented in her *Memories*: 'She had grown and I had not kept pace with her. I began to know the almost physical ache that comes with the realisation of being inadequate' (LM, p. 67).

1. *Béguinage*: The Béguinage, or Begijnhof, of Bruges was one of many self-contained lay sisterhoods devoted to charitable works. The Bruges Begijnhof was founded in 1235 and consists of a number of fifteenth-century buildings situated round a large courtyard planted with elm trees. The Begijnhof is now occupied by Benedictine sisters.

2. *a wall eye*: A divergent squint.

3. *Mendelssohn's Spring Song*: Felix Mendelssohn-Bartholdy (1809–1847). The 'Spring Song' was originally written for piano solo, one of a series of *Songs Without Words*, op. 62. Mansfield was a keen cellist, and the Trowells were keen musicians.

4. *Place van Eyck*: The Place van Eyck, north of the Markt and originally connected to it by a canal arm, is a lively residential quarter, little visited by tourists. The statue of Van Eyck in the square is by Henri Pickery and dates from 1878.

5. *Verlaine*: Paul Verlaine (1844–96), a French poet associated with the Symbolist and Decadent movements and known for the musical, fluid, evocative quality of his verse.

6. *the Venice of the North*: Bruges is almost entirely surrounded by water and linked by canals to Ostend, Zeebrugge and Ghent. It is criss-crossed by a network of small waterways, with over fifty bridges.

7. *the Lac d'Amour*: The Lac d'Amour, or Minnewater, is a quiet lake just south of the Begijnhof and was the busy inner dock of Bruges harbour during the Middle Ages.

8. *the Suffrage*: Women over thirty were given the vote in England in 1918 after years of protest which were at their height in the years immediately preceding the Great War. A. R. Orage, editor of the *New Age*, in which this story was published, and his lover Beatrice Hastings, both friends of Mansfield's, had been ardently in favour of women's suffrage, and Orage was the only man in a group of seventy-five suffragettes who stormed the House of Commons in 1907. By 1910, however, both Orage and Hastings had changed their minds, and the *New Age* ceased publishing pro-suffrage articles and became openly hostile to the campaign. The exchange in 'A Truthful Adventure' may be an ironic reference to conversations between Orage, Hastings, and Mansfield, who had never been very interested in political campaigns. Mansfield's ambivalent feelings about feminism generally are explored in the Introduction.

NEW DRESSES

This story was first published in *Rhythm*, vol. 2, no. 9, October 1912, pp. 189–92, 195–7, 199–201. Murry dates it 1910, but Ian Gordon, in *Undiscovered Country: The New Zealand Stories of Katherine Mansfield* (Longman, 1974), dates it 1911. Although in Katherine's own family there were four sisters and a younger brother, where in 'New Dresses' there are only two sisters, it seems likely that

Katherine had her own childhood experiences in mind when she wrote the story. According to Alpers, Katherine, sandwiched between two elder sisters and two babies, felt herself to be the odd one out, was neglected by her mother and became resentful and moody (Antony Alpers, *The Life of Katherine Mansfield*, Oxford University Press, 1982, p. 13). In the original *Rhythm* version, the family have German names (Henry and Anne Carsfield are Andreas and Anna Binzer, Rose is Rosa, Helen is Elena, Dr Malcolm is Dr Erb, Lumley is Schäfer, Clayton's is Brückner's, and Lindsay is Brechenmacher) and money and measurements are expressed as 'marks' and 'metres', rather than 'shillings' and 'yards'. A few German expressions were also suppressed in the revised version. The same characters appear in Mansfield's 'A Birthday', which tells the story of Baby's birth and was published in *New Age*, 18 May 1911, and then in *In a German Pension*, her first collection, which came out late in 1911. If 'A Birthday' was written in late 1910 or early 1911, it seems likely that 1911 is the correct date for 'New Dresses', which reads as a kind of sequel to 'A Birthday'. Murry changed the names of the characters when he published the story in the post-war *Something Childish*. Virginia Woolf's story, 'The New Dress', written in early 1925, contains a reference to Mansfield's story 'The Fly', and the title suggests that she may have had 'New Dresses' in mind as well.

1. *Political League*: It is unlikely that this refers to any specific group, and the reference becomes doubly vague once the changed national context of the story is taken into account.

2. *a Hamelin tribe*: In the fairy story 'The Pied Piper of Hamelin' the town of Hamelin is infested with a plague of rats.

3. *dolman*: A robe or dressing-gown, sometimes with flaps instead of sleeves.

4. The *Rhythm* version adds the following paragragh to the end of the story:

> On the following Sunday the two Fraulein Binzers in green cashmere dresses with apple green sashes and straw hats with ribbon tails sat in church between their father and mother. Elena knelt on the dusty hassock without lifting her skirt. But it did not matter – Anna quite forgot to notice.

THE WOMAN AT THE STORE

This story was first published in *Rhythm*, vol. 1, no. 4, Spring 1912, pp. 7–21. It was illustrated with a woodcut by Thompson. The story draws on Mansfield's experiences on a camping trip she made in 1907 in the North Island (see Introduction). It was this story that Mansfield sent to Murry in response to a letter from him asking to see more of her work after he had turned down a fairy story for publication in *Rhythm*. Murry was immediately excited by it and urged his and Mansfield's mutual friend, Willy George, to introduce him to its author.

Murry dates the story in the year in which he first read it, 1911. This is one of the stories that Mansfield would repudiate in later years; she wrote to Murry on 8 February 1920 that she 'couldn't have "The Woman at the Store" reprinted par exemple'.

The inspiration for the story seems to have come from a family she met at Rangitaiki, where she camped on the night of Wednesday 20 November, 1907. They were running the hotel there. There are two references to them in *The Urewera Notebook* (Ian A. Gordon, ed., Oxford University Press, 1978). In the first she wrote simply: 'Woman and daughter – the man – their happiness – forgive Lord – I cant –' (p. 46); in the second, in a draft letter to her mother that was never sent, she says: 'Well Mother I posted your letter at the Rangitaiki Hotel – and on the way out I saw the land-lord's wife – and thinking that she was a happy woman questioned her as to her offspring' (p. 61). The letter breaks off here, as though something was said, or happened, that she cannot quite bring herself to write down.

Murry introduced a number of changes into the story when he reprinted it in *Something Childish*. In the periodical version, it is unclear what the gender of the narrator is. For the collection, Murry made a small alteration which establishes the narrator as a woman (see note 14). He also altered the name of one of the characters, Hin (possibly an abbreviation of a common Maori name, Hinemoa), to Jim. It is not clear why he made these changes, although he may have wished to suppress any suggestion of sexual interest in the woman on the narrator's part, and any racial subtext. He may also have shied away from a scene in which a girl-child spies on a naked man bathing. It is hard, however, not to think that Murry knew something about the original circumstances which the story describes and wanted to cover Mansfield's tracks.

For readers interested in seeing a sample of Mansfield's original prose, the opening paragraph of 'The Woman at the Store', as it appeared in *Rhythm*, reads as follows:

All that day the heat was terrible. The wind blew close to the ground – it rooted among the tussock grass – slithered along the road, so that the white pumice dust swirled in our faces – settled and sifted over us and was like a dry-skin itching for growth on our bodies. The horses stumbled along, coughing and chuffing. The pack-horse was sick – with a big open sore rubbed under the belly. Now and again she stopped short, threw back her head, looked at us as though she were going to cry, and whinnied. Hundreds of larks shrilled – the sky was slate colour, and the sound of the larks reminded me of slate pencils scraping over its surface. There was nothing to be seen but wave after wave of tussock grass – patched with purple orchids and manuka bushes covered with thick spider webs.

1. *manuka bushes*: Flowering bush, very common in scrub country. Mansfield wrote a poem on the manuka on the evening of her return to Hastings at the end of the camping trip (15 December 1907), describing its flower as 'this blossom flaming yellow and pale gold' (*The Urewera Notebook*, p. 88).

2. *galatea*: Striped cotton, often used for children's sailor suits.

3. *wideawake*: Soft-brimmed felt hat.

4. *Jaeger vest*: Dr Jaeger's Sanitary Woollen System Co. Ltd started manufacturing woollen garments in the 1880s. They were practical rather than fashionable!

5. *duck trousers*: Duck is strong linen or cotton, often used to make small sails or sailors' trousers.

6. *fly biscuits*: Garibaldi biscuits (raisins pressed between two layers of sweet pastry).

7. *whare*: Maori for house or meeting-place.

8. *Bluchers*: Strong leather boots or high shoes, named after Field Marshal von Blucher, who fought at Waterloo.

9. *pawa*: Mansfield here is mis-spelling 'paua', or abalone shell.

10. *Queen Victoria's Jubilee*: The Queen's Golden Jubilee was on 21 June 1887, many years before the setting of this story.

11. *Richard Seddon*: Popular liberal New Zealand premier until his death in 1906.

12. *Napier*: A town in the North Island near Hastings, where Mansfield began her trip. The railway line ends at Hastings. Rangitaiki, where the original of the woman at the store lived, is on the road from Napier to Taupo, along which Mansfield herself travelled.

13. *sundowner*: Swagman or tramp.

14. '*I looked at her where she couldn't see me from*': It is here that Murry makes the alteration which establishes the narrator as a woman. The original *Rhythm* version reads: '"I'll draw all of you when you're gone, and your horses and the tent, and that one" – she pointed to me – "with no clothes on in the creek." I looked at her where she wouldn't see me frown.'

15. *calico*: Coarse cotton cloth, usually plain.

16. *sateen*: Cotton or woollen cloth with a glossy surface.

17. '*Camp Coffee*': A cheap brand of coffee mixed with chicory.

OLE UNDERWOOD

This story was first published in *Rhythm*, vol. 2, no. 12, January 1913, pp. 334–7. It is set in Wellington, where Mansfield grew up, with its prison up on the hill above the harbour. Ruth Elvish Mantz and Murry suggest, in their biography of Mansfield, that Ole Underwood's original was a vagrant who used to frighten Mansfield when she walked to school. Miss Swainson's school, which Mansfield began attending in June 1900, when she was twelve, was situated in Fitzherbert Terrace, and the tramp used to hide behind the trees that lined the road and jump out at the children. Mantz and Murry describe him as follows: 'He was a prospector – a gold-hunter from early settlement days – no-one knew just what. Swarthy – more like an Italian than an Englishman – he always wore a postman's cap; and gleaming out from his long black hair was a pair of little gold earrings' (*The Life of Katherine Mansfield*, Constable, 1933, p. 147). He also used to frequent the Chinese shops at the bottom of the hill, where he frequently had loud arguments. But, Mantz and Murry write, 'he seemed magnetised back and back again to the Terrace' (p. 148), and the girls always arrived at school scared and dishevelled. Eventually he came up before Mansfield's father, who was a magistrate, and was jailed for vagrancy.

1. *Anne Estelle Rice*: An Irish-American expressionist artist (1879–1959), whose work was published in *Rhythm*, and who remained a lifelong friend of Mansfield's.

2. *Chinamen's shops*: A large number of Chinese came to New Zealand as indentured labourers in the 1880s. Many of them ended up running small stores and greengrocers'.

THE LITTLE GIRL

This story first appeared in *Rhythm*, vol. 2, no. 9, October 1912, pp. 218–21. It was signed 'Lili Heron' and accompanied by a few unsigned illustrations. Before its reprint in *Something Childish* Murry reprinted it twice, first in his own journal, *Adelphi*, vol. 1, no. 5, October 1923, pp. 378–82; and secondly in *Collier's*, NY, vol. 72, no. 24, 15 December 1923, p. 13. In the reprints Murry altered the name of the little girl from Kass (Mansfield's own nickname within her family) to Kezia, the name of the child in 'Prelude' and 'At the Bay'. Although Kezia in the story apparently has no siblings, her original name, the setting, the presence of the grandmother and certain details about the father (see Notes) suggest that this is partly autobiographical. A couple of Murry's changes suggest that he was trying to obscure its autobiographical origins.

1. *buggy*: Light vehicle for one or two passengers.

2. *the Sketch*: A weekly glossy magazine, describing itself as 'The Best Paper for Society and Fashion', published in London between 1893 and 1959, and containing high-society gossip, photographs and advertisements.

3. *Port Authority*: In the periodical version, this is 'Harbour Board', a clear reference to the election of Mansfield's father, Harold Beauchamp, to the Wellington Harbour Board in the mid-1890s.

4. *'general'*: Maid of all work.

MILLIE

This story was first published in *Blue Review*, vol. 1, no. 2, June 1913, pp. 82–7. *Blue Review* was the successor to *Rhythm*, with Murry as editor and Mansfield as associate editor. The renaming of the magazine was a desperate attempt to keep it financially afloat. The attempt failed: only three monthly numbers were ever published. Those three numbers reflected a more conservative editorial policy than had been pursued at *Rhythm*. Murry reprinted 'Millie' in *Century Magazine*, NY, vol. 107, no. 6, April 1924, pp. 847–50, before it appeared again in the British edition of *Something Childish*.

1. *English 'johnny'*: Fellow, or idler.
2. *Mount Cook*: Mount Cook, the highest peak in New Zealand (18,000 feet), is in the South Island. It is always snow-covered.

PENSION SÉGUIN

This story and the two that follow appeared consecutively in the three numbers of the *Blue Review*. All are set in Geneva and, like 'The Journey to Bruges', dramatize little incidents in the life of a woman travelling alone. Originally the title of each story was prefixed with 'Epilogue', followed by its number in the sequence. This one was called 'Epilogue: Pension Seguin' (without the accent, which Murry added throughout the *Something Childish* version), and it appeared first in *Blue Review*, vol. 1, no. 1, May 1913, pp. 37–42. Mansfield visited Geneva in the summer of 1911, after a spell in Bruges (see notes to 'A Journey to Bruges'). In Geneva she stayed with the Yelskis, friends whom she had met during her long stay in Worishofen in 1909. In February 1912 she visited Geneva again, apparently because of bad health.

1. *the First French Picture*: This reference has not been traced.
2. *Hamlet-like apparition*: Hamlet, in Shakespeare's play, is haunted by the ghost of his dead father, who commands him to kill Claudius, Hamlet's uncle and the new husband of Hamlet's mother. Hamlet cannot bring himself to obey.
3. *the Conservatoire*: The Geneva Conservatory was established in 1835.
4. *the Appassionata Sonata*: Beethoven's famous piano sonata no. 23 in F minor, op. 57, written in 1804–5.
5. *fierce as a Gogol novel*: Nikolai Vasilievich Gogol (1809–52), Russian novelist and dramatist, author of the nightmarish and fantastic *The Diary of a Madman* (1835) and the satirical *Dead Souls* (1842).

VIOLET

This story first appeared as part of the series of three 'Epilogues' (see notes to 'Pension Séguin'). It was entitled simply 'Epilogue: II' and published in *Blue Review*, vol. 1, no. 2, June 1913, pp. 103–9. Murry reprinted it as 'Violet' in *Bookman*, New York, vol. 59, no. 4, June 1924, pp. 400–403. When it was first published, Murry wanted to cut it so that it would fit six pages, but Mansfield objected:

> I've nursed the epilogue to no purpose. Every time I pick it up and hear 'youll keep it to six,' I *cant* cut it. To my knowledge there aren't any superfluous words: I mean every line of it. I don't 'just ramble on' you know, but this thing happened to just fit 6½ pages – you cant cut it without making an ugly mess somewhere . . . I'd rather it wasn't there at all than sitting in the Blue Review with a broken nose and one ear as though it had jumped into an editorial dog fight.
>
> (Mansfield to Murry, 19 May 1913, in *The Collected Letters of Katherine Mansfield*, Vincent O'Sullivan and Margaret Scott, eds. Clarendon, 1984–93, I, p. 124)

Alpers (TS, p. 553) believes that Violet is modelled on Mansfield's English cousin, Sylvia Payne (1887–1949), whom she first met in 1903, when she came to London with her sisters to attend Queen's College for girls. Sylvia was red-haired, striking-looking and Mansfield seems to have half fallen in love with her. L. M. describes Sylvia as high-spirited and naughty (LM, pp. 27–8). She also mentions an incident which seems to have inspired 'Violet':

> I remember a letter from Sylvia, given to me to read by Katherine, in which Sylvia told of an experience of hers and sought advice. Someone had tried to kiss her. Katherine was not concerned; she felt that such a mundane consideration reduced their relationship, and consequently it changed. I do not think the letter was answered.
>
> (LM, p. 28)

1. '*I met a young virgin / Who sadly did moan . . .*': This quotation has not been traced. It may well be an ironic invention.
2. *Katharine Tynan*: Irish poet and novelist, 1861–1931, and a leading author of the Celtic literary revival. She wrote several volumes of gentle domestic verse and over a hundred novels, including *She Walks in Beauty* (1899) and *The House in the Forest* (1928).
3. *Sèvres cup*: A particularly fine bone china.
4. *piqué*: Stiff ribbed cotton.
5. *alpaca*: Coarse wool from Peruvian llamas.
6. *the Rue St Léger*: Mansfield herself stayed in the Rue St Léger when she was in Geneva. It is in the heart of Geneva's 'Vieille Ville'.

7. *the more pretentious avenues fronting the Place du Théâtre*: The garden the narrator crosses to reach the university is the Promenade des Bastions, formerly a botanical garden. The university buildings of 1867–71 stand on the opposite side of the garden.

8. *'the people in Shelley's "Skylark"'*: The allusion is to the poem 'To Skylark' (1820) by Percy Bysshe Shelley (1792–1822). The narrator is making ironic reference to line 86, 'We look before and after.'

9. *'Do you believe in Pan?'*: In late summer 1910 Mansfield met a young schoolmaster called William Orton at a tennis party in Hampstead. On the way home on the Tube Mansfield suddenly said: 'Do you believe in Pan?' The two became close friends, possibly lovers for a time. Years later Orton told Alpers that he didn't think she knew very much about Pan (Antony Alpers, *The Life of Katherine Mansfield*, Oxford University Press, 1984, pp. 118–19) who, in ancient Greek myth, is the satyr-god of shepherds and their flocks and responsible for their fertility.

BAINS TURCS

This story originally appeared as 'Epilogue: III', in *Blue Review*, vol. 1, no. 3, July 1913, pp. 181–5. It is the final story in the series of three set in Geneva. In the *Blue Review* version, 'Pfalzburg' is spelt 'Salzburg' throughout.

1. *'Honeysuckle and the Bee'*: This popular song by Albert Fitz and William Penn was a hit in Britain in 1901.

2. *Reisehut*: A 'travelling hat', apparently a word coined by Mansfield to mock the German habit of qualifying words by the addition of different prefixes. In the *Blue Review* version this reads 'Reis Hut'.

SOMETHING CHILDISH BUT VERY NATURAL

This story was never published by Mansfield herself, but Murry published it in *Adelphi*, vol. 1, nos. 9–10, February–March 1924, pp. 777–90, 913–22, before including it in the *Something Childish* collection. Murry dates it 1914 and says it was the first story she completed after their meeting, which had stopped her writing for months (see Introduction). It is probable that Mansfield wrote the story in the early months of 1914, when she and Murry were trying, unsuccessfully, to find work in Paris.

1. *'Something Childish but very Natural'*: This poem, which Mansfield has slightly misquoted, was written by Coleridge and sent as part of a letter to his wife from Göttingen on 23 April 1799. It is an imitation of a German folk-song and was later published, under the title Mansfield uses, in the *Annual Anthology* (1800).

2. *Bolton Abbey*: A ruined twelfth-century priory on the banks of the river Wharfe a few miles from Skipton in Yorkshire. The picture is presumably displayed as part of an advertising campaign for travel by train.

3. *pollies*: This word has not been traced. It may well have been an invention of Mansfield's, to emphasize the teasing, playful nature of the exchange between the couple.

AN INDISCREET JOURNEY

This story, unpublished by Mansfield, is a semi-fictional account of her journey across France to visit her lover, Francis Carco, in the town of Gray, in the military zone, in February 1915. Francis Carco (1886–1958) published his first novel, *Jésus-la-caille*, in 1914. He was an old friend of Murry's, and met Mansfield first in Paris in 1914. Many of the incidents in the story appear also, almost word for word, in letters to Murry, 20 February 1915, and Frieda Lawrence, 20 February 1915 (*Collected Letters of Katherine Mansfield*, Vincent O'Sullivan and Margaret Scott, eds., Clarendon, 1984–93, I, pp. 149–50), and in Mansfield's journal for February 1915 (*The Journal of Katherine Mansfield*, John Middleton Murry, ed., Constable, 1954, pp. 74–9). The visit was not terribly successful, and Mansfield returned to London and Murry after only four days.

1. *Burberry*: Brand-name for raincoats, known for their toughness and quality.

2. *peg-top*: Wide at the top and tapering; usually used of trousers or skirts, but here referring, apparently, to a coat.

3. *sabots*: Wooden clogs.

4. *We, Sir Edward Grey*: The official is reading out the inside of the narrator's passport. Sir Edward Grey (1862–1933) was Secretary for Foreign Affairs from 1905 to 1916, and at that period it was the Foreign Office that issued passports. It was not usually necessary to carry a passport, even when crossing national borders, but the narrator has one as a precaution because of the war. Mansfield, when she made her 'indiscreet journey', would have had a British passport, since she married the Englishman George Bowden in 1909. The marriage lasted only a day.

5. *Dodo, mon homme, fais vit' dodo . . .*: Mansfield copied out the words to this song for Murry in a letter of 8–9 May 1915. It is called 'Idylle Rouge', with words by Saint Gilles and Paul Gay and music by Georges Picquet.

6. *'Un Picon!'*: A bitter aperitif, sometimes drunk with curaçao.

7. *'Mirabelle'*: Plum brandy.

SPRING PICTURES

This story was never published by Mansfield, but an undated manuscript version of part of it survives in the Newberry Library, Chicago. A version of section two, entitled 'Femme seule', appears in Mansfield's diary for May 1915. This implies that the piece was written while Mansfield was staying alone in Carco's flat in Paris on the Quai aux Fleurs in May 1915, while he was still serving in the army in Gray. She left in a hurry, on hearing that Carco might be returning to Paris.

1. *Zeppelins*: Large airships originally manufactured in Germany.

LATE AT NIGHT

This is one of a number of pieces in dramatic form that Mansfield contributed to *New Age* in 1917, apparently encouraged by Orage, the editor who had already published many of her stories in earlier numbers of *New Age*. Two of the dramatic pieces reprinted here, 'Late at Night' and 'Two Tuppenny Ones, Please', have a war-time theme. Mansfield did not usually write in dialogue, and the inspiration for this piece seems to have come from a play Mansfield devised when she spent Christmas at Garsington in 1916 with Ottoline and Philip Morrell, Bertrand Russell, Lytton Strachey, Dorothy Brett, Maria Nys, Aldous Huxley and Carrington. Mansfield's play was apparently a great success. Aldous Huxley wrote to his brother: 'We performed a superb play invented by Katherine, improvising as we went along' (quoted in Antony Alpers, *The Life of Katherine Mansfield*, Oxford University Press, 1982, p. 227). By 1917 Orage was desperate for contributions to *New Age*, and it seems likely that he appealed to Mansfield for help. Although Mansfield never really took to dialogue as a literary form, it may well have helped her develop her own characteristic technique, which dispenses with a stable, authoritative narrative voice. 'Late at Night' first appeared in *New Age*, New Series, vol. 21, no. 2, 10 May 1917, p. 38.

TWO TUPPENNY ONES, PLEASE

This is another of the *New Age* dialogues (see notes to 'Late at Night'). It first appeared in *New Age*, New Series, vol. 21, no. 1, 3 May 1917, pp. 13–14.

1. *What's higher than a Brigadier-General?*: In the British army, the chief of staff is the highest in command, reporting directly to the sovereign. A major is above a captain, but below a brigadier-general in rank. A brigadier-general would be in charge of a brigade, comprising three battalions each made up of several companies. A regiment is a permanent unit consisting of two or more battalions.
2. *Friend. . . .*: The *New Age* version inserts the following passage between this

interjection and the Lady's speech beginning 'Oh, my dear': '*Lady*. Hasn't he! He's been most lucky – most mercifully spared . . . so far. But he's back again, you know, and "over the top" every day. *Friend*. . . .'

3. *Stewart's*: This famous baker's and confectioner's was situated at 79 Knights-bridge, in an exclusive area of south-west London.

4. *Yvette's Spring Show*: Top designers traditionally held a 'spring show' of new models.

THE BLACK CAP

This is the last of the *New Age* dialogues. Mansfield originally intended to include 'The Black Cap' in the collection *Bliss and Other Stories* (1920), but on Murry's objection that it would be 'the only thing not in actual story form', she decided to replace it with another story called 'The Second Helping' (see Murry to Mansfield, 30 January 1920, *The Letters of John Middleton Murry to Katherine Mansfield*, selected and edited by C. A. Hankin, Constable, 1983, p. 267). 'The Second Helping' was never written. 'The Black Cap' first appeared in *New Age*, New Series, vol. 21, no. 3, 17 May 1917, pp. 62–3, and was reprinted in *The New Keepsake for 1921* in 1920.

1. *linen press*: Airing-cupboard.

A SUBURBAN FAIRY TALE

Mansfield never published this story, but Murry used the surviving manuscript, dated 15 March 1919 and now in the British Museum, to publish it both in *Something Childish* and before that in *Adelphi*, vol. 1, no. 7, December 1923, pp. 570–4. Alpers (TS, p. 562) believes the story is a comment on the famine in Germany after the First World War. In January 1919 Murry had been offered the editorship of the weekly paper, the *Athenaeum*, whose sales were flagging. His task was to ensure continuity while introducing change. One of those changes was the appointment of Mansfield as the fiction reviewer. 'A Suburban Fairy Tale' was one of the few stories Mansfield wrote in the first months of 1919, since most of her limited energy (she was now seriously ill, coughing blood and newly diagnosed with an old complaint, gonorrhoea) went on the *Athenaeum*.

1. *this rationing business*: In early 1918 the Ministry of Food established a rationing system for meat, butter, margarine, sugar, lard and, in certain areas, tea, jam and cheese. The war ended in November 1918, and restrictions were gradually lifted in early 1919: margarine became freely available from 2 March, tea from 24 March, bacon, ham and lard from 31 March and so on. Some foods, like meat

and dates, were still 'controlled' in mid-March 1919 when this story was written. This story thus dates from the middle of the period at which restrictions were rapidly being lifted. The 'really over' of p. 121 reads 'nearly over' in the manuscript.

CARNATION

This story is a reminiscence of Mansfield's early days at Queen's College, Harley Street, which she and her sisters attended from 1903 to 1906, and where she met Ida Baker (L. M.). It seems that Murry's suggested date of 1917 is wrong. A surviving manuscript in the Newberry Library, Chicago, is dated 27 May 1918, and letters from Mansfield at the same period tell us that she wrote the story shortly after her marriage to Murry, when she was staying alone at the Headland Hotel in Looe, Cornwall. Mansfield wrote to L. M., urging her to read 'Carnation' if it ever came out (it was published in the *Nation*, vol. 23, no. 23, 7 September 1918, pp. 595–6): 'Its about College: Ive even put you in as Connie Baker' (Mansfield to L. M., 3 June 1918, *Collected Letters*, Vincent O'Sullivan and Margaret Scott, eds., Clarendon, 1984–93, II, p. 218). In July 1918 she described it to her painter friend, Dorothy Brett, as 'a sort of glimpse of adolescent emotion' (Mansfield to Brett, 26 July 1918, *Collected Letters*, II, p. 260). A long passage in her journal describes her days at the college and her French teacher, M. Huguenot, in terms that anticipate 'Carnation':

> I was thinking yesterday of my *wasted, wasted* early girlhood. My college life, which is such a vivid and detailed memory in one way, might never have contained a book or a lecture. I lived in the girls, the professor, the big, lovely building, the leaping fires in winter and the abundant flowers in summer . . . why didn't I learn French with M. Huguenot? What an opportunity missed! What has it not cost me! He lectured in a big narrow room . . . Below the windows, far below there was a stable court paved in cobble stones, and one could hear the faint clatter of carriages coming out or in, the noise of water gushing out of a pump into a big pail – some youth, clumping about and whistling.
> (*Journal*, John Middleton Murry, ed., Constable, 1954, February–March 1916, pp. 103, 105–6)

'Eve' is modelled on a fellow pupil, Evelyn Bartrick-Baker (whom Mansfield, or 'Katie' as she was known at college and in 'Carnation', always called 'Eve'). Mansfield was fascinated by Eve, whose unusual background (her parents were divorced ex-Plymouth Brethren) and taste for Wilde and Pater made her an exotic figure in the college. L. M. said of her: 'She was small, dark and slender, with an aloof air as though she was much older and more experienced than the rest of us. She has left me with the impression of a bunch of choice flowers – roses and carnations' (LM, p. 26). Names of some other characters in the story are also derived from fellow pupils: Katie was Mansfield's own name, Vera is the name of one of Mansfield's sisters who also attended the school, Sylvia Mann is an allusion to Sylvia Payne (see notes to 'Violet'), and Connie Baker is L. M.

SEE-SAW

This evocation of children's play echoes some of the scenes with the children in much better known stories such as 'Prelude', 'At the Bay' and 'The Doll's House'. Murry's date of 1917 appears to be wrong: Mansfield's rough draft of this story, in the Newberry Library, Chicago, is dated 24 June 1919, and she notes at the end that she sent the story to the *Nation* on that date. However, the *Nation* never published it, and it was left to Murry to bring it out, first in the *Adelphi*, vol. 2, no. 2, July 1924, pp. 125–9, and then in *Something Childish*. The original title was 'The Little Primitives'. Mansfield seems to have been undecided until the last moment about her choice of tense: a note on the rough draft says: 'When copying put it all in the present tense.' The fair copy, duly all in the present tense, is also in the Newberry Library. When he prepared the story for publication, Murry worked from the rough draft, in which the story, as in the version published here, shifts into the past tense halfway through the second paragraph. There are a number of other minor differences between the rough draft and the fair copy. For example, Mansfield changed 'He took the pickaxe and hacked a little piece out of the kitchen floor.' (p. 129) to 'The little pick-axe is hollow; he tries to blow a whistle down it.' Presumably she wished to soften the little boy's aggression.

THIS FLOWER

This story remained unpublished until it appeared in *Something Childish*. An incomplete early draft of it, in the Newberry Library, has the title 'Late Spring' (although the epigraph is included), and is much longer, with marginal comments by Mansfield. A later version, much closer to the published one and with the title 'This Flower', is in the Alexander Turnbull Library in Wellington, New Zealand. Murry's date of 1919 is wrong: Mansfield mentions starting work on 'Late Spring' in her journal on 5 January 1920, although L. M., like Murry, believes it was written in 1919 (LM, p. 135). The early draft suggests that, originally, Mansfield conceived of this as a longer story and much more explicitly erotic. She also included a considerable amount of narration from the doctor's point of view, material which is missing altogether from the final draft and survives only in sentences like: 'He gave her a strange, quick, leering look' (p. 133). The doctor in the early draft is not leering, but uncomfortable.

1. '*But I tell you, my lord fool, out of this nettle danger, we pluck this flower, safety.*': The epigraph is from Harry Hotspur's soliloquy in *I Henry IV*, Act II, Scene 3. It was later engraved on Mansfield's tombstone.

2. *Bloomsbury*: At this period Bloomsbury was a slightly run-down, Bohemian area of London. It was to Bloomsbury that the young Virginia Woolf moved in 1904 after the death of her father, much to the disapproval of most of her social circle.

3. '*Do you mind not mentioning anything of this to Mr King?*': The Newberry draft inserts here:

> [The doctor] was, on these occasions, inclined to be jocular – to swagger a bit – to make it an affair of he and she across the table with the secret between them, clinking glasses, tossing it down to 'alright, little girl. Don't you worry. You leave it to me, my dear. I'll tell him you've swallowed the kitten and want a bit of sea air to drown it in.' But the whole surroundings in which he found himself and particularly the owner of the untroubled soft voice had thrown him clean off his beat. Why the Hell had they knocked him up. Standing in the middle of the exquisite fragrant room he was so nervous he broke into a sweat and it was only while he mopped his forehead and moustaches that he discovered he'd still got his stethoscope slung round his neck.

To 'kitten' was slang for giving birth; it is possible that the doctor is attempting a jocular allusion to the woman's condition.

4. *drawing on the little purple cloth jacket*: The Newberry draft inserts here: 'That purple cloth against the pale tea rose of her arms and bosom!'

5. *warm quick kisses*: The Newberry draft, which is apparently unfinished, has a different ending:

> He kissed her quickly, quickly – warm quick kisses – until she was half stifled and cried for mercy. But still he kept his arms round her and she leant against his shoulder as though quite exhausted. He was laughing too, and she felt as though his laughter were running in her veins.
>
> 'How beautiful you are. You little beauty. Look up at me, my darling, my delight.' And she looked up at the face bent over her – at the tanned skin with a reddish light on the cheek bones, the eyes like blue fire and the rust coloured hair as smooth as paint [a marginal comment beside this sentence reads 'too much description!']. He pleased her – oh but immeasurably – and he knew it.
>
> 'What is it' he whispered, bending down to her – 'What is it my treasure.'
>
> But 'nothing' said she, shaking her head. Then 'You smell very nice. Not of cigars . . .' 'Of nuts?' he laughed. That was, peculiarly, his kind of joke. But

she did not mind it. She let him pull her down gently into the deep chair between the windows.

THE WRONG HOUSE

'The Wrong House' was the title Mansfield originally gave to a manuscript which is only a page or two long, and which is now in the Alexander Turnbull Library in Wellington. The protagonist of this fragment, much of which is illegible, is crocheting (not knitting as in the published version) mission vests. She then has a bath and has the following thoughts:

As she lay there, her arms at her sides her legs straight out – she thought. This is how I shall look in [word crossed out] how they will arrange me in my coffin. And it seemed her as she gazed down at herself terribly then that people were made to fit coffins – made in the shape of coffins.

Mansfield seems to have taken this protagonist with her premonitions of death, her name, 'Miss Lavinia Bean', and the title of her story, and woven them into another story originally entitled (in a manuscript draft in the Alexander Turnbull Library) 'A Strange Mistake'. In a journal entry of 16 January 1920 she mentions starting work on this story (see Introduction). The story is apparently unfinished, and the manuscript version adds another sentence at the end: 'After tea it was her habit to play patience until the evening paper came.' Murry cut this sentence and published the rest as a complete piece. It was first published in *Something Childish*.

SIXPENCE

In the summer of 1921 Clement Shorter, editor of the *Sphere*, a weekly illus-trated commercial magazine, commissioned six stories from Mansfield, for a fee of ten guineas each. This represented a large sum of money for her, and she felt she could not refuse, even though the *Sphere* was a fairly low-brow publication. The six stories were 'Sixpence' (the first to be published, in the *Sphere*, vol. 86, no. 1124, 6 August 1921, pp. ii, 144, with illustrations by W. Smithson Broad-head), 'Mr and Mrs Dove', 'An Ideal Family', 'Her First Ball', and 'Marriage à la Mode'. Two other fragments, 'Hat with a Feather' and 'Widowed', which seem to have been intended for the *Sphere*, were never finished. Alpers reports (TS, p. 569) that Mansfield intended to include 'Sixpence' in *The Garden Party and Other Stories* (1922), but changed her mind at the last minute, writing to the publisher: 'I have not a copy by me but I have a horrible feeling it is sentimental and should not be there.' It was duly omitted.

1. *what-not*: A piece of furniture with shelves, designed to display ornaments.

POISON

This story was written in November 1920, while Mansfield was staying in Menton at the Villa Isola Bella, and Murry, in London working for the *Athenaeum*, was engaged in a flirtation with Elizabeth Bibesco, daughter of Margot Asquith. Mansfield, although she sometimes longed to be free of Murry, was hurt and resentful. She sent 'Poison' to Murry at the *Athenaeum* on 18 November 1920, but he did not publish it. She then wrote him a long letter explaining the story, some time in late November 1920:

And about 'Poison'. I could write about that for pages. But I'll try and condense what I've got to say. The story is told by (evidently) a worldly, rather cynical (not wholly cynical) man *against* himself (but not altogether) when he was so absurdly young. You know how young by his idea of what woman is. She has been up to now, only the *vision*, only she who passes. You realise that? And here he has put *all* his passion into this Beatrice. It's *promiscuous love*, not understood as such by him; perfectly understood as such by her. But you realise the vie de luxe they are living – the very table – sweets, liqueurs, lilies, pearls. And you realise? she expects a letter from someone calling her away? *Fully* expects it? Which accounts for her farewell AND her declaration. And when it doesn't come even her *commonness* peeps out – the newspaper touch of such a woman. She can't disguise her chagrin. She gives herself away . . . He, of course, laughs at it now, and laughs at her. Take what he says about her 'sense of order' and the crocodile. But he also regrets the self who dead privately would have been young enough to have actually wanted to *marry* such a woman. But I meant it to be light – tossed off – and yet through it – oh, subtly – the lament for youthful belief. These are the rapid confessions one receives sometimes from a glove or a cigarette or a hat.

I suppose I haven't brought it off in 'Poison'. It wanted a light, light hand – and then with that newspaper a sudden . . . let me see, *lowering* of it all – just what happens in promiscuous love after passion. A glimpse of staleness. And the story is told by the man who gives himself away and hides his traces at the same moment.

(Mansfield to Murry, in Clare Hanson, ed., *The Critical Writings of Katherine Mansfield*, Macmillan, 1987, pp. 45–6)

But Murry came to Menton for Christmas as planned and, after an initial period of tension, they seem to have settled down again happily enough, although Murry, in an uncanny echo of 'Poison', was receiving letters from Elizabeth Bibesco during his stay. Murry returned to London in February, and when a letter from Bibesco arrived for Murry in his absence, Mansfield wrote to Bibesco herself:

I am afraid you must stop writing these little love letters to my husband while he and I live together. It is one of the things which is not done in our world.

You are very young. Won't you ask your husband to explain to you the impossibility of such a situation.

Please do not make me have to write to you again. I do not like scolding people and I simply hate having to teach them manners.

(Mansfield to Bibesco, 24 March 1921, quoted in Antony Alpers, *The Life of Katherine Mansfield*, Oxford University Press, 1982, p. 332)

The affair seems, not surprisingly, to have stopped there. Murry comments in the Introductory Note to *Something Childish* that 'Poison' was excluded from *The Garden Party and Other Stories* (1922) because he thought it 'not wholly successful' (hardly surprising in the circumstances). He seems to have withdrawn his objections, though, after Mansfield's death (as he says in the Introductory Note, 'it now seems to me a little masterpiece'). Presumably by then it had lost its sting. He first published 'Poison' in *Collier's*, New York, vol. 72, no. 21, 24 November 1923, pp. 10, 32, before using it as the concluding story in *Something Childish*. A corrected typescript and a manuscript of 'Poison' survive in the Newberry Library, Chicago.

1. *The Voice that breathed o'er Eden*: This is a quotation from a hymn of 1857 by John Keble (1792–1866), leader of the Oxford Movement. The hymn is called 'Holy Matrimony' and the verse in which this line appears runs: 'The voice that breath'd o'er Eden,/That earliest wedding-day,/That primal marriage blessing,/It hath not passed away.'

2. *'Had I two little feathery wings/And were a little feathery bird . . .'*: This is a misquotation of the first two lines of Coleridge's poem 'Something Childish, but very Natural', which Mansfield had already quoted in its entirety in the story of the same name earlier in the collection (see notes to 'Something Childish but very Natural'). The poem evokes a lover who, if he could, would fly to his beloved, and is in any case with her in his dreams. The lines actually read: 'If I had but two little wings/And were a little feathery bird.'

3. *'He cometh not, she said . . .'*: This quotation is from the poem 'Mariana' (1830) by Alfred, Lord Tennyson (1809–92). This is the second line of the chorus. The poem, which derives from a reference in Shakespeare's *Measure for Measure*, describes a woman vainly waiting for her lover's arrival.

4. *'The world forgetting, by the world forgot'*: This quotation is from the long poem *Eloisa to Abelard* (1716–17), by Alexander Pope (1688–1794), line 208. Pope was imitating one of Ovid's *Heroides*. Peter Abelard (1079–1142) fell in love with his pupil Héloïse, who bore him a son and secretly married him. When this was discovered, Abelard was castrated, and both he and Héloïse entered different

convents. The original letters of Héloïse and Abelard appeared in Latin in 1616. The other half of the couplet of which this is the second line is 'How happy is the blameless Vestal's lot.'